I0758260

"Those who enter the magic circle are lucky to get out."

The Magic Circle

C. F. Hayes

ACKNOWLEDGEMENT

My heartfelt thanks to Marshall Salazar, whose kindness, helpfulness and patience never gave out during my frequent need to consult him. Thanks, too, to his expert team at Book Publishing Pros, who helped make this book possible.

To Suzanne and Doug

ABOUT THE AUTHOR

C. F. Hayes grew up in Los Angeles, and graduated from University of Southern California with a degree in philosophy. She currently lives in Newport Beach, California.

The madness of love is the greatest of heaven's blessings.

Plato, Phaedrus

Now of the heaven which is above the heavens, no earthly poet has sung or ever will sing in a worthy manner. But I must tell of it, for I am bound to speak truly when speaking of the truth. The colorless and formless and intangible essence is visible to the mind which is the only lord of the soul. Circling around this in the region above the heavens is the place of true knowledge.

Plato, Phaedrus

What does it matter who you have orgasm with or how, so long as you have it.

Father Malcolm,
Bachelor of Sacred Theology

PART I

"Pity the woman who cannot have multiple orgasms. Blessed, most blessed is the woman who can. If it is to my father that I owe this great blessing, then I do forgive him his sins."

***

This is from the diary of my childhood friend, Mary Armstrong. She died last year in a car accident on the 5 Freeway. You might have read about it in the papers because she was the daughter of Senator George Armstrong, a powerful Republican who was Chairman of the Appropriations Committee for many years, and had also run for president twice. I'm sure you will read about her again, once this story is published. And the Senator too, once the truth comes out. Why, he may even have his statue, the one that was recently erected in Spain, taken down.

Of course, I didn't know this, I mean about her father and the orgasms, until I read her diary. I knew Mary kept one; when we were kids we had both started them, but whereas I eventually grew tired of mine, she continued hers to the end of her short life. When the funeral was over, her partner of the last couple of years asked me if I'd like to read it. "There were," he said, "some very interesting things inside it."

I jumped at the chance. Why? Because of the things she would tell me and then clam up about and wouldn't tell me. I felt that all the mystery—and I was sure there was a mystery unless there wasn't and it was just my imagination—would be cleared up in the diary. Well it was, but not in the way I'd expected.

They say curiosity once killed a cat. Well, not being a cat, I'm still alive but just barely. (You must excuse the dramatics—it's part of my nature, thanks to a German grandfather.) What's that other saying? Fools enter where angels fear to tread?

But that could also be said of Mary. I always think that if she hadn't gone to Germany and sailed down the Rhine looking for the Magi she'd be alive today. But then, when one learns what the circumstances were, how could she not have gone looking?

What she wrote, even so, was more than I'd bargained for, and my first thought was to consign the diary to flames—well, give it back to John. But when the initial shock wore off, I knew that I, as her friend, owed it to her not to; the events of her life, the ideas that proceeded from it, were too extraordinary not to be brought to light.

In rendering her diary into a story, I've followed, on occasion, the randomness at which her entries appear. Sometimes they are only a sentence or two long; these I call epigrams although there might be a better term for the many terse observations that appear throughout. Some of the entries appear to have been written when she was quite young, but this I'm not certain about because nothing was ever dated.

For this reason, I've had, at times, to jump around. That is, things (events) that came before sometimes come after, and things that came after might come before. You may think it's sloppy writing, and maybe it is. But it does, eventually, all come together and I guarantee that you won't be left in the dark.

Her interior thoughts I've wrung from the diary, and scenes I could not possibly have witnessed come from first-hand accounts by those who did. To make the narration run smoothly, I admit I've taken a few liberties. But as a writer by profession, it comes naturally. And since Mary and I grew up together, I feel that I know her as much as myself, even more so, perhaps, since she revealed herself in the diary more than I would ever have dared to reveal myself.

As for my own thoughts and perceptions, I have occasionally— well, more than occasionally—interjected them in order to make more sense of it all and, hopefully, slow down the reader's rush to judgment.

I'm sure that will happen: Mary's view that God and the church and orgasm are all one—is not going to please everybody. But if you are able to see that everything was endemic to the magic circle which she speaks of so frequently, and to keep in mind that religious law has taught us to cringe, you will see that she's not as heretical or unhinged as you might think.

To start from the beginning, Mary and her three sisters were, as children all touched by their father's magic wand. Of course this was his penis, but Mary referred to it that way occasionally, and you shall see why. Now whether or not this wand of his caused the sisters to have the outcomes they had—Margaret's strange death, for instance, Alice going insane, and Barbara becoming an exotic dancer at a strip club, well, that is a hard one to decide. Mary was the only one to lead a normal—well, sort of—life.

Her father, George Armstrong, was, like mine, an attorney. In fact they both worked at the same law firm—Matheson, Morley, and Weinstock—until George got into politics and became a senator in the Republican party. He ran for president twice and withdrew twice, the second time after Barbara was arrested. But neither instance affected his popularity, and he continued to remain a strong presence in politics.

After reading Mary's diary I searched my mind to see if there were any clues as to his part in what Mary often referred to as the magic circle, but I could find none. Nor to borrow a phrase from the Roman poet Catullus (who I decided to read after seeing the strange part he played in Mary's life), when the Senator undid the zone of each daughter.

***

Diary: When I have an orgasm now and think of my father, I should despise him, but I don't. It was all too beautiful. I excuse his betrayal— what other word is there?—and blame myself and can't forgive myself even though I was only a child. But why, I wonder, is that? Who was I then bothering, me, a young child, simply enjoying such bliss?

***

And bliss it was indeed, so for many years she pondered over the question—why were the consequences of this childhood transgression often so dire? Something big—really big—had to be behind it. The answer came one day as she was sitting under a palm tree at Santa Monica Beach, trying to avoid being soiled by the seagulls that were flying about in great abundance. As she watched the rowing motion of their wings, one of the gulls took aim. As the whitish goo hit her head, a flash of light went off and, in that moment she knew that the magic wand, the penis, was only the tip of the iceberg. Beneath it, in the frigid waters of hate and fear and murder and torture and ignorance and blight and cruelty and other horrors mankind inflicts on itself, was God Himself!

Now, this was no Biblical Job-berating-God sort of thing. I'm sure you'll be as surprised as I was to learn why she decided that He was the problem. Or maybe, more to the fact, that His identity was the problem. This is because she came to believe—thanks to the magic circle—that orgasm was God, and God was orgasm. Now, a few hundred years ago she'd have been burned at the stake for this heresy, and me, too, perhaps, for being her friend and for thinking, sometimes, that maybe she was right because having an orgasm always makes *me* think of God. But maybe that's because I'm grateful to Him for the experience. In Mary's case, it's quite different. It was that tool which George had used for breaking and entering her.

Diary: My father was like a god to me, and when he touched me, I knew he was God.

***

But despite her sentiments, her heresy if you will, I think it was religion, ironically enough, which kept her intact—the magic circle does tend to impair people. Consider all the many people who are troubled or in trouble—perhaps there's no difference—and go to prison (penitentiaries to do penitence) for things like murder, robbery, pedophilia, white collar crime, and the like—who turn to religion.

5

But why not, since religion, with all its guilt-inducing "thou shalts" and "thou shalt nots" is, according to Mary, what made them think they were bad even before they committed their crime. Naturally they will try to make peace with these commandments, the source of their crimes, in hopes of untangling themselves and beginning anew.

"One of my father's clients," she wrote, "in San Quentin on death row for murdering his business partner, earned a doctorate in ministry and, before his execution, was ordained a minister. Well, it doesn't always help, but these undertakings are apropos if religion is, at bottom, a skewed idea of God and the source of their anguish.

"But others who have become holy have, at the last moment, been granted a reprieve. That shows you how embedded religion is; even the parole board is taken in when there is a show of piety."

Yes, religion is very powerful. It drew her, among other things, to a man who had once been a Catholic priest, and it was this very fact that helped Mary keep from following in her sisters' footsteps. That he had once been addressed as "father"—Father Larson—didn't at all act as a deterrent, but rather the opposite. Indeed, that is what kept her with John longer than with any other man. As Gertrude Stein might have said, "A father is a father is a father."

The Senator was at first displeased with her choice—he was Protestant and his wife Helen was a Southern Baptist. But I was glad to know that Mary had finally found someone she was happy with, and I hoped that the many desultory relationships she'd been having had come to an end.

"Well, if you've never read *The Red Shoes*, you wouldn't understand," she said on an occasion when I brought the subject up. I had, at that point, counted about ten.

"I have, but what does"—I almost said slut, the word her sister, the one who went insane, Alice, used to use all the time—"have to do with a girl who gets her feet chopped off because the magic shoes she wears to church won't let her stop dancing?"

She didn't answer, and of course now I know why. How, otherwise, would she have known so much about God?

***

John Larson was never defrocked because he left the church before he could be. Being a sensitive, perceptive man and also very handsome, many women turned to him for spiritual guidance. The confession box was always in business, and his social obligations outside the church were many. He, being intelligent, and surrounded by so much sexual symbolism (the magic circle accorded Mary many such insights), such as votive candles (phallic) and aspergillums (also phallic), knew that someday he'd give into temptation, his vows of celibacy notwithstanding, and he resigned from the priesthood in good faith, no pun intended.

***

Diary: John says it's the aspergillum that finally got to him. Every time he walked down the aisle with this tool that looked like a penis and sprinkled its contents out like semen, he felt aroused and knew he had to quit. Celibacy was canon law.

John grew up in Boston and received a degree in Linguistics at Boston University. He had been searching, he said, for something (he knew not what), and before entering the priesthood, he had decided on a career in linguistics. But after giving it a go, after studying the structure, the sound, the meaning, use, and development of language, all the mysteries, the unanswered questions that lay in his heart still lay beyond his grasp—dissecting language and finding the meaning of words hadn't helped him find out who or what he was, which was, apparently what he wanted to know.

Then his mother, a devout Catholic, had said, "You will find the answer in God," and because so many boys from Boston become priests, he believed her and entered Our Lady of Grace Seminary. Eventually he was ordained and assigned to a nearby parish where, as I noted before, he was immensely popular.

But the linguistics had done him in. Knowing its pedigree (the aspergillum's)—in Sanskrit, "it breaks, or bursts forth," and the Latin, "to scatter, strew, sprinkle," and the Ecclesiastical, "a perforated globe"—was he not scattering his seed all over the place every time he used it?

When he left the priesthood, he came to Hollywood. A cousin lived there, Frank, an aspiring actor. But aside from the convenience—Frank was eager to share the rent—the move somehow seemed appropriate: the drama of the religious rituals and the drama of the movies would, John hoped, help smooth this major transition in his life. Hollywood, of course, includes Los Angeles (where Mary and I grew up), and that's where their paths crossed.

It was at one of Barbara's parties. I was there with Mary. Frank was there, too, and John, who he'd brought along. His introduction as an ex-priest made him at once a person of interest, and he soon found himself surrounded by several women, including Mary. Not yet used to real drinking—only the occasional wine left over from the Eucharist—after a few shots of this and that he asked if anyone knew that the Old and New Testaments and a man's testicles had the same meaning. I could see Mary tense up.

"How do you know that?" she asked. Her hand was starting to shake, and you could hear the ice cubes in her drink clinking together.

"Oh it's easy," he answered. "Both words come from the same Latin root, *testis*, meaning a witness to virility. So in a sense, one is related to a man's virility, and the other to God's."

Well, this confirmed what Mary had already known about both. She blushed and asked him what else he knew. He answered jovially that the penis and the Roman gods of the household, the Penates, were both derived from the Latin *penes*, meaning within the innermost interior, more or less.

It wasn't long after the party that John lost his virginity. Perhaps in a delirium of aspergils, he was more than ready. From the diary the night it happened:

"Right now I feel we are both at the gates of paradise," he said moments before.

Scarcely had this euphemism for God escaped his lips, that I answered, "Well, as long as we got that far, we might as well go right in."

And so we did.

John says it's the aspergillum that finally got to him.

***

If linguistics hadn't helped John in other ways—in his search for the meaning of life and understanding of himself and all that, it was the opposite for Mary. Once he got her started on it, her enthusiasm for finding the roots of words never stopped. And I'm glad it didn't, because how else would I have known that language evolved, as Mary later explains, in the grunting and groaning of copulating hominids?

As for John's attraction to Mary, well, he really couldn't explain it, but there it was—a sort of wildness about her, and mystery, too. (And because mystery is so endemic to religion, I'm guessing it was mostly the mystery.)

***

The magic circle was the forbidden intimacy between father and daughter. It was all magic—the phallus, the orgasm, the first breath of sexual life. In her imagination, it was a circle girded by fire which she had entered and, in my opinion, contrary to hers, never left because, perhaps, it was impossible to escape.

Not that she didn't try. The fact that her father kept appearing as God, and John had been thinking about Him since childhood thanks to his strong religious upbringing (Rose, his widowed mother, would attend a local church during the week where the Novus Ordu, the new Mass was given in English, but on Sundays, would drive with her son thirty miles or so to another church to hear it in Latin) really helped to ground her.

She and John talked a lot about God and thought about Him even more—this is apparent from the diary—and John seemed to understand her even if she didn't always herself. They had great sex because his knowledge of theology, plus his past submersion in tall Paschal candles, small votive candles (there is a size for everyone, he said) and aspergillums all came to fruition in the bedroom. And the best part of all was that he, unlike her previous boyfriends who fled the moment she intimated (on purpose?) that her childhood hadn't been quite normal, did want to hear about it—in fact, seemed dying to hear

11

about it.

Then why did she hesitate? Especially after discovering what was to become the turning point in her life—i.e., that breaking taboos or even coming close to breaking them had not been confined to such dissolute bounders as Nero and Lot, but to the likes of Gaspar, Melchior and Balthasar themselves, the Three Wise Men who went to Bethlehem to worship the infant Jesus.

Yes, believe it or not, they—the Magi, the ancient priests of Zoroaster—were themselves into taboos, and extolled the practice of next-of-kin marriages. The Persians called it *Khvetukdas*, and according to the Magi, a marriage between father and daughter, brother and sister, and 'son and she who bore him' was not only normal, it was the best kind you could have.

The truth is, when Mary first heard about *Khvetukdas* and the Magi, she grabbed at the revelation as a drowning man grabs at straws. The revelation seemed to liberate her, open doors, assuage her guilt, justify her sins and exonerate her father. How exhilarating it was to be in the same company with the Magi. She especially loved the phrase *son and she who bore him*—they seemed so poetic, so sublime. And there was no doubt that the Magi's way was the surest way of getting into heaven.

What an eye-opener, that *Khvetukdas*! Was it really true? She must learn more about this strangest of doctrines. Had some other people promoted it—the Romans, for instance, or the Greeks—it wouldn't have struck such a cord. But it was the Magi themselves, the Three Wise Men, the Three Kings, who had followed the star to Bethlehem.

Besotted with this intoxicating knowledge, she soon learned that there were still many Zoroastrians around, and Zarathustrian temples, too. To her disappointment, no one ever brought up *Khvetukdas* at any of the many services she attended. But through this new religion (for her, that is) came her knowledge of Mithra, the Zoroastrian god of light. The Christians had thrown him under the bus over two thousand years ago, but Mary, not to be deterred, hanging on to her new discovery like a police dog to his unfortunate victim, immersed herself in Max Mueller's *Sacred Books of the East*—the *Gathas* (17 Avestan hymns composed by Zoroaster), the *Zend-Avesta* (the religious texts of Zoroastrianism), the *Bundahis* (Zoroastrian cosmology), and the *Bahman Yast* (his apocalyptic scriptures). By the time she turned the last page of the eighth volume, Mithra was not only well embedded in her soul, but she had found what she wanted. She could tell the world—or at least John—about her father, and not be ashamed.

***

Diary: Tonight I had intended to expose the magic circle, and it was there on my lips when John interrupted.

"This is sure not what they teach in seminary," he said. He was reading from *The Book of the It* by Georg Groddeck, something his friend, a priest named Father Malcolm, had sent from Boston. It was written by a contemporary of Freud's named Georg Groddeck, and was called *The Book of the It*. "According to him," John continued, "the Crucifixion is all about one certain sin, not sins in general. I wonder why Malcolm sent it."

So did I. A cold chill ran down my spine.

"Listen, here's what Groddeck wrote: 'Look upon the cross with its outspread arms, and you will agree with me. The Son of God hangs and dies upon it. The Kreuz (cross, or os sacrum) is the mother, and upon the mother we all of us must die. Oedipus! Oedipus!'

"Boy, if my mother ever read this, she would die. Imagine if this man is right. It would put a whole different spin on things. I wonder if Malcolm believes it. I know he has his own ideas, but this seems a bit far out even for him. But it is interesting to think that the Christian religion is warning us against forbidden love. Which would mean that the moral to the story—the Crucifixion—is that it's not worth sleeping with your mother if it means getting killed for it."

I wondered if that included one's father. Well, it probably, did because to be at the top of the heap only to tumble down to the bottom—like God throwing Lucifer from heaven—is the pits. You're way up there with Him, but then you go shooting down, head-first, and blaze out like a falling star. And pay for it just like Jesus did. I wonder if that's why his father abandoned him, just like mine. For isn't Lucifer the devil, the same star as Venus, goddess of love?

***

If the one revelation—the Magi—had given her the idea that maybe she was not such a sinner after all, the second one—and indeed, Groddeck's was a big one—told her that nothing short of her own crucifixion would rid her of her guilt. Yes, her father's abandonment had been no less traumatic than the Son of God's.

If only George hadn't been so loving in other ways—good, decent ways. Then, being tumbled from heaven might not have been so bad. But that was not the case, assuming that the many gifts he'd showered on his daughters—all the trinkets that children like—came from his heart, the heart of a loving father and not a dirty old man luring children with candy. (A father, Mary wrote, doesn't need to use candy; being a father is delicious enough.)

Included in his good heart were the funny stories he'd spin out on warm summer evenings about enchanted princesses and wicked queens whom they all knew was their mother; it wasn't always about being fiddled in his office.

The resentment she felt was palpable; many of her entries seethe with it. I suppose that's why she so often embarrassed the Senator in public, though why he continued to let her—that's the mystery; was it his way of demonstrating contrition? A sheepish look would often cross his face at such times. But Mary was scared, too, and often vented against God instead of him. Why not? They were the same, weren't they? Her father and God?

It must have been brutal being kicked out of heaven. Even I felt the chill when George ran for office. What did he think? That I as Mary's friend knew what had happened? Well I didn't, but wouldn't you think that the teachers in grade school, whenever they discovered her drawing pictures of penises (we all used to snicker), might have started to wonder, and not just sent her off to the principal's office to be reprimanded?

Still, her early interest in art had its rewards. Whenever the Armstrongs dined out, Mary, either on paper placemats, if there were any, or paper provided by the Senator, would start drawing pictures. This helped keep her mind off her stomach which was, too often, ready to heave up its contents: thus, unlike her sisters, hardly ever was she rushed outside to throw.

***

Diary: Even with paper and pencil in hand, it is really a trick not to. That's because it isn't easy to digest your food when you're in a room crowded with people—waiters, diners, maitre d's who know, you are sure, what's been going on with you and your father. But if you don't succeed, and you do have to regurgitate, well, that's okay, too, because then some of the guilt comes up with the food. And that's the main point of it all. What more perfect penitence is there than to regurgitate a perfectly good dinner, especially if some of it comes off on your mother?

***

The happy couple had taken a duplex in a colorful part of old L.A. It was a charming little place, a stucco in the Spanish style, near Wilshire and Fairfax. There was Canter's delicatessen on Fairfax, the La Brea tar pits on Wilshire, Farmer's Market on Third, and LACMA across from the tar pits. For Mary, the art museum was a veritable entry into the world of orgasm—i.e., art being its visual expression, she said—but more of that later.

She and John spent many afternoons at the tar pits. This is where thousands and thousands of years ago, such animals as mammoths, dire wolves, saber tooth tigers, and giant sloths would come to the pits to drink water, get caught in the tar, and die. Their bones had been excavated, and there were many life-size replicas of the animals shown in their hopeless struggle to escape. While Mary sketched the animals,

John sat in contemplative silence. The pain they both felt, contemplating the horror of the ill-fated animals, was delightful.

One group in particular caused a catch in both their throats. It was a family of mammoths, all doomed, apparently, even though the father, at the moment, was the only one struggling—a futile struggle—in the tar pit. The mother and child, still on shore, watched in horror. This you could tell, said Mary, by the expression on their faces. Even so, she and John knew it would be only a matter of time before they followed.

"According to St. Augustine, everyone, even elephants, must someday meet their Calvary," said John gravely.

Knowing nothing about St. Augustine: his name, his sentiments inspired her, and some of Mary's best pictures—drawings, actually—are of the mammoths. And the way she has captured the thick gooey tar bubbling up and oozing around the father—you can almost smell it, the sulphur, and expect the devil to rise up at any moment. Who knows what great works might have been produced if the seed for her art had not been planted in such impossible circumstances?

***

Diary: Today John unpacked the final box of his belongings that still sat unopened in the living room. As he was putting the articles away in a drawer, he paused to look at a photo which seemed to amuse him. He laughed and handed it to me.

"Those are all plebs at the US Naval Academy."

"But what are they doing?" I asked, looking at a large gathering of men circled around an obelisk which had been greased up with vegetable fat. Dressed only in shorts, the men had formed a sort of pyramid, and enabled one of the men to climb near the top and cap it off with a hat.

"It's their rite of passage," John answered, "which marks the end of their first year at the Academy. The boy on top is the son of one of mother's friends at her parish. According to her, he will, supposedly, be the first admiral in his class."

I handed the photo back and, after a moment's thought, seeing how it seemed to please John, decided not to say that, with the grease streaming down the obelisk's sides like semen (or vaseline?), and a cap at the top resembling the glans, didn't it look like the pleb was climbing up a penis?

But before I could stop myself, these words burst from my mouth.

"Wow! What an unusual way to worship the Word of God!"

"They do it every year," said John. Whether he heard me or not, or had simply decided to ignore the remark, he continued to admire the scene. "We are but a link in a chain," was inscribed at the bottom. A chain to what? I wondered, but decided to say no more.

***

George Armstrong had been born with one leg shorter than the other. Not many people knew about it, but as a child it was common knowledge among his schoolmates. They often made fun of him, and the special shoe he wore only added to all the ribbing and bullying. The deformity caused much grief, but instead of retreating into his shell, he learned that by being a clown and making people laugh he could still make friends. He also learned that playing the pity card sometimes came in handy.

At a young age he decided to become a lawyer. The outsider feeling he'd acquired as a child never went away, and while it might have put him on the path to becoming a public defender and helping the poor and downtrodden, he decided to become a corporate lawyer or a tax lawyer or any kind of lawyer who could become rich; screwing the system was his way of getting back for his deformed body.

Thus he had gone to Yale Law School, and during one of his spring breaks had taken a road trip through the South. It was there, in Mississippi, at a Civil War re-enactment of the Battle of Meridian, that he met his future wife, Helen Mulligan. She was one of several women dressed in antebellum clothes. He was not only impressed with her beauty and what he perceived as charm (she reminded him of Scarlett

O'Hara), but also with her lineage which went back to a John Mulligan who had sailed from Ireland to America in 1760. For his services in the Constitutional Army, he had been awarded 500 acres of land in Virginia; over the next 200 years, the Mulligans spread throughout the South, but mostly in Mississippi. Helen was from Decatur.

George fell in love, and over the next several months saw her often but couldn't seem to get anywhere. While he was handsome enough and good company, the other men she dated, all boys from the South, she liked better: they were still ingrained with the principles the old South had fought for. But they didn't have George's leg. As a last-ditch attempt, he revealed it; and Helen, overcome with guilt for her cavalier treatment, said yes.

They were married in a ceremony attended mostly by Mulligans, but his sister Lucille was there, and several friends from Yale. Everyone was careful not to mention his leg, but just as the newlyweds were about to leave, a KKK member took George aside and said that if anyone ever bothered him, he had friends in Huntington Beach who would be glad to take care of it.

After the couple returned to Los Angeles, George went to work for Matheson, Morley, and Weinstock as a tax attorney. A year or two later, one of his favorite specialties was setting up off-shore accounts. That was how his sister met her future husband, a stockbroker and Wall Street investor named Donald Pryce. Indeed, so good was Pryce at knowing when to buy and sell—he spent whole days and evenings at it—and so good was George at saving him money—that within a year or two after Pryce's marriage, he and Lucille bought a grand estate in Beverly Hills and a country villa in France where they spent their summers, often with Helen and her daughters.

If his rapaciousness in the stock market was ever criticized, he would say, "Predatory capitalists are a great improvement over predatory animals, don't you think?"

This went for George, too, and his knack for helping people evade taxes naturally brought him to the attention of powerful people.

Although he'd had no prior experience in politics, his outgoing personality and good looks were such that he was courted to run for the Senate. He won on the Republican ticket, and he and Helen moved to a house in Hancock Park, just down from Nat King Cole's old house.

Excited by this new life, she threw lots of parties and made the most of her Southern charm. This is why—at least according to my mother—the famous artist Thomas Bruell, begged to paint her portrait. He was the son of Walter's cousin Shlomo, and so besotted with her that, after finishing her portrait he went on to the Senator's and then, after a time, to Margaret's, Barbara's, Mary's, and Alice's. You can see that, through his art, he had a very long relationship with Helen.

The hired help were all Black. There was Derrick Clay the gardener; Marcus Bell the butler; and his brother Martin, the chauffeur. The cook, Bertha, was Black, too. Helen told my mother that it made her feel like she was still in the Old South, which is why she called them Negros.

***

Diary: We used to ask Mother if she'd had a mammy when she was growing up, and she'd say yes, all little white children have mammies in the South. We believed her until her cousin Jessica told us there was only a maid who came each day to clean.

My sisters and I liked Marcus and Martin very much: they both had soft, gentle eyes—sad, I thought—and when they spoke to us, they were both very kind. I don't know about my sisters, but it meant a lot to me. I also had the feeling they felt sorry for us, but I was too young to know why, and now I'm too afraid to ask.

Derrick would cut roses for me because he knew it was my favorite flower.

***

The supposedly rational need for the Senator to distance himself from his law firm—i.e., from Walter Weinstock who was Jewish—

during his first run for office to make sure that, even though the surname Armstrong was Gentile enough, no one would associate him with the conspiratorial bankers and Zionists who intended to take over the world was, Mary thought, bullshit. Like the sea anemone that instinctively closes its tentacles as soon as it's touched, George, with his many transgressions all rooted in his disobedience to the Old Testament laws, was just as instinctive. And because the Jews are so deeply connected to these laws, he laid his own guilt at their doorstep and acted accordingly.

This was Mary's own idea, of course, and in wanting to formulate it, she decided to use Walter as a sounding board. He had been forgiving of Walter, and wanted to remain friends with his former partner in spite of all the slights: being a Jew, the expediency of George's actions were totally understandable, Walter said. Of course, in discussing her ideas with him, she could not tell Walter where her inspiration came from. But even so, there was so much fertile soil on which to expound—not just her immediate family but the whole world in general.

For instance, the Mulligan clan themselves had gone to great lengths to hide the fact that there was Jewish blood in their history. Even the progeny of the great-great aunt who had married a Jewish doctor, and all their subsequent progeny, never claimed to be anything but Baptists. Was it because they harbored the same guilt that had made George distance himself from Walter?

Why not? If the Jews were persecuted for killing Christ, and if his crucifixion was, in fact, all about forbidden desires as Groddeck had proposed, then maybe that's why they were hounded and why people froze up and denied their Jewish blood. With Christ's death there was no more access to magic circles—a dead man on a cross stood in the way. Perhaps that was why Jews were not just Jews but "dirty" Jews because sex was itself deemed to be dirty. Yes, it was all about sex, and forbidden sex at that.

"Well, I don't know," said Walter finally, looking at her with a blank stare. "You might be right," he said, "and then again you might be wrong? Who is to say?"

(And who of us can, without experiencing God the same as Mary had?)

***

When the suggestion was made that George run for president, he was at first hesitant. With all the inadequacies he'd felt as a child, how could he be Leader of the Free World? But Helen and others pointed out that many past presidents had done lousy jobs, and the more he thought about it, envisioning himself in the highest office in the land, the less stigma did he feel for having a bum leg.

His campaign got off to a good start. He was charismatic and humorous. With his charming wife and four pretty daughters, he was obviously a good family man. But shortly after he began stumping across the country, an ad appeared on television with the picture of a club foot and some ugly platform shoes. His opponent, actually from the same party, had said, "Do you want these platforms on YOUR platform? What platform is he really running on?"

George thus explained to the world that he didn't have a club foot, only a foreshortened leg. But fighting back was too much. All the pain he had felt as a young boy returned, and he decided to withdraw from the race. It was the outcry from the public and the sympathetic press that made George decide to run a second time. But when Barbara was arrested, he opted out again.

Helen's disappointment turned into a life-long grudge. Mother says that Helen never forgave him, not only for his shortened leg but for his premature withdrawals as well, and would have left him if it hadn't been for the presence of the children's riding instructor, Baron Wolfgang von Clapp, who had, for a long time, been indispensable to them both.

***

Helen loved to ride. Riding did something for her that George was never able to do. Thus her disappointment to learn, after settling in Los Angeles, that the old bridle paths in Beverly Hills, the ones the movie stars used to ride in, had been dismantled in the '60s, about the time she was born. But the 4,000 acres of wilderness in Griffith Park still had many paths, and she rode as often as she could. This is how she met the baron. He had a riding academy in the park, and the two were often seen taking his horses out for pleasant rides on the Old Zoo trail.

When her children were old enough, she told George that it was imperative for the daughters of a senator to ride. You never knew, she said, when they might be invited to go on a fox hunt in England. The baron's academy was where the girls tried to learn. It was not easy.

"We were so afraid of everything," Mary wrote, "why shouldn't we be afraid of horses?"

Alice, the youngest, who may or may not have already fallen from grace—Mary wasn't sure—was the only one who seemed able to keep her saddle.

"Ja wohl, ja wohl!" the baron would say each time she completed a successful round in the ring. But that was only when he was watching and not lost in conversation with Helen. This is how it was when Margaret's horse—a big gray gelding—began to gallop madly around the ring. It wasn't for the first time, but she fell off anyway and lay crumpled in a heap.

During the next several months that she spent with a cast on her leg, von Clapp tried to make amends by becoming a frequent visitor. And thanks to Helen, he and the Senator got along splendidly. It wasn't long before George discovered what a boon the baron was at political events in Orange County. To the rich constituents in Newport Beach, always on the lookout to meet the right people, von Clapp impressed them with his name. For the poorer people in Huntington Beach, well, von Clapp being German was, by association, a good enough reason to endorse the Senator.

Almost at once the baron took Helen's place on the hectic drives to Orange County. Which was fine with her because she was tired of hearing the same subjects discussed over and over—money, the stock market, and women's breasts.

But von Clapp, who loved it, would often say to his wife, Baroness Gretchen von Clapp, "Ja, ja, meine Schatz, you are so big, I want to take you to Newport and show you off."

And though it was embarrassing to the Senator, how von Clapp would burst into loud laughter when the audience at Segerstrom Hall applauded between symphonic movements (you could even hear him when the concerts were broadcast), no one ever mentioned it.

During his visits to the Armstrongs, the baron liked to bring marzipan and strudel cakes made by his wife, the baroness. When he was invited for dinner, he brought her, too. On one such occasion he gave Margaret a copy of his favorite boyhood book, *Struwwelpeter*. Indeed, it was still, it seemed, his favorite.

"Ja ja," he said as he and Gretchen were dining on lobsters, "Schiller is great, Heine is great, Goethe is great. But Heinrich Hoffmann, dear friends, the author of *Struwwelpeter*, is the greatest of all. Whenever the baroness is acting up I bring out *Struwwelpeter*: 'This is what happens to bad little children,' I tell her. Not that she is a child, but she knows what I mean, ja, Schatzie?"

He threw Gretchen a loving glance and patted her plump hand, which was not easy to do since she was sitting across the table next to George. She pulled her hand away and said, "Wolfgang shouldn't have given it to your children. It's the worst book ever written."

***

Diary: As a tree blows in the wind and rain falls from the sky, is it just as natural for people to climb the ladder and meet the right people as they strive to be at the top? Or are they in unconscious over-drive to prove to themselves they are not worthless beings still running from the dark thoughts and forbidden desires they've secretly harbored since the days in their mother's womb?

And for those that are, the lucky ones will go to their graves never knowing why they struggled to be at the top, while the unlucky ones like me, who know why, will never get to the top.

***

Once again Walter became Mary's guinea pig. Unable before to convince him—why everyone hated Jews and criticized them for everything except going to the gas chamber—she decided to try again now that she had new proof, Franz Cumont's *The Mysteries of Mithra.*

This was the third revelation in her life, *Khvetukdas* and Groddeck's Crucifixion being the first two. In pursuing the Magi—the allure of *Khvetukdas* shining as brightly to her as the star of Bethlehem had to them—she had come across Cumont, and gained further insight into their behavior.

In their religion, light and darkness represented the battle between good and evil. This played out in Mithra's struggle with a wild bull. When he overcame the bull with his sword, an event that was celebrated as the tauroctonous—bull slaying—wheat and vine sprang from the dying bull's body. The sacred drink made from this vine was part of the mysteries and rites.

Jesus had even more in common with Mithra. They were both born on the same day, December 25th, and like the bull, Jesus was sacrificed to purify men's sins. The tauroctonous and the Eucharist used the same ingredients—wheat and wine.

"What does this have to do with me?" asked Walter listening patiently.

"Well, the bull was very good at wiping away men's sins, especially when they bathed in the bull's blood," Mary said. "People were happy and left the Jews alone. But then Jesus came along, and it was determined that if you sacrificed a man instead of a bull, and the wheat and wine come from a man's body instead of a bull's—a body that only another bull could identify with—more people would join the religion. That was the genius of the new religion. But in seeing a dead god instead of a dead bull, it was harder to atone for one's guilt; and since

24

the Jews killed Jesus, they were blamed for setting up the Crucifixion and making it so hard. In revenge, the Christians have made pogroms ever since."

"I don't suppose there's any way to go back to the bull?" Walter asked.

Mary thought maybe it wouldn't be, since Europe and especially Germany already abounded with mithraeums and tauroboliums, the vaults where converts were baptized in the blood of a bull and their sins forgiven. Perhaps that would end all the anti-Semitism in Europe?

But the crux of her argument was still to come. Since Mithra was the god of the Magi, and the Magi believed that forbidden love was the highest good of all, wasn't that all spoiled when they came to Bethlehem to worship a new god and start a new religion? And since Jesus was King of the Jews, hadn't the Jews spoiled *Khvetukdas* for the new converts to Christianity? Was the visceral hatred of Jews, expressed concretely by the Nazis, rooted in *Khvetukdas*—in the forbidden desires of magic circles? If the violence didn't begin in the gonads, in orgasm, in the reptilian brain that was still alive and well, then why was there always this sexual connection with the Jews— WWII cartoons of Jewish men raping Aryan women, Jewish men with big phallic noses? Why that continuing search, even as the war in Germany drew to a close, to snuff out any lingering pockets of Jewry? So visceral it was—it couldn't have been just because the Jews killed Christ. Or could it, if the Crucifixion was, in truth, Oedipal?

Even if FDR was President and had political things to consider, couldn't his reluctance to let the Jews escape from Europe, and the military's refusal to bomb the railroads going to the concentration camps, have come from those same visceral, vicious, snarling roots—a primitive, gonadal instinct for lawless sexual freedom? And wouldn't that explain why the entire world shut its eye to the Final Solution? It was not, in fact, a question of it failing to understand what was going on, but of understanding it only too well.

Once again Mary's argument fell on deaf ears. Although he wasn't a religious person, Walter refused to believe that it all started in the gonads and that God was orgasm and orgasm was God.

"You cannot," he told her, referring to the holy nickname of God, "change 'I am what I am' to 'It is what It is' or 'It is what It isn't' or 'It isn't what It is,' because that would be sacrilege."

***

Alice's obsession with Rigoletto began when George took the family to see Verdi's opera at the Dorothy Chandler Pavilion. He had intended it to be a lesson for his wife and children—who had suddenly stopped showing him any respect—to see how much people with deformities (Rigoletto is a hunchback) tend to suffer, and how a deformity can affect one's personality. Alice was still very young, and by the end of the opera, when the deformed father leans over his daughter's body (whose death he is more or less responsible for), Rigoletto left an indelible impression on her as did the curse that he speaks as the opera ends.

The following evening the Weinstocks had dinner at the Armstrongs. Like everyone else, they ate lobster. It was George's favorite food, but because Bertha balked at the idea of cooking the lobsters alive—"No way am I gonna scald them poor creatures to death"—it was the Senator who dropped them into the boiling water.

The Weinstocks had also attended the opera, and to George's discomfort, they began to talk about it.

"What a pathetic creature," said Sarah, Walter's wife. "He was not only deformed physically but mentally, too. A very cruel man, I would say."

"Not all deformed people are cruel," said Walter as he dipped his lobster into a well of melted butter. "I have a client who is cross-eyed, and he is very nice."

"Was Rigoletto really such a bad person?" Alice ventured shyly. "After all, he was really just trying to protect his daughter from the duke."

"Yes, but some people thought his daughter was actually his mistress," said Margaret. "I mean, isn't that kind of weird, like Rigoletto's really into fucking his daughter?"

"Please don't use that language," said Helen.

George, who up until now had remained uncharacteristically quiet, said in a vehement tone, "He was under that damn curse. What was it? Maley... maley..."

"Maledizione," said Marcus helpfully as he refilled their wine. Everyone knew that Marcus loved opera and often acted as a super. Only last week he'd appeared in Aida carrying a spear. Walter snickered.

"I suppose your favorite opera is Othello?" he said.

"No, it's Nabucco," Marcus replied.

As he left the room, he began to hum *Va Pensiero*, the Chorus of the Hebrew Slaves.

After a few more comments about Rigoletto, like why did his curse make such a powerful ending? And other things, like why, in other Verdi operas, there was a destructive father, and why, in operas in general, the women always died—was it to show the composer's sympathy for them, or his antipathy and contempt?—the conversation went off in another direction.

***

I know I'm getting ahead of myself, but it seems like the right moment to include the following entry because of what stayed in Mary's mind most that evening. It was the memory of Walter and Marcus mixing it up. She liked them both and was puzzled by what, over the years, was an apparent dislike not only between them, but between Jews and Blacks in general. In pursuit of her own redemption, of course it had to do with God and orgasm. You may not agree with it, but it does seem to make sense.

Diary: Blacks blame Jews for creating a Bible that equates darkness with evil, and Jews blame Blacks for being the earthly manifestations of that evil. So, like everything else in the world of humans, it comes down to the gonads. But neither party knows this because it began so long ago, perhaps with the hominids and their magic, that transformed orgasm into God.

***

As the sisters grew older, they tried their best to fit in with the crowd, but it wasn't easy thanks to George's monkey business; the secret they shared took its toll on their ability to make friends. Margaret was the most successful, having discovered how much fun she could be under the liberating influence of alcohol. Barbara and Mary, on the other hand, undertook pursuits that didn't entail social interaction—Barbara with ballet, Mary with drawing, and Alice with singing.

Though it was not really known at the time, she had begun to train her voice in hopes that she would someday become an opera singer and sing Gilda's famous aria, *Caro nome*—Gilda being Rigoletto's daughter. After school she would hurry home and practice her scales. Whether it was a natural misfortune or something else, her voice was horrible. It drove everyone to distraction, and some of the family thought she was doing it on purpose.

I overheard Marcus on occasion, telling his brother how lucky he was to be away most of the time, driving around town with Mrs. Armstrong. When Alice's voice began to take on a mannish quality (Mary told her she sounded like a water buffalo), she started singing arias written for tenors. One of her best was the duke's aria—Gilda's lover—*La Donna e Mobile*. Bertha became concerned.

"Poor child," she said. "You'd think somebody would start wondering, wouldn't you?"

But other than being annoyed by the sounds that came from Alice's room, no one else was. If only there had been a gypsy in the house who could foretell the future.

28

It began so long ago, perhaps with the hominids and their magic that transformed orgasm into God.

✳✳✳

Good and evil, darkness and light. How much of a part did they play in Mary's life! The magic circle—the defining moment of her childhood bathed in incandescent light—was countered by all the darkness it brought afterwards—multiple orgasms, aside. Had she confronted Helen earlier on and not waited until the last minute when it was too late, she could, perhaps, have extracted and purged Helen's darkness from her own. But would there, then, have been a diary such as this? Where all the dots she connected—Helen, slavery, the Civil War, vaginas, orgasm—make for such good entertainment?

"For instance, The Civil War," she wrote, "was really not fought for economic reasons. Truth be known, it was fought in order to keep the darkness from overtaking the light. It was the deep South's literal interpretation of the Bible, of good and evil, darkness and light. And by setting dark-skinned people free, would that not set evil loose to run rampant everywhere?"

Of course, this all was connected to the gonads and the magic of religion. "But to show how stupid the South's campaign to fight for woman's honor was, all you had to do," Mary wrote, "was look at her mother." Here was this perfect example of Southern womanhood—charming, refined, legs always crossed, who was nurtured in the soil of God-fearing, Bible-thumping white men who would rather lynch a Black man than let their own Magus go unchained.

Had Derrick and Martin and Marcus and Bertha been employed to remind Helen of how sacred she was? But that was all tied up with orgasm, wasn't it, with God dividing light from darkness? Helen came from that, and with such a sacred vagina, she must have thought how unfortunate it was that the only way to have children was to grin and bear it and let a man use it. But when she had all the children she wanted, she closed the sacred entrance off, and the Senator had to seek his pleasure elsewhere.

Now I ask you: how many people can connect their mothers to God, orgasm, and slavery in the Old South? Not many, I suggest, outside the magic circle.

***

Diary: Like the fiery furnaces of Baal awaiting to devour little children, the yawning chasm of mother's vagina was just as deadly. In my childhood nightmares, I was the squirrel that got crushed under a falling tree; the tree frog that was cut in two by a pair of large shearers; a figurine seal made of porcelain which I handed to Mother, as if it were an offering, after it was shattered.

Yes, my early immersion into abandonment and guilt—Father, why hast thou forsaken me?—had a lot to do with her. Perhaps I should not be so hard on her. Jesus died in his mother's arms, and I died in my father's.

But what a beautiful sin it was, and so magical. Worth being crucified for. Ecstasy is death, too, isn't it? I wonder if Jesus knew this.

It's too bad He died and could not relive the same magic. When John pleasures me (or I pleasure myself), I'm able to relive it over and over. A sense of nostalgia often accompanies it. Could it be the source that defines that ineffable magic of childhood? A source rooted in the blocked-out memories of orgasm and not the long days of irresponsible play?

When I think of Margaret and her alcoholic stupor, Barbara and her clients, Alice and the doves—perhaps that was their way to avoid returning to the circle.

God was created to protect sons from their fathers (like Isaac from Abraham) but not daughters from their fathers. This does seem curious, does it not? But then, when you think about who God really is, I guess it's not curious at all.

***

There were many times throughout the diary when I came across what Mary said were insights she gained from the magic circle. I suppose they could be called axioms or homilies. But because of the special relationship between Mary and God, the one that began in her childhood, I think it is not inappropriate to call them canons or canonical edicts like those issued from Rome.

I'm hoping that I've not done a disservice by sometimes lumping them together. Not only does this make the journal easier to read, but also helps, I think, to show the great heights the circle took her. Some are not as profound or audacious as others; and some, I confess, though never having been in such a circle, I found myself to be in agreement with.

CANON I

"Orgasm is the wellspring of creativity, the genesis of the creative impulse."

"If you need detectable evidence that God is real, just have an orgasm."

"Of course God is manifest in everyone. It just takes an orgasm to prove it."

"The secret garden that only children can see is but a metaphor for orgasm; it must be kept secret because it is so dangerous."

"People fear sex because God has taken it over. Indeed, He IS sex, and because we fear God, we fear sex."

"To experience the convulsions of orgasm is to experience the sacred."

"Are we created in the image of God or an explosion of orgasm?"

"The verisimilitude of God comes from the reality of orgasm."

"Why are we all God's children? Because without the phallus we could never be born."

"Just as we reach for orgasm, so do we reach for heaven."

"The hostility of religion to science is easily explained: religion doesn't want us to know that orgasm is just orgasm, and not God."

***

I used to wonder (but not anymore!) why Mary never missed a chance, if opportunity arose, to embarrass the Senator. One occasion sticks particularly in my mind.

She had invited me to a dinner party at the Senator's house. Seated at the dining room table arranged with candelabra and flowers were many of George's biggest supporters, including a well-known professor from Chapman College with whom he had become friends. The consomme had just been cleared away, and Marcus was bringing in the salad when the conversation turned to Billy Graham, who had recently died. After there was unanimous agreement that he was the best evangelist ever—who else could show that God-given liberties should be preserved against government intrusion, or advocate the rule of law, free markets, and fiscal liberty, and spread the Christian message at the same time, someone said:

"I never heard anyone talk about conservative values with such inspiration."

"That's because they are inspired by Aphrodite—or Venus as the Romans called her—the goddess of love," said Mary. A hushed silence fell around the table until someone said, "And what, pray tell, do conservative values have to do with the goddess of love?"

"Well said Mary, it's not so much what they have to do with her, but what she has to do with them. The passion she produces in men, not only for sexual desire and pleasure, also produces the passion for everything else that wells up in the human heart—things like warfare, civic affairs, and politics. Disraeli thought that political parties were only organized opinion, so if the ancient Greeks were right, and Aphrodite is behind it all, then the Conservative opinion on orgasm is to keep on repressing it."

"If that's so," said someone, "then why did Billy Graham leave behind forty-one great-grandchildren?"

Despite the seeming contradiction, it brought some at the table to Mary's point of view, especially when she said that Aphrodite had risen from the foam of the sea after Cronus severed the genitals of his father Uranus, and threw them into the sea. Which was probably a metaphor for the frothy foam of semen.

The professor could see that his friend was feeling uncomfortable. So, coming to his aid, he said to Mary, "Does your passion for denigrating the conservatives, also come from Aphrodite?"

This, she wrote, scared her because it was not only Uranus' balls, but her father's too, that had given her passion. So she quieted down and went back to her salad, but not before saying that people voted from their gonads, not their brains although what, on the other hand, was the difference, if the brain was, as is said, one big gonad?

Then there was this other time at another such gathering, when the gonads were brought up again. But this time it was started by the same professor. I think he had not liked the idea of being connected before to the goddess of lust and procreation—he was still at forty-nine a bachelor—which is why, just after Marcus had brought in the lobster, and the wine glasses had been switched to a different size and a different wine, and Mary was thanking Marcus as he poured her glass, the professor, who was watching, turned to the Senator, and said: "A couple of Proud Boys just enrolled in my political science class, and I have to say that their arguments about the superiority of the white race actually make sense. Yes, I know it's not politically correct, but when you look at what goes on in the African countries, it's possible they're right."

"I don't know," said George. "That organization is a little too far to the right, even for me."

"Of course. You have to stay a more moderate course. But these boys brought up an interesting point about Francis Scott Key. He was a lawyer, you know, and in one of his cases, he said that it wasn't slavery that was morally evil, but the Black race itself; otherwise they never would have had that dark skin color."

"The composer of the *Star Spangled Banner* said that?" George asked, surprised.

There was immediate excitement.

"The Proud Boys must be very proud to know that a racist wrote our national anthem," said someone sarcastically.

Ignoring the sarcasm or not catching it, "Oh yes," the professor answered, "and they get very upset whenever they hear someone crack on the high note. The student from Huntington Beach said he would shoot the next singer who does that. The other students all thought he was kidding, but being from Huntington Beach, you never know."

In his excitement, the professor's wine glass slipped from his hand and some of its contents splashed onto the table. Even though it was protected with varnish, Helen looked worried and rang for Marcus. The professor, looking pleased as he watched Marcus' white-gloved hand deftly wipe up the wine, said: "When Rudyard Kipling spoke of the white man's burden and those who bore the task of it, he knew there was a sound moral basis for it. It was the Empire's selfless moral duty, he'd said, to manage the affairs of non-whites and have control over them."

"Control over their gonads, you mean."

It was Mary, of course, unable to control her own any longer. And before anyone could stop her, she dived into her favorite subject, the dichotomy of darkness and light, good and evil, and how it all came from the gonads and man's fear of God, transmitted to people of color. What, she asked, was the white man's burden anyway, other than to keep the dark races out of the white woman's vagina? Wasn't this what slavery was all about, keeping the dark side of mankind chained up— i.e., controlled? And for the same reason, what was giving the police the immunity to shoot down Black people on sight? That blue stripe going across the black police flag—what they called the thin blue line—wasn't that how they thought of themselves—officers standing between good and evil, order and chaos, right and wrong?

And in the same vein, was modern gun culture really spawned by the proliferation of weapons at the end of the Civil War? Or was it spawned by the white Southerner's terror once the Black man, who represented evil, was no longer enslaved? And why were there still conflicts over how slavery, the Confederacy and the war should be taught in classrooms and history books, if the terror wasn't still there?

But could you really blame the Bible for its message of light and darkness ? For making life good for white people and dangerous and sad for people of color? For shooting them down just for being Black? For being the promoter, promulgator, and disseminator of racism?

Well, you could, but what if the testicles of men were what was really behind the whole thing?—something that was started with the hominids and their magic—controlling the gonads by turning the testicles into a dichotomy—the ball on the right good, the ball on the left bad.

As Mary stopped to catch her breath, the professor wanted to know if that was why ball games were so popular, why someone had to win and someone had to lose, and on which side would they be on— the right testicle or the left? The ridicule stung, but her belief that there was a collective memory that went all the way back to the hominids— fortunately, she left it there and didn't pursue the memory back to the slugs in the primordial sea (think of the ridicule then!)—never wavered in regard to just who started it all. She was about to answer that the looser was always the left testicle. But just then, Marcus brought in the baked Alaska flambé so heavily doused with rum that everyone gasped with delight, and the dinner concluded without any further discussion of the gonads.

***

How she came to believe, and with such certainty, that men were afraid of the blackness of their own souls, she also struggled to understand. Though she credited everything—her insights, visions, canons, axioms—whatever you want to call them, to the magic circle, did that really explain it? There had to be a "how" to it all, like how did the magic circle provide the insights? Was the evil—i.e., the Biblical darkness—the taboo itself? Or was it the guilt? What inspired a white man's passion for a Black woman? Was he delving into the dark side of his subconscious and hoping to have orgasms that came from his forbidden desires? If only she could remember the teacher's name, the one back in grade school who was always, it seemed, singling out the only little black boy in class, and ask her if she paddled him more often than the others because of something going on in her vagina.

The Darkness and the Light—Good and Evil—all that came from the gonads. But was the darkness from the forbidden act itself or from the guilt one felt afterwards? Was Good not just good, but also how good the forbidden act felt, how good to be free of the taboo? But the Evil that came later—were people evil because it felt so good? Was that where evil—the concept of evil came from? Was it evil to feel so good? Did Good and Evil (just like God and orgasm) come from the same coin? And would she ever, she wondered, be able to figure it all out?

***

Diary: Have the orgasms I connect with my father caused me to connect and confuse orgasm with our Heavenly Father? But if they have, maybe I'm only following in the path, well-trodden, of people long, long ago. For instance, how did this whole idea of God as the Father come about in the first place? When you think about how things might have been a million years ago—and that's when some experts think that our ancestors began to speak—and you know that in the animal kingdom, a male lion will kill his young if he thinks another male is the real father—and a million years ago there must have been a lot of lions running around and setting the example—why wouldn't those hominid fathers do the same thing—kill their young—if they were not sure? By witnessing such malevolent power, wouldn't others have pause before confronting such a beast?

When you see how a newborn looks into the face of an adult—I'm remembering Margaret's twins when they were born—it's all wide-eyed in seeming wonderment. But terror is expressed that way, too, so maybe it's thinking, who is this monster? I remember how her babies would cry if she looked at them without any kind of expression—which, sad to say, was quite often. It even scared me, it seemed so unnatural. So if a face without expression can do that, what did the faces of the earliest gods do, the ones in Mesopotamia with the faces of monsters? Faces so inhuman, not only to warn children to honor their father, but also to confuse him with the gods? And since this was—is—all mixed up with sex and procreation, why shouldn't orgasm have morphed into God? Or, putting it another way, why couldn't God—i.e., the hominid father making sure of his power—the monster whose face the newborn hominid looks into—have morphed into God the Father? Strange thoughts and happenings must have gone on in those days, and if it didn't start with the lions, it had to start somewhere.

***

I know it took courage to say the things Mary would say at times around the Senator. It wasn't the subject matter per se—the gonads and such stuff. She was always trying to make people see and understand what she had learned in the magic circle. But multiple orgasms aside, she was very frightened of her father, and I imagine her speaking out on occasion was her way of trying to get over the fear. Of course she had good reason for this fear, but what reason have I? That I, too, am scared of my father has no sound basis. He has always been kind to me. Is it possible that, maybe, all women are, in some unfathomable way, afraid of their fathers? A terror that reaches down or rises way up from somewhere in the clitoris, as Mary seems to think?

But wait. Here is another reason—actually two—why she never missed a chance to instigate controversy and embarrass the Senator. I would never have guessed it until I read the diary. Yes, there was the fear, but there was also anger. Not because he had molested her, but—get this—because he'd stopped molesting her. And she was angry at herself for being angry that he'd stopped. Which leads me to think something as outrageous as, "Well, if it was as great as all that, maybe the Magi were right after all."

Sometimes I wish I had never known her. Her thoughts and her ideas lead me to places I feel so uncomfortable in. But I still love her and loved her back then, and having her diary makes me feel like she is still here. Indeed, the more I read it, the less uncomfortable I become with her thoughts, and many of them really don't seem all that threatening—unusual, perhaps, but not threatening.

***

After college Mary tried to make a living as an artist and free herself from the largesse of her family. To her disappointment *and* mine—I so wanted her to succeed—she wasn't able to; the art galleries, even the ones in Laguna Beach, said no, and although he tried, the Senator was unable to persuade them otherwise. (Not surprising: Laguna was the only city in Orange County that didn't vote for him.)

Her paintings, though well-executed, were uninspired, and her sculpture was no better. The clay figures she'd made of nude models in a sculpting class were so flat that the instructor had put his hand on her shoulder and shook his head sadly.

"Have you ever considered ceramics?" he'd asked.

Yes, she dared not transmit her passion, her sensuality, onto canvas or clay. It would be too revealing, where the source of glory came from. No, that must never be expressed in public. But there was even more to it—a second element—that explained her mediocrity. Not only was her inability to touch the creative process due to George, there was also Helen—the dangerous rival, the powerful enemy who could, with the swipe of her paw, wipe Mary off the face of the earth, or incinerate her in a mouth that breathed fire. Childish fears? Yes, but twenty years later, the danger still lurked. No way could Mary sound out her clitoris and express herself through its beauty on canvas. Not as long as Helen was alive—or any woman, really. Was she not afraid of them all? Even, she told me, of herself? And especially herself?

But was her fear only an isolated case of a neurotic, pathological mind? Or was there an historical precedent? If the Chinese practice of drowning newborn daughters, and the ancient Roman one of throwing them in wells, had originated not because girls were expendable, but because they were future rivals to their mothers, then maybe Mary's terror, coming from some ancient strand of DNA, wasn't ungrounded after all.

Oh well, whatever the case, when she realized that she could never be anything other than a well-trained hack, a painter of pictures destined for the walls of a dentist's office, John suggested she try teaching. By chance, a position for an art history teacher had just opened at a Montessori school in Los Angeles. Mary had studied the subject in college, so she applied and was hired. How excited she was! Here was the perfect avenue in which to mold young minds and pass her insights to others—insights you'd never get from Vasari or Berenson. She had no doubt that they would be well received, the school being known, as such, for its progressiveness and open-mindedness.

"I don't know," said John, still unaware of Mary's childhood. "Some of the programs are for infants and toddlers."

But Mary assured him she would only be teaching the secondary students who ranged in age from twelve to eighteen. There was no doubt that the eighteen-year-olds would get it, she said, and the way kids were today, with all the X-rated movies and such, so would the younger ones, too, perhaps.

Compianto sul Cristo morto by Niccolo dell'Arca, 1462. With a nod to Groddeck, this sculpture was to be Mary's centerpiece, or at least one of them, in her discussion of Renaissance art. What better example of orgasm's influence, even in terracotta, which is what the sculpture was made of. Hence the life-size figure of Christ lying on his back, his hands lying across his genitals, placed as demurely as a shy maiden's; his lips, slightly parted as much in pleasure as in death; the three Marys, horrified, yes, but by his death alone, or by the come-hither look of a figure in provocative repose? And finally, the Apostle John and Joseph of Arimathea who didn't look particularly saddened. Was it because it's not manly to show one's feelings, or because Christ's pose was, well, just "manly?"

In vino veritas, "in wine there is truth." But why not also in Groddeck? Perhaps dell'Arca *knew*, she said, without *knowing* he knew. Anyway, it would be interesting to hear what the students thought.

(On learning that I was writing this memoir, the school was kind enough to send me transcripts of Mary's lectures' notes. Next to her notes on dell'Arca she had written, "Include? Maybe, maybe not, I'll think about it. John says no.")

Like the fiery furnaces of Baal awaiting to devour little children, the yawning chasm of mother's vagina was just as deadly.

CLASSROOM — Day One

"Just as orgasm can be transubstantiated into God, paintings and sculpture can substantiate it into vision. This grand idea, possibly conceived of even before the cave paintings at Lascaux, captures the fleeting experience of orgasm through color and texture onto a permanent fixture which one can hold onto for eternity. Art museums can be described as an orgy of visual orgasm.

"Of course music and dance can do the same thing, transporting us into a world of subconscious desire, but we are here only to talk about art. Albrecht Durer said that an artist has to have insight in order to extract what is beautiful in nature. Well, since nothing is more beautiful than orgasm—which I'm sure some of you already know— the insight must come from the gonads, and those who have this insight will produce good art, while those who don't will produce the art that winds up in a thrift shop. Not that some very sweet things can't be found there, but that's all they are—saccharine expressions of repressed passion.

"In studying the history of art, of this wonderful transubstantiation of orgasm into vision, we are also able to learn how we have changed our views on orgasm. In classical mythology, both Greek and Roman, it was viewed as a struggle between men and gods—the friezes at Bassae are a beautiful example—the gods, of course, representing the power of orgasm. This was also true of Egyptian art, so inseparable from magic spells and rituals. These, by the way, are as transmutational as the art.

"But when the stilted academic style of any art is loosened, it's an indirect sign that our sexual taboos have also been loosened. When one style of art is superseded by another—the relative flatness of Medieval art, for instance, by the dimensional paintings of the Renaissance—it means that church, God, and His hold on orgasm have also transitioned.

"Vittore Carpaccio was quite aware of that. Look at all the broken rods which, in his painting 'Betrothal of the Virgin,' the rejected suitors of the Virgin have thrown on the ground. Only Joseph's rod remains upright—it's actually flowering—why? Because we are talking about penises and sex and how it must be approached through religious authority.

"Yes, people were beginning to get it. If there are no sexual overtones to the Crucifixion, then why did Caravaggio paint St. Francis in a state of ecstasy as he receives the stigmata from a sexy-looking angel? A rather compromising position, don't you think?

"Indeed, any artist who has painted the ecstasy of anyone—saint or otherwise—was thinking of his or her own orgasm. One could even say that the real value of art is in its ability to allow us to see in which direction our relation to orgasm is taking us.

"Such was the Renaissance; it owes its awakenings to the upheavals going on in the church and, ultimately, with God and orgasm. Humanism, the Reformation, the debates and conflicts, the revival of neo-Platonism and other ancient philosophies—all had a profound effect on contemporary thinking and theology and the relationship between man and God, man and gonad.

"And don't we see a lot of that in the works of Michelangelo? In his erotic drawings of male bodies straining and twisting and turning, are they not visions of virtual orgasm?

"Fast forward four hundred years, the artist continues to express, stroke by stroke, color by color, the deterioration of God's hold on the gonads.

"Yes, from cave paintings to the gods, to the medieval saints and angels, to abstract art at times not more than a blur—what a journey orgasm has had!"

CLASSROOM – Day Two

"Whatever is perceived as spiritual in art may also be perceived as the direct experience of orgasm. In his Surrealist Manifesto, Andre Breton said, 'Anything marvelous is beautiful, in fact only the marvelous is beautiful.' What is more marvelous (or beautiful) than orgasm? Or stranger and more bizarre than Surrealism's attempt to capture it?

"In Kandinsky's attempt, he talked about rhythmic visual experience in his paintings. What could be more rhythmic than the in-and-out movement of the male organ? That colors caused the human soul to vibrate, what better way to convey the depths of human emotion erupting from orgasm?

"But the Russian revolution may have gone one better, allowing its rejection of the church and its embrace of modernism in the arts was an unconscious desire to worship orgasm without God.

"No wonder people shy away from modern art and make fun of it. Likewise with conceptual art. No longer is orgasm sublimated through any kind of permanent medium; it is now overtly realized through the physical movement of the artist himself and the fleeting nature of the art work. We are experiencing the artist's orgasm directly as he is vacuuming a rug, for instance, or slithering about on a platform or burning up a car in the desert, its orgasmic moment permanently captured on a non-fungible token.

"Yes, that is really what art is all about, the flouting of old conservative values and an FU to those who bandy up under the banner of Conservatism, that safe haven which says that the traditions and customs of the past are the true bearers of wisdom—i.e., a safer place for orgasm to take place. What is the concept behind fifty cans of Campbell's soup other than to poke fun at our taboos and fight to eliminate them? In the old days, men expressed orgasm through religious art because they believed in a Supernatural Being. Now, because God has become amorphous, He can be expressed by blowing up cars. That's about as close to a real orgasm as anyone can get.

"By the way, it may interest you to know that commerce and trade didn't just appear out of nowhere. It came from the need to turn pigments into paint so that the artists could honor Eros visually; that today we have trains and tankers and banks and the Internet and billionaires and drug cartels and everything else under the sun, we can thank the gonads for.

"Before ending today's discussion, which I hope has taught you how the substance of visual art magically transforms orgasm onto the canvas, I'd like to give you an example of how writers can transform it, too, through the magic of words. This poem by John Keats is one of the most famous examples of all:

> 'A thing of beauty is a joy forever: It's loveliness
> increases; it will never pass into nothingness, but still
> will keep.'

"Class, could anything have inspired those words other than orgasm? By the way, it's quite natural to compare works of art in different media—paintings with buildings, sculptures with gardens, poetry with symphonies. One only needs to hear the love theme from El Cid—the slow rhythmic cadences which capture the rhythmic movement of the penis as it slides back and forth inside the vagina, to know what inspired it. I almost disintegrate each time I hear it."

CLASSROOM – Day Three
Canceled

Yes, there was no third lecture. Mary, who was going to start it with a discussion of the artist Inness, "who saw manifestations of the divine in nature, and who, in the iridescent hazes of his landscapes, sought to commune with God by capturing Him in the transitions of twilight, sunrise and sunset which, of course, boiled down to the correlation between the convulsions of nature and the convulsions of orgasm," never got the chance.

The problem was that not even Montessori's sophisticated secondary students understood much of what she was saying, except for the word orgasm. Her probing of its transformation into art had fallen on deaf ears, but not deaf enough that their parents didn't get wind of it.

Yes, even though the school was famous for its open-mindedness and informal curriculum, an emergency meeting was called of the Board of Directors. I guess there is a limit to everything, and Mary's explanation that the movement she was talking about in regard to Kandinsky was a popular movement known as synesthesia and wasn't at all dirty, wasn't enough to settle the twelve members' nerves. Matters were made worse when one of the parents produced a print Mary had passed out in the classroom of Fra Angelico's painting, *The Annunciation*. Her caption read: "Why did the Renaissance painter Fra Angelico paint angels in robes of pink? Because pink is the closest color to the genitals, and does not divine power—orgasm—come from there?"

Another example was produced: William Blake's painting, *Satan Passing Over Eve.* Pointing out that Satan looked suspiciously like the artist, the caption read: "Blake could never have made this picture unless he had very explosive orgasms."

And then there was Walt Whitman. Knowing that she thought he knew a lot about orgasm, it wasn't surprising to find this in her diary. "After I recited Keats, there were many students looking at me with blank expressions. So I decided to recite one by the great American poet, a poem called 'O hymen! O hymenee!' Why? Well, since Hymen was, in ancient Greece, the god of marriage—hence consummation— surely a more visceral example would be more easy to understand, how poets are inspired by orgasm."

Here is the poem which she recited extemporaneously to the class:

'O hymen! O hymenee! Why do you tantalize me thus?

O why sting me for a swift moment only?

Why can you not continue? O why do you now cease?

Is it because if you continued beyond the swift moment you would soon certainly kill me?'

Aghast at hearing herself being called a pervert by one board member whose son was now wearing his sister's pink t-shirts, and unable to explain why she was not a pervert (i.e., how the beauty of the magic circle had changed her perception of the entire world) Mary resigned. I'm sure it would have made her feel happy and maybe even vindicated to know how much a class could miss a teacher who had only been there for two days, but that didn't come out until her memorial service, and then it was too late.

***

I hope I haven't given the impression that the Senator was crass or boorish. He went to operas and symphonies and took the family with him. But once inducted into politics, it's understandable why, as a politician, whenever he was campaigning in Orange County, he went around in Reyn-Spooner shirts, a short-sleeved cotton shirt popular in

Newport, its repetitious patterns of boats, fish, planes, automobiles, people—i.e., anything and everything—usually placed in big or little squares indicative, Mary said, of how their fans perceived the world. But her father and von Clapp were always ready to listen in on such favorite topics—noted once more—as money, the stock market, and women's breasts and the puerile jokes that were told about them.

Unless Helen was there. She was very cool to people she felt to be beneath her—which was most everyone—and what gave her this sense of superiority was the fact that she was a direct descendant of a slaveholder who had owned a plantation in Mississippi. His name was John Adams Mulligan, and in a privately printed genealogy of the Mulligan clan kept on a coffee table (their claim to be descended from an Irish king named Brian Boru was never proven despite the coat of arms), there was an entry Helen had marked in red:

"John claimed and proved up on some 3,500 acres of what is now the Oakland community, north of Decatur. He bought slaves, planted cotton, and prospered... Just before the Civil War, John bought up extra slaves for a bargain expecting to sell them after the war and make a profit. The slaves were freed so he lost the slaves and the money he paid for them."

"You'd think she'd be less proud of it," my mother had said. It wasn't often she found fault with her friend. Yes, despite Helen's shortcomings, Mother was quite fond of her. Helen's childishness and immaturity, which Mother attributed to a deep insecurity, was often disarming. And at times when she was drunk and vulnerable, she was even more likable.

But if what Mary says is true (and according to her, there is only truth to be gotten from the magic circle because it is the only place on earth where lies cannot be told), then Helen was proud of her heritage because slavery was rooted in the sweetness of all that's forbidden. As were the haunting melodies, said Mary, of Stephen Foster.

***

Diary: We were supposed to go to the Getty Villa tonight and see John's cousin who is acting the role of Agamemnon in Euripides's play, *Iphigenia in Aulis*. But John has the flu, so we've canceled. Thank God! I mean, how embarrassing would it be if I had to again run out of a theater, just like I had to at a revival of the movie version a couple of years ago, because I didn't want anyone to see me breaking down in tears which I did during the scene where Iphigenia is pleading with her father for her life? I mean, what else is a girl to do when she sees a father luring his daughter with promises of great happiness into his hold, and then betrays her? And just so he can get his ship to sail and win the Republican office?

***

"If orgasm is God," John said, "then that would explain why people talk about Him so much."

This observation, which Mary thought was brilliant, followed on the footsteps of another fundraiser for the Senator in Newport Beach.

"I guess their husbands aren't doing such a great job at home," she replied.

"Maybe so, but I'm tired," he continued as they made their way home on the 405, "of hearing these old ladies with blue hair talk about their church and the cookies they make for the church bazaars."

Mary didn't like it either, all the attention John got, but she could no more stay away from these events than the spider from the fly. She could only suck in her breath and ignore the lascivious looks the women gave him, especially when he was hard-pressed to explain why he had given up the priesthood.

But it was just these looks, this attention, noticed by the Senator, that made him believe John could be as much of a boon to his campaign as the baron.

This last event had been held at the Lido Isle home of George's good friend from Chapman college. It fronted the harbor, and had its own private dock. The professor was in the midst of telling a Polish joke when someone noticed that a sea lion had climbed onto the dock. With a round of profanity, he rushed out and squirted the poor animal off with a hose.

"Who do they think they are, anyway?" he said, returning. "I wouldn't mind if they cleaned up after themselves. But they never do. That's the trouble with animals. You know, those penguins in Antarctica are really cute, but boy! do you have to hold your nose!"

His wife joined in.

"My husband used to use his bb gun to get them off, but he stopped when he found out it was illegal."

"Most unfortunate, because that got them off *right* away."

When it was time for the Senator's speech and pledge of allegiance, Mary had, as usual, wanted to stay seated. How could she pledge to a flag that was really her father's penis? Well, not just his but every man's on the planet—penises in general—and thus give allegiance to man's power? But to not stand up, would that not give her away, and the magic circle, too? Thus her courage had left her; there were too many God-fearing people about, people who, to paraphrase Stanislaw Lem, would rather explore other worlds than find out what lay behind doors which they, themselves, had closed and sealed tight. No wonder the professor's father and others on the island had, many years ago, put their houses on the market when it was rumored that Reggie Jackson wanted to buy one!

***

Diary: How frightened I used to be when, if no one came to pick me up from elementary school, I had to walk home. I'd run and hide behind trees or buildings because I thought a man was following me. But since I never saw him, I'm thinking now that it was only the bogeyman. Ah, foolish child!

***

With this entry, I became curious. Having, I'm sure, never been in a magic circle, why had the bogeyman been so frightening to me? Well, did you know, thanks to Wikipedia, that he began in the 15th century as a demon in the form of a bear who ate small children for misbehaving? This, to me, seems worse than the bogeyman jumping out from some hidden place, like the closet or under the bed. But who knows what little children were doing six hundred years ago. Maybe they deserved to be eaten? Back in those days, didn't families all sleep in the same room or the same bed? And if the bogeyman is all about sexual guilt, maybe they all deserved to be eaten?

But did I deserve to be frightened out of my wits for such incursions as not eating spinach, for instance, or refusing to go to bed when it was time? Well, picking up on what is in the diary about St. Augustine and 3D ultrasounds of babies masturbating in the womb and Original Sin, could that have something to do with it? Especially if the memory is still in my subconscious?

***

What was happening to John? Instead of lightening up now that she had taught him who God was, he seemed to be more uptight. Instead of being eager—she thought he would not mind being painted in the nude, she'd had to wear him down until he finally agreed.

The John who had talked about testicles and Testaments, penises and Penates—where was he now?

"I had two friends," he said one afternoon as they sat by the tar pits, "both priests, who were brought down this way. So unfair!"

He was reading in the L.A. Times about a priest who had just been accused of abusing several women. The man was facing a severe punishment.

"I've told you how they used to come on to me. But why do they want to have sex with us? Is it because we are holy? And directly in line to God the Holy Father? To holy orgasm? I know that's what you think. It must be a real turn-on. I'm glad I got out of it."

A hardness in his voice and a nasty expression as he looked at her was chilling. Why, she wondered, was he glowering at her? But minutes later, his voice softened. He took her hand and kissed it.

"You really are, you know, the most beautiful woman in the world. I'm so lucky you're not one of those female vultures ready to take down a man of God (ex- or not ex-)—because of the lure of forbidden desires. Forbidden desires be damned!"

That night, while they made love and he groaned with pleasure, she wasn't able to climax—a rarity indeed.

CANON II

"A woman's dreaded power originates in her vagina."

"Decipher the cryptography of religion, and the results will be amazing."

"If adults perceive orgasm as an unbearable pleasure, how can a child ever begin to process it, or process the taboo, which it seems to know by instinct? No, it cannot; the child is lost forever."

"Is it God or orgasm that makes the body a temple of love?"

"The church towers, the steeples that rise up toward heaven, toward God: are they but penises that are reaching for heaven? And the tallest ones get the biggest charge?"

"If sexual rejection increases a fruit fly's desire for alcohol, why shouldn't it increase ours?"

"Were the sweat glands of our ancestors developed for chasing after prey or chasing each other, and was there any difference?"

"The divinity within, which transcendentalists such as Emerson believed was shared by all people, is rooted in the gonads."

"Orgasm is real, but God is magic."

"If the morphing of God began millions of years ago at the beginning of the hominid's reign, why is it so hard to believe that it actually happened?"

"If good and evil can only be defined by God, then they, too, are born in the convulsions of orgasm."

"All the goodness in life comes to fruition in orgasm. Is that where are concept of good comes from?"

***

Mary's portrait, the one painted by Bruell when she was five, hangs in the hallway of the Senator's house; it is admired by everyone who sees it. Unlike his other portraits of her sisters, Helen and George, the traditional kind where the sitter is placed in the center of the canvas and is surrounded by a non-descriptive background, Bruell instead painted Mary sitting in the leafy boughs of an apple tree. She gazes into the distance, her lips parted in a smile. She is holding a ripe apple, and just to her right there are two birds perched on a nest of young fledglings. In the background, soft white clouds float in a blue sky.

I supposed there was no mystery about it, why he painted her that way. But a passage in her diary in which she mentions that the only memory she had of the sitting, was a large painting leaning against the studio wall, of three life-size nuns in black cowls, their expressions severe, and it had me curious. So I decided to call on Bruell at his studio. He was reluctant at first to see me even though, both of us having been in and out of the Armstrong house for years, we were well acquainted. He finally agreed when I said I was writing a memoir for our dear friend Mary.

We met in his studio off Mulholland Drive. A large window overlooking the garden was flooded with light. Was it the same room, I wondered, where Mary had sat? Had Bruell looked as he looked now in his painter's smock and black beret? He offered me a chair and a glass of wine. By the time he got around to enlightening me about Mary's portrait, telling me first about all the Who's Who he'd painted, he'd consumed most of the bottle, and I was afraid he might be too drunk to be of much help.

"Hell, I don't know. Maybe it was the song."

"The song?"

"I never knew why George sang it to her, a song about a soldier who goes off to war and writes to his girlfriend to be faithful. But his little girl liked it so much, I said to myself, so why not? Why not put her in an apple tree?"

"Do you remember the song?"

"Oh sure! It goes like this: 'Don't sit under the apple tree with anybody else but me, anybody else but me, anybody else but me.'"

Mary's portrait, the one painted by Bruell when she was five,
hangs in the hallway of the Senator's house.

Diary: Because, says Walter, I'm so interested in his religion, he thinks I should visit a synagogue, and has thus invited me and John to an organ recital at the Wilshire Temple. We went to hear it yesterday. The temple is quite beautiful. I felt like I was in a golden womb. And the organ, too, was beautiful. Was this not the perfect place for such an instrument? All those long straight pipes, and the name itself—would the harp which angels play in heaven steer the mind toward the sacred gonads nearly as well?

As we waited for the concert to begin, one of Walter's friends came over to say hello, and asked about Walter's cousin who was on a Noah's Ark to Mount Sinai tour with his wife.

"Shlomo and Rebecca are having a great time," said Walter. "They've seen the place where Moses separated the Dead Sea, and on their way up Mt. Ararat to see where the ark landed, they met a group of pilgrims going toward the summit who had heard that the Second Coming of Christ was due there this summer."

Right away I thought of my own coming. This happens whenever I hear of Christ's.

"God needs to punish us again with another flood so we can get this drought over with," said Walter. "I need more than five minutes to take a shower."

Ah, here was another chance to express myself, share my secret without really divulging it. In a low voice I asked him why, even if there was a flood, it couldn't have been used as a metaphor for something else such as a flood of fluid coming from the penis? And what if the earth—Mother Earth wasn't really inundated with rain, but inundated with semen? Was there not a better way to wipe out Paganism than to denigrate it in a flood of its own making—i.e., ungodly sex, ungodly orgasm?

"Maybe yes, maybe no," said Walter, "but if the Flood was real, you can't deny that Noah was very lucky to have a boat."

Sarah, who had been reading the program notes, spoke up excitedly.

"Did you know that the pipe organ in today's recital has 4,102 pipes? But according to the notes, to capture the essence of God, you really need a big organ."

Of course, I thought of my father's, and felt relieved when the concert ended. It was hard to levitate on the sacred church music of Bach and Telemann. Later that evening I was duly chastised.

"In the house of the Lord," said John, "you're only supposed to levitate on the sermon, not on the rapturous music of a Rachmaninoff. Christian hymns and Gregorian chants are there to put a lid on everything that, in your words, is gonadal, and connect us, instead, to the spirituality of sacred music."

Ah yes, I thought, but to bring out the spirituality of the music, wouldn't it be better to hear bombastic music that rips through the cathedral ceilings, and expresses the sacred explosions of orgasm? Then he dropped a bombshell.

"You may think that Gregorian chants are boring, but practically the whole brain—the temporal lobe, the frontal lobe, the cerebral cortex—lights up with the incantation of words."

Incantation? Wasn't that but the chanting of magical spells and rituals that had their origin at the beginning of time? But why not, if it was all about the phallus, the Word of God? Might the Gregorian chants have had their beginning in the incantations—the chanting— of ancient priests in Egypt? With so much electricity going on—the brain seeming to work overtime—might it not indicate how much the gonads were still fighting against their need to be tamed?

Christian hymns and Gregorian chants are there to put a lid on everything, said John.

***

Besides their riding lessons, Helen immersed her daughters in ballet. Unlike my mother, Helen thought it was beneath her to be a soccer mom. So every afternoon after school, she had Martin drive them to a dance studio on Hollywood Blvd. This was okay with Mary because, as I think I said earlier, she didn't feel comfortable around her schoolmates, knowing as she did, that there was something wrong with her. I imagine her sisters felt the same way. So in going along with their mother's desire to show what superior children she had, they were not unhappy to spend hours practicing at the bar.

After a while it became clear that only Barbara was good at it. The other three seemed to fall down, doing their pirouettes, as often as they'd fall down from their horses. But how could any of them have succeeded, what with the baggage they were carrying? You can't climb the mountain if you're weighted down with chains. If the world had ever been their oyster, how could the hobbled painter, the hobbled singer, and the hobbled mother ever gain it? That Barbara got as far as she did—far enough to audition for the ABT—was a miracle. And when she did the audition, despite her muscular thighs and calves—a result, supposedly, of the Vaganova method of teaching—she was right away accepted.

She was, actually, exceptional. Her talent went beyond technique. The director perceived this, something he could only describe as a spiritual quality—how, he asked a colleague, could anyone be a Mary Magdalene and the Virgin Mary at the same time? Mesmerized by this strange magical quality, he took her from the corps de ballet and promoted her to soloist. This was unheard of, but she did not disappoint. At her performances, tickets were sold out ahead of time, and many a scalper was able to upgrade his car, thanks to her.

The day came when a production of the Firebird went into rehearsal. Naturally Barbara was the lead. It was then that she began to show up late for rehearsals, or miss them entirely. Everyone was terrified. Even Barbara was bewildered. But no matter how much pleading and remonstrating, she couldn't bring herself out of it. The unhappy director had no recourse but to take her off the lead, even though the wardrobe mistress had already started to sew the beautiful red feathers onto Barbara's tail. From that point on, she began to trip and fall on stage, and the director, bewildered and heartbroken, was forced to dismiss her from the company. Even putting her back in the corps de ballet was, the Board of Trustees said, out of the question.

A few days later, she fed the squirrels in Central Park for the last time and returned to L.A. After a few gigs in various nightclubs, she was hired to dance in private clubs. Her talent was such that she was soon living in a ritzy apartment near Sunset Boulevard (which is where Mary and John met). But the magic circle had left her with an inability to say no, and when the vice squad eventually learned that her services had veered beyond dancing, she was arrested and hauled off to jail.

***

Diary: Today I visited her at the detention center for women in Lynwood. As we communicated through a glass partition, I asked her why. Why did she louse up the ABT? I'd have given anything to be in her shoes, bleeding toes and all.

She didn't want to answer, but I persisted and finally drew the story out of her, some of it, anyway. It had happened right after mother, who had been staying for a while, in the Capitol with dad, came down to New York to visit Barbara. They were in the middle of lunch at the Russian Tea Room when Barbara hurled her wine glass onto the floor. As Helen signed the check, she looked at the distressed waitress, with a perplexed expression.

"All I said was, 'I'm prettier than you.' What's wrong with that?"

What an idiot, I thought, after Barbara finished, letting such a silly remark by our stupid mother spoil her life. Yes, it did hold the ear markings of Snow White's step-mother asking the mirror if she was still the fairest of them all. And for me, it might have held—it would have held—a lot of terror. But for Barbara?

63

"I can't believe," I said, "that that's what did it."

"I know. But after I walked out of the restaurant, I didn't want to dance anymore. The thought of me being a soloist—what I had wanted to be ever since I started lessons—seemed terrifying. How could I dance in front of all those people? I'd be thinking of dad the whole time. That's when I realized why I was there in the first place. All I wanted to do, really, was dance for him."

Wondering if that was why all little girls want to be ballerinas, a strange thought came to me. Could Barbara have been in the magic circle, too? Never had I dreamed it, and even now I dared not ask her. I wanted to, but I was too afraid.

Our time was up. We threw kisses through the glass, and I got up to leave. There was one more thing she said.

"I didn't make it to the top, but I made it to the bottom."

I wondered if she was referring to the yawning chasm of mother's vagina, and as afraid of it as I was.

***

"All I wanted to do, really, was dance for him"

I'm prettier than you.

Can you believe it? Those words sending Barbara down the rabbit hole? Or conjuring up, as it did for Mary, Snow White's wicked step-mother, the poison apple and 'Who is the fairest of them all' business? So much for the magic circle! You can have it, screw the multiple orgasms.

***

The Senator knew about a symposium being held in Washington for the International Psychoanalytic Association. Thinking he could get some insight into how people vote, he decided to attend. By pure chance it was on the day that the topic of incest was being discussed. He was given a warm welcome—everyone being impressed that a politician could be interested in things of the mind, especially the part that nobody knows about. It turned out that he and one of the psychoanalysts, a man from Vienna, had a mutual acquaintance, the baron. Thus the Senator was not entirely surprised when Dr. Strauss one day appeared, as von Clapp's guest, at one of George's Los Angeles gatherings.

Mary was there, of course, and lost no time in asking him if he'd ever heard of Georg Groddeck.

"Ah," he cried, "Oedipus! Oedipus! On the Cross, the mother, we all must die!"

"Is that why Jesus started calling his mother 'woman' instead of 'mother?'" asked Mary excitedly.

"Yes!" said Dr. Strauss. "And why he says, 'Woman, behold thy son,' and 'Woman, what have I to do with thee.' It's because he naturally doesn't want anybody to know that he has a thing for her."

Ignoring the consternation he had caused, he continued with his own evaluation of the story. Were not her three transformations all part of it?—Mary going from Virgin to Mother to Woman—because the whole thing was, really, all about sex, not about Jesus being the Son of God, and being there for the entire world, not just his immediate family? Wasn't that why he was naked on the cross, and why he spoke

66

to his mother as he would to a lover? She, no longer the pure virgin mother, but the figure of Oedipal desire? Who in their right mind would say to their mother, 'Hello, woman' instead of 'Hello, mother?'

"Yes, yes!" cried the Senator. As everyone looked at him in surprise, his face turned a lobster red. But suddenly there seemed room for redemption. If Jesus could do it, why couldn't he?

***

Every year in Decatur, Mississippi, a Mulligan and Allied Families reunion took place at the Decatur Country Club. It was fortunate that not every Mulligan attended because the country club was too small to accommodate all of them at one time. For several years after her marriage, Helen would go. This, so that she could throw in a ride with the hounds and see some of her old beaus. But after George became a senator she was advised against it. Not the riding part (although now that fox hunting was illegal, it wasn't so much fun), but the other part. This made it imperative that she be visited by cousin Jessica. They'd grown up together, and it was comforting to have this touch of the Old South in a city full of Yankees.

At the moment, Jessica was giving Helen the latest news as they sat in the garden drinking mint juleps. Mary, who was gathering a bouquet of roses with Derrick, could hear every word.

"We just had the Bobby Addy Memorial Hog Tournament," Jessica said, recounting what was going on at the country club.

"I know, I saw it on Facebook," Helen replied.

"Have you read this yet?"

Jessica handed her a letter from cousin Magnolia. As Helen read it, her face turned white. One of the cousins in Tennessee had been caught cheating on her husband. The paternity of their youngest child had come into question, and on doing a DNA test, to the husband's relief the child was his. But the test also showed that there was "hidden" African ancestry in the little girl. The father had insisted on further testing and, once again to his relief, learned it came from his wife's side.

Helen was stunned. Wasn't this cousin an offshoot of an uncle whose sister was connected to a family that was connected to the line of John Adams Mulligan? She hurried into the house and came back a moment later with the family genealogy. With a sign of relief after fingering many pages, she saw that their lines weren't connected.

"Thank you, God!" she said and saluted Him with her mint julep. Jessica clicked her tongue.

"I don't know which is worse," she said, "being tainted with Black blood or tainted with Jew blood."

"Ask Mary. It's the sort of thing she loves to discuss."

Helen waved her over. The question was repeated, whether it was worse to have Black blood or Jew blood. Well, said Mary, since the fear of either one came from the same source, the forbidden desires in the gonads, it was really just a toss up, which race you hated the most.

"See? I told you," said her mother.

After Mary left, Jessica continued to fill Helen in with the latest news. Eventually she got around to what had happened when a leader of the Proud Boys had come through on a speaking tour. He had drawn a big crowd, and signed up several new members. This had upset the local Ku Klux Klan who thought that the men who joined the Proud Boys should have joined the Klan. The scene had grown ugly and led to a fight.

"Can you imagine?" said Jessica. "I mean, they both have so many of the same values, why start to fight?"

This news inspired Mary to write the following story. I know for a fact that she sent it into the Decatur Daily Democrat, but whether or not it ever got published—that I can't say because she never told me.

TALE OF THE TESTICLES
by
Mary Armstrong

Once upon a time there was a little boy named Tom who lived in Mississippi. Being a boy, he was naturally born with a penis and two testicles. Every Sunday he went to church, and as he grew older and felt all kinds of things going on in his testicles, things he was uncomfortable with, he realized that all testicles could be either good or bad, and that the good and bad in the Bible was really about the two testicles. The one on the right was the good one, and the one on the left was the bad one.

When he became a Senator in 1960, he used his influence to keep the Jim Crow laws in place. What, after all, was White Supremacy other than the good testicle reigning over the bad testicle? From what his testicles were telling him, he knew how important those laws were, because that was what segregation was all about. And because he knew his testicles, he always ran his campaign with the slogan, "Know your testicles." Of course, the people in his state thought he meant "Know your Testament"—that is, the Bible, and was probably suffering from aphasia. So they gave him a pass and voted him in and kept good faith with the Bible and its message of good and evil—that is, the Light (White Supremacy) over the Darkness (Black Inferiority).

Eventually he grew old and died, but the White Supremacists carry on his flag to this day, knowing that he was right all along about segregation—that is, the testicles, his and everyone else's.

***

The Senator's attempt to free his daughter compounded the lifelong embarrassment of being deformed, so he didn't try very hard. Barbara was sentenced to sixteen months, and sent to a women's work camp off Hwy79 in San Diego County. It was located in a peaceful wilderness of gentile mountains, California oaks, manzanitas, mule deer and wild turkeys. Only occasionally did someone get bitten by a rattlesnake, of which there were many. But by keeping peacocks on the grounds, to eat the snakes, their population was kept low.

Mary thought it was no coincidence that it was *Puerta La Cruz*— Door to the Cross. With her newly acquired obsession with words, the fact that the cross was, in the Spanish language, of feminine gender— the article was *la* instead of the masculine *el*—gave additional proof to Groddeck's argument that the Crucifixion was Oedipal, and the cross "on which we all must die" was the mother. And since most of the inmates were minorities, she wondered if women of color were also a threat to the white race, thanks to the Holy Scriptures.

***

Diary: But now, I think they are helping Barbara with her own dark issues. She has come out—actually we both have—both disappointed, I think, to learn that the magic circle was not ours alone. Now we are wondering if we shared it with Margaret and Alice, too.

Because there are so many Black women here, I can see why Barbara speaks so often of mother. If the drive from L.A. weren't so long—it's over two hours—I'd come more often: it's so peaceful just to sit under the oak trees, watch the squirrels play, listen to the birds sing and marvel at how much every newly-formed leaf has the same shiny quality as a baby's skin.

I was there today. It was very hot, but sitting in the shade of the trees, it was quite pleasant. At a little distance, we watched a small flock of wild turkeys scratch the dirt, looking for insects.

"They make me think of the pilgrims' first Thanksgiving," I said. Barbara nodded.

"They make me think of the one when mother was helping Bertha with the turkey, and just before they put the stuffing in, I reached into the cavity and mother slapped me hard on the face. Wham!"

A yellow Monarch flitted by, landed on a leaf and flew off again.

"Did mother ever tell you to watch out for men with yellow teeth?" I asked. She didn't answer but said instead, "You have plenty of time to think here. It wasn't just the Russian Tea Room thing, it wasn't just the scarlet costume. I couldn't, you see, distinguish between Koschei the Immortal and dad."

A squirrel came over, and Barbara handed him a piece of her sandwich.

"It was the whole fantastical story about the Firebird," she continued, watching the squirrel as it sat on his hind legs chewing happily. "Here was this wicked sorcerer—Koschei—who had put a magic spell on all these young maidens, and it was only through the help of the Firebird that they could be saved. But this could only be done by destroying the magic egg where Koschei lived. But how could I destroy it, how could I kill him? That would be patricide, wouldn't it, even if he did live in an egg?"

I wondered why she didn't have the same problem with Swan Lake. When she danced Odette, didn't she put an end to the evil enchanter who had turned her and many other girls into swans?

"Well, in that case, as the swan, I had to die, a just comeuppance, I thought, for killing him."

I patted her hand consolingly. I could definitely see the confusion. In fact, I felt it, too, although I wasn't really sure about how wicked the sorcerers. Perhaps they were only trying to play out the forbidden desires of men? And why there are so many other ballets where young girls—maidens—are put under magic spells? And why so few get out?

When the PA announced it was time to leave, we got up and shook the leaves off our clothes. I was turning to go when Barbara put her hand on my shoulder.

"If only those glorious childhood convulsions could leave me alone," she said wistfully, "I know I could dance the Firebird forever."

***

Yikes! From drowning insects to the majesty and glory of God—and now, sorcerers who live in eggs—the magic circle takes you all over the place! Even preordains people to go from childhood ballerinas to grown-up call girls. But apparently it was easier for the two to discuss their father in terms of sorcerers and magicians in tights rather than a father who has fucked up his daughters. Oh well, who knows? Maybe that's the only way they could, coming as they did from a childhood where orgasms were magic.

At this point, I think I should confess that I have read the diary more than once—many times, in fact. Maybe it's the subject matter—it's hard to resist. Is there a certain voyeurism, a certain envy? It's not the guilt of being molested which haunts people, but the guilt, Mary writes, of having enjoyed it so much. People find it hard to forgive themselves. I find myself thinking about the magic circle and wondering what it's like to be in it, to experience God, as she puts it, at such an early age. I doubt she could have conceived any of her ideas, had it been otherwise.

***

Despite her fear of being discovered, Mary decided at the Senator's next pledge of allegiance to spill the beans. When it was over, she asked the elderly gentleman next to her, whose trembling, wrinkled hand had been pressed hard to stay over his heart, if he knew for a fact that it was not only his penis he was pledging allegiance to, but also to orgasm and the Word of God.

"Eh?" he said, cupping his hand to his ear, "You have to speak louder."

This was asking too much. No, in no way could she shout out that the flag was a phallic symbol, and the phallus was symbolic of the Word, and the Word was the incarnation of God, and God was the

72

transubstantiation of orgasm. Her bravery, for the moment, was silenced.

Yet every so often she herself had doubts. "Have I raised my father up to the glorious heights of heaven, or denigrated God to the lowest depths of hell?" she wrote at one point. This, I think, could be attributed to John and his frequent harping on the idea that she'd come to believe that God is rooted in orgasm because she mixed up the two fathers, the one on earth with the one in heaven. At such times, she begins to doubt and lose faith.

But then she remembers the photo on the Senator's desk in his office. It was taken when he was a little boy. He is dressed for Sunday school, and holds a Bible in front of his crotch. There is a cross emblazoned on the cover, and he holds it in such a way that the transverse horizontal part of the cross resembles the scrotum, and the vertical beam, the penis. In other words, the cross appears to be an extension of his genitals.

What further proof was needed? And her faith returns.

***

Well now. If Mary is right, there are a lot of scrotums on the covers of Bibles. But what of Groddeck? He says the cross is the mother, and upon her we all must die. But that being the case, why can't it be both? Mother *and* scrotum? But then, that's mother and son, too, isn't it? Be that as it may, I for one am ready to give up an agnostic point of view, because some of her arguments seem pretty sound. I especially like the one about the Supreme Being springing from the Supreme Moment. Orgasm for me is definitely a supreme moment.

***

Yes, transmutation was never far from Mary's mind. Obsessed by the once controversial idea that species could change over time, why could not orgasm, too, change over time—from the real thing to an imaginary thing? But if she was right, could one ever reconcile the Bible to this scientific fact? This was what worried John. How many people, he wondered, would otherwise lose their jobs? Maybe the entire body of the church!

She decided that John was right. To think of Father Malcolm out of a job was terrible. And look how confused John himself was. Because when the Senator said to him one evening during a discussion of the testicles and the Bible, "How did you ever become a priest," whether an answer was expected or not, John couldn't give one.

"In light of all the things you say your father did to you," he told Mary later on, "to serve God really didn't sound right. By the way, shouldn't George be in jail?"

Oh how crushing! Not the part about jail, but his remark about what she *said* her father did to her. Did he not *believe* her?

***

Diary: Oh well, look how he has given me this powerful tool, the origin of words. Already he has taught me how the etymology of religion: *re-*, back; *ligare,* ligament, defines religion: 'to bind back— fasten man's faith to God'. I wonder whether or not real ligaments could have once been torn from the bodies of hominids to frighten them into believing in God.

I've also learned from him the etymology of the Tongan word tabu (English taboo): *ta,* to mark, plus *bu,* exceedingly. So anything that is exceedingly marked becomes sacred. Well, since it's hard to mark orgasm per se, I guess you have to mark certain places or things, like people's vaginas, for instance. Those would be easy to designate as such. And once that's done, might not orgasm, also exceedingly marked, become God?

***

If art is the visual expression of orgasm, and music is the auditory expression, then it is no wonder that Barbara, evil enchanters aside, was felled by dance, the primordial culmination of all three. So was Alice at Dr. Niedlhauf's private clinic.

The doctor had once thought of becoming a dancer himself, inspired by the great men in ballet—Diaghilev, for instance, who had transformed his ballets into creations of great sensual beauty; and Balanchine, who probed the transformation of love into art. But instead he had become a psychiatrist.

Now, in the hope of helping his patients through dance, Niedlhauf hired Miss Sheinbaum, a modern dance instructor. To the beat of a drum, she led the patients around and around the cleared recreation room, in all sorts of movements such as crouching and springing and swaying.

Unfortunately, the amalgamation of all three expressions of orgasm—sight, movement, sound—proved to be too much for most of them. Many collapsed on the floor, Alice amongst them. She was not ready, Mary wrote, for Balanchine's probing nor, even more, for confronting the physical expression of her own orgasm.

***

I wonder whether or not real ligaments could have been torn from the bodies of hominids to frighten them into believing in God.

Diary: But now she is much better and has stopped singing *Caro nome* during her therapy sessions. I found her sitting in the garden watching the doves. It was a beautiful day, there were many around—some in the trees, others on the ground. Alice was listening to their cooing.

"I can hear what they say," she said happily, and as their little necks pulsated in and out, she began to translate.

Hhhooo-hoo-hoooo was '*Catch the ball, catch the ball.*' *Hoo-hoo-hoo-hoo* was '*That's five dollars.*' *Hoo-hooo-hoo-hooo* meant '*Right here, right here,*' *hoo-hooo-hoo, hoo-hooo-hoo* meant '*My child's dead, my child's dead,*' and *hooo-hoo-hooo-hoo* was both '*It's my birthday*' and '*Deeper, deeper, deeper, deeper,*' the latter coo heard most often early in the morning while she was still in bed.

Later, when I'm about to leave the clinic, the Matron says that Dr. Niedlhauf wants to see me. He shows me some of Alice's drawings. They aren't very good, just mostly stick figures. One shows a girl shooting a man. In another, he is falling backwards, and in another, he is already dead. The word *bang* is written in a puff of smoke.

Doesn't it seem curious that there are no bicycles in the drawings?

***

The usually locked gate off Hwy 79 and Fink Road was open. Rather than return at once to L.A.—Barbara was out fighting a fire—John decided to turn in and see where it went. After about two miles the paved road dead-ended, but a dirt road appeared at a cattle guard and went on for several miles, eventually bringing them up to a beautiful wooden gate. It was closed but unlocked, and ignoring the private property and trespassers will be shot signs, they parked the car and let themselves in.

The scenery was as idyllic as the work camp just up the road—oak trees, meadows, birds and wildflowers. They wandered around for some time. The mule deer seemed tame and didn't run off at the sight of them. After a while they came to a heavily gladed area where a creek ran between a thick line of oaks, cottonwoods and firs. There were two chairs placed near the water, and they decided to sit down. It was the perfect spot to commune with nature. After a while, Mary broke the silence.

"That tree reminds me of the Senator."

She was looking at a big dead tree just opposite them. It was dead as a door nail, its roots having been exposed over time from the high water mark. But how imposing it still was, what with its outstretched arms and its trunk soaring into the sky. And fascinating, too. Fascinated by the thought one day it would fall, and anyone sitting where she was sitting would be crushed—visualized it falling and destroying her—ah, what pleasure, this fascinating thought! Like the snake who is hypnotized by the sound of the flute, she couldn't take her eyes away.

Eventually this reverie came to an end when a skunk appeared out of nowhere and waddled toward the creek. He was very fat, and seemed to be old. Sniffing the air and seeing no one even though he was quite close, he went down the bank and began to drink. How exciting was this?! Excitement which seemed to parallel, at the same time, the excitement of the tree.

But more was yet to come. By the time he had finished drinking and licking his paws, the shadows had begun to fall. As they passed through a grove of manzanita trees on the way back, they saw the skeletal remains of a deer. Something had eaten it, and all that was left were its rib cage, its spine and a leg bone still attached to the pelvis. Could one identify with anything better than this? A beautiful creature being brought down by a carnivorous, merciless monster? Well, the mammoths at the tar pits, maybe.

What had started out as a dismally disappointing day had turned into a day of triumph.

***

Alice had stopped eating meat or, as she put it, anything that had

79

once had a face or a heart valve, long before she tried to kill Joe. But when Dr. Niedlhauf was informed that she had also stopped the soup, he was worried that she would shrivel up and fade away like the boy in *Struwwelpeter*. She had mentioned the book so many times that the doctor had bought a copy. The subtitle, *Merry Stories and Funny Pictures*, were perplexing. How, he thought, could stories about children going to hell, mostly, just for misbehaving, be amusing? Yet why *did* children like the stories? Certainly all the Armstrongs had, from what he could gather.

***

Diary: When I was waiting in Dr. Niedlhauf's office, I noticed that his copy of *Struwwelpeter* was opened to the picture of Augustus, the boy who refused to eat his soup and died five days later.

"I can't understand that," said the doctor a few minutes later. "All children love soup. I loved it, I still do."

As he thumbed through the pages, I recalled von Clapp's hearty laugh, and Bertha saying that only a German could find the humor. Dr. Niedlhauf paused at the picture of the boy who goes out in a storm and flies into the sky when his umbrella gets caught in the wind.

"That is impossible," he said. "Certainly an umbrella can, in a heavy wind, turn inside out. But carrying a child into the sky? That's nonsense!"

Not, I thought, if the umbrella is your father. As the doctor turned to another page, I continued to think of the boy and the umbrella—a red one—who flew so high up he was never seen again, and remembered the day I came into dad's library and saw Alice lying flat on the floor. She had recently started her periods, and I thought maybe she has cramps. But her eyes were squeezed shut and her body was stiff. When I asked her if she was in pain, and she didn't answer, I grew worried and decided to wait. It seemed a long time before her body began to relax, and I wondered if she had been having a fit.

When I promised I wouldn't tell mother, she described the attacks, how this feeling started in her cheeks starting in her cheeks and followed by a loud buzzing in her head, then a crushing pressure; the floor was the only safe place to be until the pressure had passed—sometimes it took several minutes—and she was able to get up.

"Well, I've had tougher cases than this one," said Dr. Niedlhauf, snapping the book shut. When I left and walked passed the doves, I wondered why I wasn't locked up like Alice. I guess I had only God to thank for that.

***

The two were sitting by the tar pit with the struggling mammoth when a figure emerged from behind a tree. It was a woman, and as she approached in the blinding sun it was difficult to make out her features. As John squinted, he jumped up in surprise.

"Mother? Is that *you*?"

It was. The two embraced and, after being introduced to Mary, the three sat down. Almost at once Rose became aware of the sulphorous vapors coming from the tar pit.

"I think I smell the devil," she cried, clutching John's shoulder.

"Oh, mother. These are the famous tar pits I wrote you about. You remember that picture Mary sent you of the mammoths? This is where they died 11,000 to 50,000 years ago."

"Not according to the Bible," she replied.

Mary was about to speak, but John threw her a warning look not to.

"I hope there is a church nearby," Rose continued, "I had to miss Mass this morning in order not to miss my plane. Perhaps that is why Mephistopheles is here."

"This is a Jewish neighborhood, mother. There probably aren't any."

"Anyway, once you know who God is, you don't need a church," said Mary.

John laughed nervously, and said in answer to his mother's quizzical look, "Mary is very spiritual and believes God is everywhere."

"Oh yes," said Rose knowingly. "It's called Pantheism. Father Conklin has warned us about it."

"Father Conklin?" said John, surprised. "Isn't Father Malcolm still at the parish?"

John and Father Malcolm were friends. They had known each other since college. Rose shook her head.

"Father Malcolm left, it was all quite sudden."

***

In Rose's sudden rush to the airport—a last-minute panic attack had made it necessary to see the ten cats she'd left with her neighbor one more time—she had left her rosary beads behind. So the next day the three drove to Olvera Street. Rose purchased a new one, and after stopping to eat at La Golondrina, they took her to the nearby Lady of the Angels Cathedral, a modernistic structure made of beautiful alabaster whose pinkish tone reminded Mary of a woman's skin. How, she wrote, could a material as hard as stone look so soft and senuous?

Unfortunately, the noon mass was already over. Why, then, was the room still crowded? A parishioner approached and urged them not to go. A group of Benedictine monks was about to give a special performance of Gregorian chants. They had come all the way from St. Ottilian Abbey in Germany.

"Oh how exciting!" said Rose, clutching John's arm and Mary's, and leading them as close to the altar as she could. The monks came on stage, so to speak, and after a nice introduction by the Archbishop, they began the chanting. It was a large group, and as she listened, Mary's eyes focused not on their long black robes, but on the men's foreheads. Since there were so many lobes and cortexes involved, she wondered whether there was enough electricity going off to light up a city.

82

Meanwhile, whether it was the hypnotic effect of the chants, or the long day Rose had had and all the stress, leaving the cats and rosary behind, it wasn't long before she fell asleep and began to snore. When they came back to the duplex, she collapsed in the spare bedroom on which she'd been counting.

***

During the next few days, John took her wherever she wanted to go. This included Universal City, San Diego Wild Animal Park, the Los Angeles Zoo, Chinatown, Hollywood Boulevard, and Grauman's Chinese Theatre. A day at Disneyland was supposed to be the climax. But as they neared the Mickey and Friends parking structure, they were stopped by a cordon of police cars and ambulances. A group of people were standing near a tarp that covered a body. John walked over to see, an employee told him what had happened.

"It's another suicide. A man jumped from the top level."

As they both gazed off toward the covered body, the employee said, "This is the third time since I've been here. The people have jumped from that same structure. Makes you wonder why they chose Disneyland to end it all."

Because of Rose's tight schedule, the visit to Disneyland went on as planned. But the man's comment about previous suicides had, in Mary, struck a nerve and caused her to wonder if the Magic Kingdom, the Magic Key—the pass that led into a world of fantasy and make-believe might indeed be a pass to something else. What was it people were supposed to make-believe in? When she was little, all this make-believe was possible. But now, why did it smack of something else, like a clever decoy for things that lie beneath? Wasn't there something in the Bible about the keys to the kingdom of heaven? Had they been transmuted into a pass called the magic key so that one could spend the day in a kingdom where there were castles and drawbridges and all kinds of things to help you gain heaven in a child's world of make-believe? Was Disneyland itself but a simulacrum to God's kingdom, a kingdom of forbidden desire? Was that what all the make believe was

83

about? All the magic? Making-believe one was going to have things one could never have outside the magic circle? Was Disneyland a simulacrum for magic orgasms? And when certain desperate people knew it was all a hoax and they could never have them, they jumped? Or did they jump in hopes of entering the Kingdom of God through the magic of Disneyland where all magic came from—the Magi and their doctrine of *Khvetukdas?*

* * *

Even though I'm Mary's friend, it's hard to believe that Mickey Mouse and the Magi all come from the same place. But maybe there's something to it. I mean, hardly a day goes by without the word magic coming up. I mean, it's like it's stamped in our brains—newspapers, T.V. quoting someone saying that something was magic or magical, to express some joyful experience. Because of the spells and incantations of the church, is magic in our blood? And all because of *Khvetukdas* and the magical orgasms of childhood? That's what the diary says, anyway. And then it goes on to wonder what the world would be like without magic—i.e., the worship of orgasm. I quote:

"If magic is something that makes something happen in the brain to make it believe something is true which isn't true, make it believe in a reality which isn't reality—a rabbit pulled from a hat, a coin pulled from an ear—could it not also have made people see many eons ago, a god pulled from a vagina?" In other words, are the roots of magic to be found in the electric signals and neurotransmitters that cause orgasm? And is that how God came to be? Because what is more magical than orgasm?

* * *

Rose was disappointed to learn that John and Mary had no immediate plans to get married. At the airport she gave them both a hug, and as she boarded the plane, told them not to forget what the Bible said about Original Sin. Later that evening, John said that maybe they should get married. Mary, who felt she had already experienced it—Original Sin, that is—demurred. Wasn't the snake, the apple, the

Garden of Eden only an argument against *Khvetukdas?*

What was the Garden of Eden anyway, if not a metaphor for the delights of forbidden love? Was not a garden—that magical place of flowers and fountains and fruit trees—but an enclosure whose root, *gher,* "to grasp, enclose," was a metaphor for the vagina as it grasps and encloses itself around the penis? Why else did Ezekiel refer to the Garden of Eden as the Garden of God?

As for Original Sin, when you dissected *that* apart, paring origin down to its IE roots, it meant "to set in motion," (*er*) and "arise and cause to be born" (Latin *oriri,* origin). Was this not as good a description as any for the penis as it arises (becomes erect) and sets itself in motion and nine months later something new is born?

"The pupil has surpassed the teacher," John said, hiding the fact that he was feeling uncomfortable. It wasn't about the evidence she had just come up with—it did set one to thinking. But now he wasn't sure if he had given up linguistics because it was unfulfilling, or because there was some other reason. And after a restless night and strange dreams, he woke up in a foul mood.

"That woman is driving me crazy," he thought as he was shaving. After nicking himself twice, he called up Father Malcolm who, he had learned, was now staying at a monastery in Oceanside, and went off to join him for a week.

***

Diary: The Senator is pleading with mother not to wear her fur coat to the lighting of a Christmas tree over on the Westside. His committee has told him there could be some animal rights people there.

"If you tell her that prairie dogs can talk, elephants can cry, sheep can dream, and flies can take naps, maybe she'll change her mind," said one of his more liberal-minded staffers.

Even so, what if it's not really the prestige of a fur coat, but an ancient DNA reminder of the old days when people lived in caves, wore animal skins, and didn't have to worry about God? Or even before that, when their own bodies were covered in fur and they didn't have to worry about anything because they were still swinging from the trees?

If only a cat or a dog could give Mother the same pleasure. Couldn't their furriness substitute for the Fall? I wonder if the stock market does the same thing for men as furs could be doing for women—i.e., taking men back to those same prehistoric days; every time Uncle Don makes a killing, isn't it at the cost of someone else? Doesn't someone else have to take the fall?

Oh, it's all so confusing. I mean, why did the hominids, 100,000 years ago, begin using shells and sharp stones to scrape the hair off their bodies? Could this have been an act to defy nature? To distance themselves from the animal world? Castigate the gonads and begin their subjugation?

When I visited Alice today—it's Christmas eve—Dr. Niedlhauf said she was again under sedation. He gestured helplessly and led me to the recreation room where a Christmas tree had been put up and many packages placed underneath. When she saw them, she began kicking at them and tried to pull down the tree.

"It took several attendants," he said, "to restrain her, and all the way to her room she kept crying out, 'He wouldn't do what I wanted!' Have you any idea what she wanted?"

By now I was sure it was the Senator. The Christmas presents would indeed be a poor substitute for what he could give her. Instead I shook my head and went off to peek in her room. Her window was open, the doves outside were cooing. As I stood there listening—*hoo hooh hoo, hoo hooh hoo*—it sounded awfully like, "He wouldn't, he wouldn't."

***

The day after her visit—Christmas day—for the first time in history—at least according to her diary—she "came" not with the usual ecstatic visions of God or her father, but with a beautiful vision of candy canes, gingerbread houses and tiny gingerbread reindeer.

They were placed beneath the green branches of a Christmas tree, just where the Christmas gifts were placed in her childhood. The sweetness of the vision held the glory of Christmas, and it was hard to let it go.

***

With Mary's discovery of the true meaning of Original Sin, she thought she understood why linguistics had failed John in his search for the reason of his own existence. He just hadn't gone deep enough. Nor, she thought, had the philosophers who, back in the 1920s, were searching for a single language that underlaid all the thousands of languages that now exist. Like John, they just weren't looking in the right place.

But if language *did* originate in the grunting and groaning, shrieking and squealing, huffing and puffing, howling and snorting of two people in the throes of gamogenesis—i.e., love-making—then here was the answer to Heidegger's, Wittgenstein's and other philosophers' search. Here was the one language underlying human speech—speech being that which defines the human form of life. And for those who had, back then, doubted there could be this one deep structure shared by all languages, maybe now they'd change their minds and see that language, like everything else, originated in the gonads.

CANON III

"As saccharin is to sugar, so is religion (God) to orgasm. Prime example: the exquisite relief an orgasm brings to the soul is mimicked by the spiritual relief it brings to God."

"It's as hard to put an end to a roll of multiple orgasms as it is to not eat up a half gallon of ice cream, once you've started."

"God is a man because God is a penis."

"God is the earliest word in cryptogram form."

"How beautiful the temples of God, where suppliant thighs await the faithful."

"I give my soul to heaven every time I have an orgasm."

"In the animal world, do those whose orgasms are the most explosive, become the ones who are the fittest?"

"What a different world it would be if all could have sex without guilt."

"What is man's greatest pleasure, to have a personal experience with God or a personal experience with orgasm? Or is there any difference..."

"In the final analysis, might the ends to which all words serve—be they recipes for cookies or equations to send rockets to the moon—be in order to keep orgasm at bey?"

"The concept of God's love being universal is not to be scoffed at, the reason being that orgasm is also universal."

"That His love is more powerful than fear or hatred is also true, since neither fear nor hatred have the power to levitate us outside our bodies as does orgasm."

***

It was only after they became adults and began sharing notes that the sisters (except for Alice) realized why they had never gotten along. The magical umbilical cord that tied them to George, had led to the jealousy and rivalry and other emotions that excluded any kind of sisterly love.

This was especially obvious with Alice. Sensing she was the weakest and most vulnerable, the sisters vented on her the most. This caused her to overeat and grow so fat that von Clapp, at one point, refused to put her on his horses. To ride again, she became bulimic.

Ironically, Helen blamed the weight gain on George.

"Whenever she spends the day with him," she said, seeing Alice sitting against a stall and crying as she watched her sisters ride by on their horses, "he buys her hamburgers and French fries."

"Dear lady, you mustn't blame your husband," the baron replied. "In Germany, everyone drinks so much beer and eats so much sauerbraten, knockwurst and schnitzel, there's no room for fast food. But they are fat anyway."

Was it wrong then, to malign MacDonald's and Taco Bell and all

89

the other fast food places for Alice's obesity? Especially, Mary wrote, if her wolfing down the food was a compulsory, subconscious, reptilian disorder built not in the stomach but in guilt, disgust, and fear of the magic circle?

***

Mary's obsession with her father's penis—hence, all penises—led to a truer understanding of all penises in general. Almost any topic could throw a light on them and lead to some truly amazing discoveries.

For instance, taking Walt Whitman's cue that God's highest work was the human body and that people should stop worshiping kings and queens and start worshiping their bodies instead—the heart, he said, of democratic politics and human understanding—Mary took to mean that, in singing its praise, he had, perhaps, insights similar to her own. Was not his poem, *I Sing the Body Electric*, but a paean to the electrical impulse of orgasm?

Had he, too, seen the connection between the king and God and sacred orgasm? A connection that went way back to when? To the king's divine right to rule? But how did that idea ever come to be? Where and how did this connection come from, this notion of a king's connection to God—hence orgasm?

Lo and behold! Learning the true meaning of Original Sin was nothing compared to learning where the divine right of kings came from—although since everything was rooted in the gonads, why be surprised that the divine right came from the penis? This is how she explained it.

From the Indo-European root *reg*, meaning a movement straight from one point to another, i.e., a movement along a straight line, comes the Latin word 'regere,' meaning to guide or direct in a straight line. And from that comes the word 'rex,' meaning a king.

Now what better description of a penis is there, than a movement which is guided and directed straight into the vagina? Why should one

90

not, by use of this definition, become "a true guide, a powerful chieftain" and "have direction and command over people?"

Regal, rule, erection, rectitude, rector, righteous and rectum—all rooted in *regere*, all rooted in the penis. And the same thing in other languages, too—Germanic, Spanish, Portuguese, Sanskrit. In Greek it was *oregein*, meaning to stretch for, to reach towards, and *oretic*, meaning to reach, while the English word *king* came from the notion of begetting.

Was this not proof enough? All this stretching and reaching towards something, that men ruled the world because they had this big sausage? No wonder this penis erectus—this phallus—became the Word of God! So much power! The conception of royalty and rectors and rectitude and righteousness—morals in general—all from the penis. Well, if this was where world order started, no wonder there was so much chaos.

But would it have to be? Would Robert Conquest's "great impervious dream on which the world's foundations rest," still be so impervious if this were all cleared up?

And the Untouchables in India—i.e., the lowest rung of the caste system—would they still be so untouchable if people stopped mixing them up with *reg*—the moral authority which celebrates the triumph of good over evil, light over darkness?

And Black men and women. Would they still be dangerous, their dark skin still symbolic of evil and man's forbidden desires—and be persecuted and killed?

Wow! Can you believe all that came from her father's big sausage? But I liked her arguments, and that the etymological proof she gave was very ingenuous, if nothing else.

***

Diary: Tolstoy argued that since the divine lives inside us (no argument there!), we must honor that divinity through our actions. But by sanctifying the most basic and primordial part of our biology and instincts—an act that goes totally against nature—does that not explain why man's actions are so cruel?

***

Easter for Mary was not, naturally, about Jesus and the Crucifixion and Resurrection, but about magic penises being swallowed in the mouth of a fish. This is why she loved Easter and had so much fun helping Bertha color the Easter eggs. Her dream of a wild ride on the Word of God (I've set it all down for you below) came the night of that last Easter she and I would spend together.

The Senator had thrown open his doors to a large gathering of friends and supporters for a traditional Easter brunch, and had John start it off by explaining the significance of the Easter meal. The lamb represented the sacrifice made by Jesus, the Lamb of God. The spices in the hot cross bun represented the spices used to embalm Jesus, and the orange peel signified the bitterness of His time on the cross. Was there a more ingenious way to ingest his suffering?

Alas, thought Mary, if only we were celebrating Mithra instead! Then we could be eating roast beef or hamburger instead of lamb. Who likes lamb, anyway? Then a happy thought occurred.

"Why not eat hot dogs to signify the Lord's penis?" she said.

Unperturbed by the sudden silence in the room, she continued. Wasn't Easter all about its resurrection? Fertility, rebirth, new life? How close to the magic of it all could you get? Why had the egg, since ancient times, symbolized death and rebirth? Why had the early Christians in Mesopotamia used the egg with its three parts—the shell, yolk and albumen—to represent the Holy Trinity? Saw the hard shell as the sealed tomb, and the cracking of the shell as Jesus' resurrection? Was this not a good way to resurrect their own death and rebirth story, and distance themselves from pagan fertility and resurrection stories, such as the one the Egyptians told about their god of fertility, Osiris?"

Of course, the Senator was embarrassed. Who wouldn't be? But since the baron was eager to hear the story, as were many others—the blood of Jesus, that is, the red wine, had lightened everyone up, Mary told how Osiris was killed by his brother and thrown, piece by piece, into the Nile. Right away his penis was eaten by a fish, the one said Mary, that you see on the back of people's cars. But Osiris's wife, Isis, who was also his sister and the goddess of fertility, magic, and health (as Queen of the Gods, she was as venerated then as the Virgin is today), collected all his parts except for the one that the fish swallowed. Then with her great magic, she was able to resurrect a new penis for her husband and bear him a son named Horus. Even so, for the Egyptians, the loss of the phallus was symbolized by the loss of the Word. But when John said in his Gospel, "In the beginning was the Word, and the Word was with God, and the Word was God?" was it not resurrected again, said Mary? And could one not connect the magic birth of Horus with the magical birth of Jesus? If the great Egyptian goddess could conceive a child with the help of a disembodied penis, why shouldn't the Virgin Mary be able to conceive a child with the help of a disembodied spirit? Fair was fair, after all, and what was good for the goose was good for the gander. Magic was magic, was it not?

Just then, a loud blast of music came from Alice's room. It was so loud that Bertha, who was bringing in more buns, dropped the plate, scattering them all across the floor.

"That is Parsifal," said von Clapp, recognizing the music at once, "Wagner's opera about a young man—his name in Persian means idiot—who finds the Holy Grail and the Holy Spear. A perfect choice for Easter, ja?"

"Not if you're Jewish," said Walter.

"There are Jews here?"

It was one of the Chapman professor's students who had spoken. The professor and his wife had brought him as a guest.

"I saw no one with a big nose," the guest continued, picking up the fork he had momentarily laid down.

When the meal was over and Marcus had cleared away the last plates of Bertha's dessert—a simnel cake she had decorated with the customary eleven balls of marzipan that symbolized the eleven disciples who had not betrayed Jesus—the children ran outside to hunt for Easter eggs—or, as Mary put it, hunt for Osiris' missing penis. It was such an innocuous way to worship the phallus!

The fertility of the gods, the fertility of the rabbits—who knew? But the hypocrisy of it all—teaching little children to worship the phallus this way—didn't seem to bother her. But then, why should it? Wasn't that what Mary herself was doing? I mean, was there any difference between Osiris' and her father's? Wasn't one just as magical as the other? Or did it boil down to the magic of orgasm, and what the people in Africa were trying to express when they were carving designs on ostrich eggs 60,000 years ago?

THE DREAM

"It was the day before Easter, and Isis who looked like my mother told me that Osiris was waiting for me in the kitchen. She had just pulled him from the water, and was now going to show Lucius the Ass where the roses were in the garden. He trotted after her and I went into the kitchen. An ostrich egg that looked like Humpty-Dumpty was lying in pieces on the floor, but after the Holy Trinity put him back together, the Word of God told me to get on. I was very angry when a few minutes later, the Word told me to get off. But Helen wanted to use the kitchen to show Jesus and Alice how to color Easter eggs, so I went outside and played with the Easter Bunny. When he hopped away, I followed him to Walter's synagogue. There was organ music being played, and he went inside to listen. I decided to wait for the sunrise service and watch the sun god Ra rise from behind a hill topped with a cross that glittered in sparkling blue stars. Afterwards I went to eat with the pope. He'd prepared some pasta so that Alice wouldn't bang her head on the Holy Cross he wore around his neck. The spaghetti dripped with a marinara sauce that tasted like cotton. But a lot of people were there and they ate it anyway. Afterwards everyone but the pope climbed into a bus that was covered with roses. They were from the Rose Parade, and Isis had stolen them to feed to Lucius the ass. As the bus drove off a cliff, a lot of Easter Bunnies threw rocks at us.

"I was laughing when I woke up, but in my mouth was the unpleasant taste of cotton."

***

"So I went outside and played with the Easter Bunny."

So much for the glory of Easter. You can't fault the Crucifixion alone, nor George who had imbued her with the illicit waves of pleasure. No wonder she clung to the Magi. They were her only means of escape. Salvation lay not with Jesus but with the Magi and their magical doctrine condoning the glory of orgasm in little children.

Now, if this magic phallus was the standard by which she measured all men, no wonder she had trouble even, as it turns out, with John, finding permanency in any sort of relationship. No wonder it led her, like that poor girl Karen, to dance in *The Red Shoes.*

It was not, as said before, just the aspergillum that had decided John to give up the order. It was also the fear of breaking canonical law, those ecclesiastical edicts which preclude murder and a priest not being celibate. Imagine Mary's delight when John, showing off his knowledge of words, said that canon came from the Greek word *kanon* meaning a straight reed. Well. The way she grabbed at that reed, she might have grabbed, same way, John's penis and guided it straight in. This was revelation indeed. This clue as to who and what was ruling the world was even more direct than the straight measuring rod of rex the king. A rod was a rod, no?

Canonical law, yikes! Here was the reason, she wrote, why the fairy tale *The Red Shoes* was still haunting her. It was a canonical edict for sure, not to wear red shoes to church. But how could you not if they were magic? And how could you ever forget the magic, if your feet kept dancing even after being cut off?

***

Margaret had, unlike her sisters' personal dreams of glory, only wanted at an early age to have a family. The Senator was helpful in her achieving it. No, it's not what you're thinking. What I mean is, what with the political circles he ran in and his wide circle of acquaintances, she was bound to meet someone sooner or later, right?

She fell in love with a state assemblyman named Jack Nordstrom—no, no relation to the department store—and, after a short engagement, they were married. Because the legislature was still in session, their honeymoon was delayed several months. When it ended, they flew to Athens and, after cruising the islands, rented a car and drove from Athens to Thessalonica. They took their time, Margaret was already pregnant.

On the way to Thessalomica, they came to Hypata, the city where Lucius had applied the wrong ointment and been transformed into an ass, not the soaring bird he had expected. (I guess Mary wasn't the first to come in contact with Apuleius' tale of magic and transformation!) The couple had dinner at the Golden Ass Cafe, and decided to stay overnight. In the souvenir shops, there were jars being sold as the same magic unguent which Lucius had used. When the shopkeeper laughed and said they might only transform wrinkles, she bought several jars.

✱✱✱

As her womb expanded, Margaret began to panic. For some reason, she had lately become afraid that her child was going to be born with a pig's tail. Yes, *One Hundred Years of Solitude* had been George's favorite book, but what did that have to do with her?

Diary: I flew to Sacramento to try and calm her. This talk of the pig's tail, where was that coming from? But suspecting where it might, wouldn't a little talk about the Magi be helpful? While we sat in Starbucks, Margaret poured bourbon into her coffee from a flask she had in her purse.

"Maybe Alice is right. She says the world is already too full of people, and that's why she's not going to have one."

I pictured how impossible that would be, her fear of the gaping chasm and all. I guess Margaret had never heard Alice's mutterings about women having babies just to prove to themselves they are women and not men. How could she be a man if she was having a baby? I think that despite all the stuff she does with Mother, she still doesn't want people to think she isn't a woman even though she herself isn't sure whether she wants to be one or not. But if she becomes a mother, that kind of leaves no room for doubt, does it?

"God, Mary, I hope that's not why I'm doing it, especially if it comes with a pig's tail—or even two heads? I think about that so much, maybe I'll will it to happen."

Strangely enough, there were indeed two heads that showed in the ultrasound, but that's because she was going to have twins—twin girls—and she appeared to be relieved that she wouldn't have to name either of them after George. The magic circle appears to have a way of confusing people about gender, does it not?

***

Diary: "A man's good book is irrational his whole life."

This is what Alice had written on the dining room wall with a can of spray paint. Even though I didn't know what it meant, it seemed to make sense. Dr. Niedlhauf thought so too, which is why he hasn't had it removed. He says the patients all like trying to guess what it means. One man, for instance, who was getting treatment for a gambling addiction, said it had to do with bookies. Another said it was the Bible.

Everyone was happy until a patient who thought he was Goethe angrily accused Alice of plagiarizing a line from his novel, *Faust*: "A good man, in his dark urges, is well aware of the right way."

Alice had jumped on him at once. It wasn't necessary, she said, to turn an old man into a young man just so he could seduce a young virgin. Older men can do the same thing, and if she'd wanted to, she wouldn't just change a sentence or two, she'd change the whole book.

I looked at Dr. Niedlhauf. Did he now know what was wrong with Alice? Should I tell him that, next to Rigoletto, her favorite opera is Faust, and how she loves to sing Marguerite's aria, the *Jewel Song*, as much as *Caro nome*?

I decided not to, and went to her room where I found her asleep. There was such a beatific expression on her face that I decided not to wake her and end the peacefulness. She was lying on her stomach, her hands cupped under her pubis. Well, why not? It needs protection, too, doesn't it, in sleep as well as wakefulness? Little kids know that from the start, I'm sure that's why they lie that way.

Just before I'd left his office, the doctor had once again thumbed through the pages of *Struwwelpeter*. He stopped at the story of the boy who terrorized animals—pulled wings off the insects, killed birds and threw a kitten down the stairs. I thought of Iphigenia being led to the altar. He shut the book and sighed.

"There's nothing here that gives me a clue why she won't eat meat. Well, maybe something will turn up. She talks a lot about the family's trips to Glenbrook, and all the roadkill she saw—'animals tossed helplessly to the side of the road and left to rot.' I feel that she is identifying with them, but I don't see how that's all connected. Do you?"

As I listened to the doves say, "Catch the ball, catch the ball," and watched Alice play with herself, I had this strange thought. Could the Father, Son and Holy Ghost be part of that triangle, the one Alice was touching?

***

On the drive home, her head full of flies and maggots and the doctor's profuse thanks for helping, Mary wondered why she was not locked up like Alice. She should be, should she not? Maybe it was from tearing the limbs off her dolls that had saved her? She knew they were bad. Could their punishment have propitiated God, put her in His amazing grace? She'd also cut off their beautiful hair and hers, too. Poor Marcus, he hadn't been able to unlock her door in time.

If only Alice had understood that God and orgasm and fathers are all tied up in one, she wouldn't be where she was now.

***

Now, I know I'm getting ahead of myself, and in recounting her life, she has not yet met Father Malcolm. That is coming. But because this seems like the right moment, because of Alice and roadkill and all that—roadkill? That's even more graphic than Iphigenia. Hard to believe that Mary could still think she was her father's one and only. Or did she. By the way, should I confess how fixated I've become on those decals with the fish symbol?—to bring him up. I will just say that, after she met him at the Sanctuario de Chimayo, he had given her a book about a man who is turned into an ass. She liked it so much that she read another version of the same ass in a volume of stories by the Greek writer Lucian.

Well, I'm guessing it blew her away. Not the story about the ass, but the one about love. It was not God, said Lucian, who created the world. It was Eros who, when "brought forth by the earliest source of all life," created the world and ended the chaos and the void.

> *"For you gave shape to everything out of dark, confused shapelessness. As though you had removed a tomb burying the whole universe alike, you banished that chaos which had enveloped it to the recesses of farthest Tartarus... Spreading bright light over gloomy night you became the creator of all things both with and without life."*

If only Alice had read this version of Genesis instead of the Bible's! Would she then have been so fragile, Mary asked, if the West had chosen Eros—a God of love not in the Christian sense but in the organic sense—instead of Jehovah? Or would it not have made any difference which book she read, since people everywhere in the world seemed similarly conflicted? Like in India where, for some yogis, wasn't it all about having great orgasm, while for others it was about not having it at all? Wasn't it like there were two different divinities who created the Universe—one who welcomed sex and one who didn't? Which was why some mystics held out an arm or stood on a leg for hours or days at end in order to gain occult powers? But maybe, as this practice held back the semen, they were only trying to figure out which was which?

But did anyone know? When Lucian wrote about the execution machine commissioned by the tyrant Phalaris—a bronze bull in which the condemned man was locked, a fire lit underneath, and, as he roasted to death, his cries sounded like a bellowing bull, Mary wondered where such cruelty (and all such cruelty which history abounds with) comes from. It must come from somewhere! The answer, which for her came naturally, she put in the form of a question: "Do we torture each other because our gonads are in such torture?"

***

Diary: John always seems amazed whenever there's a headline about a sex scandal in the church. I don't think he will ever see that sex is religion and religion is sex, and never the twain shall part. If that were not the case—if orgasm were not at the heart of religion—then why do spiritual leaders have such an easy time coercing there followers into having sex? Do nuns wed Christ because marriage is a sanctified way to experience orgasm? Do priests take vows of celibacy so they won't think about sex? But how can they not, when the church itself is but a yawning chasm of orgasm?

"But this time it's Father Malcolm!" he said excitedly. "The nitwit! He should have left the Order when I did."

"But aren't they all nitwits?" said I. "I mean, they are just people too, and nitwits enough to be spewing out their pearls of wisdom from a theology they learned based on the penis. Can you believe it? Getting wisdom and counseling from the penis? But I guess that's why there are so many believers: What's more exciting than to be in the realm of such a God?"

John, looking crestfallen, shook his head.

"Father Malcolm is different. You'll see when you meet him."

***

"Do priests take vows of celibacy so they won't think about sex?"

When Rose had visited, Mary learned that he and John had known each other since they were altar boys, and had shared the same dorm room in college and attended the same seminary. In preparation for the priesthood—this had been his heart's desire ever since he and John had carried the tall processional candles to the altar—Malcolm had studied classical history, and could read the Latin and Greek classics in the original language. He could even read the ancient magical papyri found at Thebes in its original demotic Greek. John found his company compelling, and many a happy evening they'd spend together as Malcolm recited some of the love poems of Catullus. But they were not all about love. Poem 90, for instance, was about incest and the Magi. Lucky for Mary that John had remembered this, even down to the number which made it easy for her to find. There was this one:

Too Much!: To Gellius

Let a Magus be born from the sinful union of Gellius and his mother, and learn Persian soothsaying: since a Magus ought to be born from a mother and son, if the impious religion of the Persians is true, so with acceptable chants he'll pleasingly worship the gods melting the entrails in the greasy flames.

And then there was this one. She went back and forth not knowing which one she liked best:

Let there be born a Magus from the unspeakable coupling of Gellius and his mother, and let him learn the Persian art of divination. For if Persia's impious religion is true, a pleasing Magus ought to be begotten from mother and son so that, when the chant has been learned, he may worship gods while melting the fat innards in the sacred flames.

Perhaps John remembered Catullus' poem about his friend because it was, he said, the first time he'd heard the word Magus.

"But those are the Magi," Malcolm had said, surprised, and gone on to explain why their reputation was well known in the West. It was excruciatingly hard for Mary to hide her excitement. *Finally, somebody* who knew what the Magi were traditionally known for. Ah, here was an opportunity to share the greatest document that had ever been written (I hope she didn't mean that!), share the ancient passages—passages she had found as if a finger of fate had led her to them—with an erudite man like Malcolm. Perhaps he already knew them, and had read the passages straight from the Persian!

The consummation of the mutual assistance of men is Khvetukdas… That union is that with near kinfolk, and, among near kinfolk, that with those next-of-kin; and the mutual connection of the three kinds of next-of-kin—which are father and daughter, son and she who bore him, and brother and sister—is the most complete that I have considered.

When the millennium is about to dawn, 'all mankind shall perform Khvetukdas, and every fiend will perish through the miracle and power of Khvetukdas.' The first time a man practices it, 'a thousand demons will die, and two thousand wizards and witches… and when he goes near to it four times, it is known that the man and woman become perfect… Whoever keeps one year in a marriage of Khvetukdas becomes just as though one-third of this world had been given to him… unto a righteous man… And when he keeps four years in his marriage, and his (funeral) ritual is performed, it is known that his soul thereby goes to the supreme heaven; and when the ritual is not performed, it goes thereby to the ordinary heaven.' The good deeds of those who observe Khvetukdas are a hundred times more efficacious than the same deeds performed by other pious men; and the penalty for dissuading from it is hell.

Yes, what beauty in those lines! What opportunities for redemption for those who have fallen! And, she wrote, there were pages and pages of it, in that most beautiful book, the *Dinkard*. Yes, wouldn't it be delightful and exciting to discuss this with a real priest? But there was also a sense of urgency to do it in case he was defrocked. They should invite him to L.A., and John would be happy, too.

***

Diary: Margaret has asked me to critique a short story she has written, and plans to send to the New Yorker. It seems that being a wife and mother isn't enough, even in Sacramento. Which is too bad, because the story is, to me, rather silly although there are, I think, a few exceptions. I quote one, verbatim, that appears near the beginning:

"An old man and a young girl of fourteen stood alone in the foyer of a well-appointed house. He drew her close, and began gyrating his hips against hers.

'Do you like it?' he asked.

Since she was his daughter it was an awkward moment. Dare she hurt his feelings by saying no?

She answered evasively (and also truthfully): 'I don't know.'

The gyrating went on for another minute and then stopped. A mixture of hurt, anger and disappointment passed over his face, and she grew afraid. You didn't cross this man, he had a bad temper."

But the rest of it is kind of a letdown. The above experience leads the girl later on to study the mating habits of animals. Her insights are so good that she receives a stipend to study their habits in Africa. But the story ends tragically when, shortly after she is almost killed by a stampeding herd of wildebeests, she tries to save a baby zebra from a Nile crocodile, and gets eaten herself. Thus she is never able to prove her doctorate thesis that there is no incest taboo in the animal kingdom.

But how fun it would be if, in the story, there was, and a baby elephant was born with a pig's tail!

***

CANON IV

"The idea that there's a connection between religion and capitalism isn't new—the fundamental need of wealth is necessary to strengthen the hierarchies established by the ancient priests. But a connection between capitalism, crashes in the stock market and orgasm? Now that IS new."

"If people could see that our cultural differences are merely the different approaches to our worship of orgasm, they would also see that the fear and loathing we have for other cultures is a great indicator of how much we fear God, orgasm, the penis and the vagina."

"Whenever we copulate, there is a divine voice that lives inside us."

"Racism and conquest are ubiquitous in politics because they are Biblical in origin. All racist tropes are rooted in man's fear of sex."

"If our fear of orgasm (hence God) wasn't so great, why, then, is the Western world run by white men (hence good over evil, light over darkness)?

"What ARE those hidden treasures we seek in our dreams?"

"To all you Conservatives who believe that tradition and custom are the true bearers of wisdom, let me remind you that the original bearer of wisdom was Aphrodite, goddess of love. From her groin springs every structure of human life.

"And since you are as much a part of her as the poet Sappho, why keep fighting her? You are only fighting against yourself, and no matter how many laws you legislate against her, you will never win because she and you are the same."

"'Eros,' said the ancient Theban, "'is the only general that has never been beaten.'"

"There is no better place to experience God than in the holy womb of the church itself."

"By transforming orgasm into God, we have created an illusion that seems more real than reality. God, who is to be feared, has jurisdiction over our greatest pleasure. No wonder we believe in the religious laws which rule our sexuality."

"As body, mind and soul swell up together in that euphoric moment of climax, I am filled with love for all mankind. I wonder: is orgasm the source of our belief in mercy and forgiveness?"

"Here's a conundrum: How can the bad feel so good, the wrong feel so right, and the horror of it all feel so glorious? Does the answer to this mystery lie somewhere in the magic of childhood?"

***

Dr. Niedlhauf had asked Mary to have dinner with Alice. "A man's good book is irrational his whole life" was still on the wall. While they were eating, two women with disheveled hair came up to them and looked disdainfully at Alice's plate. It was heaped with mashed potatoes, peas and carrots.

"You should be eating meat, dear," said one of the women, emphasizing *meat*. Her companion nodded.

"For the protein, I suppose," said Alice patiently.

"No, because animals are bad," she answered.

"That's right," said her friend. "They have sex in the open, and the best way to punish them is to kill them and eat them."

"But why not forgive them their sins and not eat them at all?" Alice replied. "That's why I'm eating my peas and carrots."

"Oh no, my child," said a man who had just joined the other two. He was dressed in a toga, and introduced himself as Callimachus, priest of the ancient Amazighs— more familiarly known as the Libyans.

"They must indeed by punished. Why, when we sacrifice to the sun and the moon, we first cut off the ear of the animal, and then kill him by twisting his neck. Then we eat him. It is the tried and true way of getting rid of our own carnal instincts."

"And it's no coincidence," said the other man, "that Christ was crucified on a Friday—the fifth day of creation when God made the animals."

The woman's eyes lit up cruelly.

"Can you ever forgive your instincts?" she said to Alice, emphasizing *your*.

Callimachus perceived how frightened Alice looked. His eyes softened.

"Dear child," he said gently, "continue eating your peas and carrots, and refrain from eating the birds of the air, the fish of the sea, and the beasts that creep and crawlith upon the earth. I give you special dispensation."

"But you are quoting from the Bible," said Mary.

"When you have been on the earth as long as I have, you know everything. And to atone for our sins, we need to go back to sacrificing bulls instead of those insipid Thanksgiving turkeys with their scrawny little necks. No self-respecting priest would ever waste his time."

"But their stuffing is delicious," said the woman.

"And don't forget the pumpkin pie afterwards," said her friend. Then, turning to Callimachus, she added, "An animal is an animal no matter how scrawny its neck."

***

The baron also liked to visit Alice. It wasn't so much for his forgiving nature as it was a sense of guilt and obligation. Gretchen, the baroness, had thrown *Struwwelpeter* in his face, saying that was why Alice had gone crazy. Though he found this hard to believe, a book which, in his mind far surpassed all the other great German writers of fairy tales.

"But Liebchen," he had said in his defense, "those children *needed* it. They were always acting up, so I thought the book would help like it has helped many German children throughout the years." As an afterthought he added, "If the girls were horses, I would have known what to do."

"Ja, naturlich, no more sugar."

On one of the evenings with Alice, while listening to Callimachus discuss the merits of bulls over Thanksgiving turkeys when making sacrifice to God—an omen, the baron thought, that his new endeavor would succeed, he paid little attention to a minor raucous going on out in the hall. It was Moses—a patient who had come down with Jerusalem syndrome (more on this later) and had never gotten over it—who was now, as usual said an attendant, very angry when the rod he carried wouldn't turn into a serpent.

"Why not, why not?" he shouted, whacking his staff on the ground over and over. "Am I not the greatest magician within the sect of magicians I alone started—me and Iannes? If I were not, would a magical book bear my name—*The Sword of Moses*? Would Strabo rank me high as a magician, and Artapanus the Jew think that I was the music teacher of Orpheus? Would the Egyptians include me in their magic spells? How could I have carved God's name on my staff if I were not a magician? Even the Lord knew I was, and my brother Aaron, too.

"'Go unto Pharaoh,' the Lord said to him, 'and take your rod and cast it down before Pharaoh, that it may become a serpent.'"

Moses swept his hand in front of his eyes.

"I can see it now, how my brother cast down his rod before Pharaoh, how it turned into a snake, how Pharaoh summoned his own priests, how they also cast down their own rods, how they, too, turned into snakes."

He stopped. "What happened then?" asked an attendant.

"My brother's snakes ate their snakes. We had to leave quickly."

As he was led away, Mary turned to the baron.

"I had no idea!" she exclaimed.

"What, that people are crazy?" he said.

"No, that Moses was a magician. I always thought of him as the prophet who led the Israelites out of Egypt."

This was news! Here were men turning their rods into snakes to see which rod was better. It was all so phallic, wasn't it, this talk about rods and magical staffs? And Pharaoh's priests—did they not worship the phallus of Osiris, the word of God? But with the magic of Moses and Aaron triumphing over theirs, had the Israelite God overcome their God? Could this war of the rods be, in fact, the Judaeo phallic rod triumphing over the Egyptian, thus imposing a new, revolutionary transformation, a new word of God that would have no graven image?

Had Walter understand more than he thought when he'd said, "So the stigma of being a Jew is that we stopped pagans from enjoying themselves—I mean, enjoying the word of God?"

***

Diary: Margaret still thinks that a pig's tail could start any minute. All this stuff she is still putting on the twins' little behinds will prevent it, she says. It's something she bought in Greece. I ask her what it is, but she won't tell me. It has a nice fragrance, and when she's not looking, I put a little on my hands.

***

Let us be generous and say that in Mary's case, it wasn't a Messiah complex that possessed her, but a clear desire to keep people from winding up like herself and her sisters. By proving that orgasm was God and God was orgasm, wasn't that one way to do it? There would always be magic circles, and for people caught in them, wouldn't they be happier if they knew who the Almighty really was? Certainly the world would be better off if people didn't keep killing each other over religious differences and all—that is, how they were worshiping orgasm.

Always reading, always searching. Always finding examples of it surfacing surreptitiously (or not) in people's minds. How could anyone miss this one from the mind of Henry Adams, descendant of two Presidents? (No one was safe!) "The greatest and most mysterious of all energies," he had said in deference to the goddess Diana. Nor were other religious roots lost on him when he compared Christianity, the Cross and the Virgin to the electric forces and dynamos on display during his visit to the Paris Exposition in 1900. Zounds! Or miss this:

Quae quonium rerum naturam sola gubernas—For you alone rule over

the nature of things.

"These lines from Lucretius' *Invocation to Venus* were," said Adams, "perhaps the finest in all Latin literature." And when Dante had used the same lines to invoke the Virgin, what more proof did one need?

Yes, whenever there were paths leading toward salvation, she was there to take them. Like this book, *The Origin of Consciousness in the Breakdown of the Bicameral Mind*. (Wow, what a mouthful!) I think it was way above her head, but she made use of it anyway (God help us). But

112

who knows? That an ancient divine function of the right hemisphere—a vestigial godlike function—had a genetic basis for it going back to the Pleistocene era when the progenitors of man first appeared, could Mary really have been on to something?

On the other hand, even if this *was* the same side of the brain that has been identified as the source of sexual pleasure, was it really a further proof and "great explanation" as to how orgasm became the source of God? Even if A equals B, and B equals C, does A always equal C?

But never mind. If true that our progenitors were having great orgasm, and that lots of chaos was the result of it, I suppose it could follow that God's metamorphosis, if in fact there was such, began in an ancient divine vestigial godlike function of the right hemisphere. And if the Pleistocene era began over two million years ago, and Mary's transmutation thing didn't happen overnight, well, who knows? Don't they say that anything's possible?

Why draw the line? Why not pounce on the idea, as Mary did, that when the Pleistocene era ended, which was only about 11,000 years ago, shortly there after, according to Julian Jaynes, author of the book, consciousness evolved as people began to obey the voices of gods, voices which were hallucinated from—yes, the right side of the brain.

Well, why not? It was as good as anything she'd come up with, if not better, to end John's conviction (which she was getting tired of), that she had mixed up her earthly father with the heavenly one. And if it wasn't, well then what, if anything, was?

But even if she had—mixed him up, that is—hadn't other people, too? Was she not in a long line of such people—augurs in ancient times divining good only from the right side of things; the Scriptures honoring those who sat at the right hand of God and the right hand of Jesus; the policies of the political right being less fearful than those on the left? Even right-handedness in people, from when prehistoric men were using their right hand to kill? (This from the evidence of prehistoric skulls with deadly fractures on the left.) Did their testosterone-laden love make us all right-handed? And turn the left into something sinister—*sinistrum,* on the left?

***

"I think I know," she said that evening while John was working on the latest jigsaw puzzle his mother had sent, "why right is never wrong."

The puzzles had started when Rose, after her visit, had sent one depicting Michelangelo's *Fall from the Garden of Eden.* They both laughed and spent half the night piecing it together. But then a second one came, *Virgin with Angels,* and a third, *Lost Lamb.* Was Rose trying to send a message? Or was it just a coincidence when Botticelli's *Adoration of the Magi* arrived? Well, whether it was or not, or whether Rose knew things or not, it was, for sure, hard to spend any quality time in the bedroom when these puzzles kept coming. At the moment, John was working on Durer's *The Adoration of the Trinity.*

"Eh?" said John, hardly listening as he tried to force the wrong piece into God's crown.

"It has to do with the right temporal lobe."

She had a vision of herself sitting on the right hand of Jesus, and feeling a slight movement of his fingers. Well, why not, if Jesus and forbidden desires were all tied up in one? And why shouldn't that be, if it all came from the right temporal lobe, all framed by the hallucinated voices in the divine right hemisphere?

But lo and behold! Here before her very eyes was John himself proving Jaynes to be right. For as the puzzle progressed, illuminating Durer's vision of God the Father, his crucified son, the Virgin, the pope, the emperor, the saints, the people, the heavens above and the hills and lakes on the earth below, the cherubim with colorful wings, and the dove hovering in a cloud of gold, was there any denying that the artist had been inspired, not by the church but by the vestigial function in his own right hemisphere? And why the picture was so beautiful?

***

114

Jack Nordstrom, having been re-elected for a third term, was on a mission with several other senators when the plane they were on went down. There were no survivors, Margaret closed the apartment and returned home.

How Mary wanted to tell her not to stay! The children were too young to be visited by God. But didn't Margaret already know that? Surely the pig's tail and two-headed baby were clues that she did!

To Mary's relief, a savior appeared in the guise of Aunt Lucy. She was going to spend the summer in France, and invited Margaret and the children to join her.

It was only later, after Aunt Lucy had sent her some books and Margaret's journal from Paris, that her suspicions proved correct. This entry in particular caught her attention.

"The aftermath of dad's love? My brain blew up in pieces and scattered in tatters. Why not? I was only a child, but the confusion he caused is still there. My brain is still in tatters. And so, I think, it will always be."

CANON V

"You never hear women calling themselves instruments of God; this is because women don't have penises."

"If the bicameral men hallucinated the voices of gods, are the visions of mandalas, monsters, metaphors, myths and mysticism but the mirages we see in the desert?"

"As we reach for heaven, so do we reach for orgasm."

"God is an illusion who seems more real than reality."

"If disorders of the brain originate in the divine right hemisphere, no wonder they are hard to cure."

"As long as that territory is forbidden—it belongs to God—no one dares to enter it and grapple with the disease."

"Money doesn't buy happiness, but it buys forgetfulness. The bigger the mansion, the bigger the yacht, the less we remember things that might have been but can never be."

"If Oedipus had listened to Zoroaster, he wouldn't have had to gouge out his eyes."

"What do money and God have in common? They are both collective beliefs and necessary fictions rooted in the vestigial god-like function of the brain."

"What is Armageddon but an unconscious desire to blow ourselves up because in reality we really can't stand ourselves?"

"'In God We Trust.' And what is more trustworthy than a good orgasm?"

"Why does the Shield of Trinity—the schematic diagram of the structure of God—look so much like a woman's pussy?

"Religion is the control of orgasm. But orgasm can't be controlled. That's why religion is hypocritcal and doesn't work."

***

Every afternoon after school, and on weekends, Alice shut herself up in her room and practiced her voice lessons. Even though the door was shut, the scales—the *ah ah ah ah ah ah ahs* and *ee ee ee ee ee ee ees*—reverberated throughout the house and made people crazy. Mary, bless her, thought that was what she wanted to do. Often she became hoarse from practicing too long. Her voice teacher only let her learn simple arias like *Che faro senza Euridice*, and when she practiced them at home, people were glad that the door was shut.

Unhappy that she wasn't singing *Caro nome* yet, she decided to find another teacher and auditioned for a famous one in Hollywood. If only she had listened when he candidly told her that he wouldn't give a plug nickel for her voice. Well, this would devastate anybody, wouldn't it, especially someone whose dream of singing opera and having flowers thrown at her feet and people everywhere acknowledging how great she was, was too deeply rooted and inextricably connected to

Rigoletto and George. This came to the surface after Dr. Niedlhauf had administered sodium pentothal, but the reason why it was all rooted and connected, didn't come.

"I guess there are some things that not even truth serum will work on," wrote Mary.

***

Diary: Last night Margaret and I had dinner at THE Blvd. Restaurant at the Beverly Wilshire. We were outside in the patio and saw mother and Alice coming from one of the shops on Rodeo Drive.

Margaret paid no attention; she is leaving for France next week and still worries about the twins.

"I know it's silly," she said, "but I can't seem to stop. That stuff I bought in Hypata is almost gone. But it probably won't take very long to fly from Paris to Athens."

There was a catch in her throat.

"I miss Jack so much. Sometimes I feel like a bug being washed down the drain, or an insect drowning in a swimming pool. Lately, when I see that happening—and I don't care what it is—a fly or a bee that might sting me—I always try to save it."

Mother and Alice went into another shop.

"Have you ever seen," Margaret continued, "an ant struggling in the water? They actually sit up on their hind legs to keep their little heads above water as long as they can. You can't stand by and just let it happen. That's why I'm doing my best to make sure their lives—I mean the twins'—won't be dark, and they'll never know what it feels like to be dragging around chains, or try to mask the night and make it less dreadful. It's the past that makes the present seem so dark. You know, they—I mean the twins—haven't once thrown up on hot dogs? And they love eggs. Remember how we used to hate them, especially when Bertha served them soft-boiled in the little egg cups?"

Mother and Alice continued going in and out of shops. Margaret, on her fifth vodka martini, was starting to slur her words, but I decided not to say anything. Why? Wasn't the invention of agriculture driven not by a desire for bread but by a desire for beer and wine? Twelve thousand years ago people needed to get plastered. What was that saying, about there's nothing new under the sun?

As I drove home I thought of another saying: *In vino veritas*, 'In wine there is truth.' But the truth of what?

***

Mary's brain must have been in turmoil, poor thing, when she wrote this.

"If we equate God with orgasm, then God exists because He is a biological process that can be worshiped as a provable entity. But if God comes not from an electro-chemical process but from our perception of the process and the emotions it creates, then how can I love John if God has no more substance than a shadow on the wall, a crack in the sidewalk?"

She could, in other words, love John and not treat him as she'd treated the others—i.e., kicked them out—because he, as a former priest, was a palpable connection to God. But if God *didn't* exist, if He were nothing but a puff of emotion, no more real than a hole in the ground or the indentation in a rock or the center of a donut or the line on the horizon, then was her love for John real or only a delusion?

Wow! How stupid can anyone be? Even if it was creative, this theological argument—wasn't she just trying to get rid of him? Yes, I'm sure that's what it was, and she was just reverting to her old pattern of looking for a way out of a relationship because John, even as a man of God, was unable to replace her father. But when she saw the argument was working—she couldn't help discussing it with him—and he began wearing his cross necklace and said he was going to spend a few days at a Catholic retreat with Father Malcolm, she panicked. That she would be abandoned again was too appalling, the butterflies in her stomach too unbearable.

Desperate to make things right, a new idea struck her. Even if it were true, which it wasn't, that she didn't love him, how, she asked, could he go back to the church now that he knew that God was a figment of a monkey's imagination and that man's brain evolved from the phallus and worship of orgasm? Would he not be tempted to begin or end or include any of this knowledge in his sermons? What if he tried to turn the Bible around so that Black people were good and white people were bad? He knew enough about it now, so that he might. What if he tried to reverse the colorizing of guilt so that all that is good would be symbolized by Darkness, and all that is evil would be symbolized by Light? This could get him into real trouble, especially if the police started shooting white people, and hospitals gave priority to Blacks. He would be turning the world upside down and inside out! Even if he told his congregation that their being there and listening to him was all nonsense because it had all been hallucinated in the heads of hominids whose minds were split in two when they became bicameral, would anybody believe him?

With her arms around his shoulders and kissing him passionately, she said, "Don't you think this could all slip out, even if you didn't want it to?"

***

Whether it was the argument or the kisses and a lot of time spent in bed, he put the cassocks that had just come from the dry cleaners back in his drawer. Anyway, he said, Father Malcolm was no longer at the retreat. After being severely disciplined, he had been given one more chance and was being transferred to the Sanctuario de Chimayo in New Mexico. It was a holy shrine with healing powers. The disciplinary board thought it might be good for him.

"He must have some powerful friends," said Mary.

"No, it's because everyone likes him and would hate to see him leave the Church," John replied.

Was it that, she thought, or were there too many priests who were too full of God, already up on charges? Nevertheless, for some unknown reason, she suggested they go visit his old friend, and this made John very happy. But while they were making preparations for the trip, an unforeseen incident occurred which caused a slight change of plans. A house the Senator owned in Nevada had caught fire and burned to the ground. Arson was suspected, and an investigation was going on.

The Senator was perplexed. In Glenbrook, the exclusive enclave at Lake Tahoe where he bought the house, most people were Republicans. Even outsiders who were permitted to play for pay on the private golf course, they were Republicans, too, weren't they? But now he was in the middle of a Ways and Means Committee battle, and couldn't leave. Would Mary go instead?

It was too hard to resist seeing the charred remains of the Senator's house even though this would delay meeting with the exciting priest, so she said yes. As for the house, the Senator, on the advise of his brother-in-law, had bought it as a tax haven should he ever want to retire. For several summers the family made the eight to nine hour journey to Glenbrook.

It was not easy. There was so much roadkill on Hwy 395—rabbits, coyotes, squirrels, fox, deer and even, on occasion, a cow who had found a hole in the barbed wire of fenced in pasture land. Perhaps the worst incident occurred when the Senator himself was the murderer. A vulture, who happened to be feeding on dead carrion along the road, was either too heavy from his meal or too indulged in how delicious it was, to get out of the Senator's way. Not heeding the children's screams to slow down, the car sped over him.

But why dwell on that when Highway 395 has so much more to offer by way of the Sierra Nevada range to the left (if you're traveling north) and the White Mountains to the right. Did you know that the oldest bristol cone trees are in those mountains?

The further north you go, the more dramatic they become, the Sierra Nevadas. It was not known until later, when Alice was given sodium pentothal under the care of Dr. Niedlhauf, how much they had effected her. She blamed them for wanting to make her a man. The doctor had scratched his head.

"Well," he said, "I suppose that going north instead of south can do that, especially if you're a little crazy to begin with."

I would love to have found out what pleasures the highway might have held for Barbara and Margaret, but Mary never says. But for Alice, we know, it was the roadkill and for Mary, it was the mountains, the beautiful mountains with steely granite peaks towering thousands of feet in the air—unyielding, inaccessible, impenetrable, dangerous. She liked best the craggy peak that cradled Convict Lake, and visualized herself climbing its sheer rock and entering its wilderness. How much fun it would be, wouldn't it, to climb them, get lost in the wilderness? Of course she would die, but like she did once before, wouldn't it be worth it?

While she was enjoying herself thus, John, having heard many times about the vulture, kept his eyes glued to the road, and by the time they arrived at the Ahwahnee Hotel, was exhausted. He was grateful that the Senator had made arrangements for them to stay there since you often have to book a year in advance.

It's an historic old hotel made of granite from the same mountains, and timber from the surrounding forests. Indeed, even Queen Elizabeth had stayed there when she came to America. You think they would have enjoyed it.

Diary: A terrible experience at the old Ahwahnee. Oh yes, it's a beautiful hotel and our room was lovely. But the whole thing was spoiled by an angry park ranger who came up to a group of people feeding a raccoon, and told them responsible for—get this—a thousand raccoons dying off last winter. John and I were just standing there a few feet away, watching. But he pointed his finger at us, too. Can you believe it?

Well, it spoiled our whole night. I mean, how can you make love if you have the deaths of a thousand raccoons on your conscience?

***

122

It was not really that offense though, the deaths of the raccoons, that had piqued her conscience and brought on a sleepless night. No, it was an offense that had occurred a long, long time before, and what better way to depict its magnitude than by the deaths of—not one, not a hundred, but one *thousand* innocent raccoons?

***

They were both bleary-eyed when they went to check out next morning. As John waited at the desk, Mary began thumbing through an album a guest had just left open, commemorating Queen Elizabeth's visit. She was staring at a picture of the Queen feeding a raccoon while others watched, and almost jumped when one of the hotel managers came up behind her.

"That's my father," he said proudly, pointing to a park ranger in the picture.

"I thought you weren't supposed to feed the raccoons," said Mary.

"Ah, well, the Queen, you know?"

He flipped through to the picture that was taken upon her coronation. In one hand she held the scepter, and in the other hand, the orb and cross. Ah, another proof! What more did one need? Here it was. Anyone who held the royal scepter—the penis, that is—and the royal orb and cross—the power of God and orgasm—could feed the raccoons! Did that not prove the power of the crown? Of the royal scepter and the royal orb? How marvelous these symbols were! For without them, how could the Queen become the earthly incarnation of God, or better, the Word of God, and be anointed with holy oil (semen) from a spoon with two lobes (the testicles) when she is crowned? Or keep the Word of God, the phallus erect—*"The king is dead, long live the king?"*

But as marvelous as all that was, it was even more marvelous, really, that it all started with the hominids whose brains were no bigger than an ape's, but who were already experiencing visions and burying their dead. How marvelous was that?

***

"There's so much truth here," said John, gesturing at the surrounding hills thick with pine trees. They were now in Glenbrook, and as he gazed out over the green meadows he said, "The mountains are just covered in it!"

They had finished earlier their meeting with the inspectors and sheriff, and were still standing near the charred remains on Short Road. As Mary watched a coyote chase a rabbit across the meadow, and breathed in deeply the acrid smell of smoke, she said, "All I see are trees."

"But that's just it! The Old English words for tree and truth come from the same root—*treow, treo*— loyal, trusty, faithful—'as firm and straight as a tree.'"

"Is that why there are so many religious retreats in the mountains?"

It's sweet, I think, how they went back and forth with their etymological leaning—she, finding the root of one thing, he finding the root of another. What do they call it in math, the square root of something? Mary was never good in math, but now she could find lots of roots, square or not. And, as we've already seen, attach all sorts of meanings to them that, at least for me, I'd never thought of before.

For instance, now. Wasn't the phallus of Osiris—the Word of God—also as firm and straight as a tree? Was that why the Druids worshiped trees, and the Hindus believed that trees were the origin of life, and people hugged trees and decorated them at Christmas? When loggers cut them down, did they get a thrill? No wonder it was so hard for people to tell the truth, or even know what it was, if it was all tied up with the phallus.

A guest house had been arranged for them a short distance away, but that night they slept outside—the air was warm—and made love under a canopy of trees and stars.

As so often happens in the mountains, the weather the next day made a sudden turn. On their walk back from Skunk Harbor, a

124

sheltered cove near Glenbrook, they were drenched in a freezing rain. They lit a fire in the living room and opened a bottle. Warmed and light-headed, John suggested they go to dinner in the cassocks he'd brought for Father Malcolm. The rain had stopped and the trees had begun to take on the mystery of night. Canada geese were in flight to find a safe place to sleep. As the couple walked toward the golf course clubhouse, an old codger pulled up his car beside them. His bald head was fringed with gray hair down to his shoulders. He rolled down the window and spat out a wad of tobacco.

"Say, for a minute there," he said, "I thought you two was Rita Hayworth and that singer she married—Haymes, wasn't it? Guess it's the way you're dressed, same kind of long, brown robes. 'Course they're both dead now and I weren't more than a boy, but I remember it like it was yesterday—the two of them dressed up like monks and wandering around these here woods—actually t'was over there 'cross the lake, place called Crystal Bay. Yup. People 'round here said they was like a couple of lost souls. Are you on a pilgrimage, too?"

"No, we're just wearing these robes to keep warm," John answered. The old codger spat out another wad.

"Yup, you can't keep warm in them thar slinky dresses Miss Hayworth wore in that there movie—what were it—*Gilda?*—not up here anyway. But that ain't why she was wearing 'em robes. Seems something went on betwixt her and her daddy. Whoa! Can't think of a better reason for a pilgrimage than that, can you?"

After a final spit, he wished them a good evening and drove off. Well, as fortune might have it, that evening the Turner Classic Movie channel was playing (for the umpteen time) that very same movie, and they were able to watch it comfortably from bed. That night, when Mary was finally able to go to sleep, she dreamed about a mandala, the sacred circles which Buddhist monks make out of colored sand. It was a replica of the one she had seen at LACMA, but this one wasn't just a flat design; it was a real palace that she could go into. At its entrance, she saw elaborate gateways lined with human skulls and fierce monsters. Were they there to guard the human figures that were inside the heavenly palace? Or were they there as a warning? As she wandered past them—the terrifying monsters and skulls—if this sacred enclosure was indeed a warning, could any conclusion be drawn other than this—that when a man enters a woman, his orgasm and hers now belong to the terrifying realm of God?

***

Father Malcolm's urging was hard to ignore. He couldn't wait to show them around his new premises—the Sanctuario de Chimayo, the holy shrine known for the healing powers of its holy dirt. He was also eager to meet Mary after learning of her interest in the Magi. John himself could hardly wait to see his old friend and find out what made the dirt holy. So despite the Senator's begging them to stay until the investigation was over, the couple left Glenbrook the next day and headed for New Mexico.

Because St. John's College at Santa Fe was not far from Chimayo, Father Malcolm had asked them to stop at the college bookstore and pick up a copy of *The Histories of Herodotus*. On their arrival, they were not prepared for the scene of confusion and mayhem that met them. A professor had just been shot, and the campus was swarming with police cars, ambulances and paramedics. Yellow tape was still in the process of being unfurled.

In the bookstore, which had not yet been put on lock down, everyone said it was probably Professor Barnes, a natural science teacher whose lecture series—What Is Life and How Does It Evolve—had, apparently, gone slightly adrift, and instead of sticking to the curriculum, he was teaching his own unorthodox theory of evolution. Many people liked it, but a few didn't. There are always a few, aren't there?

An excited student was happy to explain it. The brain, Prof. Barnes had said, was an organ like any other. It had developed its size due to what happened when the apes began to walk and, after some millenniums, was bombarded with the electrical impulses of orgasm.

This wouldn't have happened, of course, if man's ancestors had stayed in the trees. But when they came down from them—for whatever the reason—and began to walk, there was a drastic change in their physical structure, a change that would have monumental consequences. The backbone became straight—vertical—and was perfectly aligned with the pelvis which had now become larger—more bowl-like—in order to accommodate the upright walking. With this new alignment, the spinal cord could now conduct the electro-chemical impulses of orgasm with such a surge, such intensity that what had once been a normal animal now became a sex-crazed monster. All hell broke loose, and eventually something had to be done. For how long could these primates keep pulling the lever—i.e., like the lab mice in the experiments who literally die from all the pleasure—before killing each other off and everyone going extinct? This, then, was the catalyst. This was how the brain got its size—determining how to stop pulling the lever. To solve this problem, it grew bigger and bigger in order to learn how to talk and make rules. Yes, language was needed for the lever. And religion—that was the big one. It's all there in the Bible—metaphorically, that is—as the chaos, the void and the darkness before the light.

"I can see why the professor might have been shot," said John.

"Yes," said the student cashier. "The Archdiocese of Santa Fe has not at all been thrilled."

"If it *is* Professor Barnes," said another student, "it was probably Rufus who shot him." Rufus, he explained was the Archbishop's nephew.

Mary, whose turn it was to drive, almost ran over a policeman, she was so excited. If she'd had any doubts before, they were now swept away. Yes, why not? This linear development—brain, spine, pelvis—was an excellent catalyst, indeed, for God. So much orgasm—electrifying, all-powerful, out-of-body orgasm; wouldn't the hominids be too primitive to know where it came from? If she as a child, whose mind was yet to be formed, had identified orgasm with God, why wouldn't the unformed mind of a hominid identify it likewise? Not necessarily God, but a spirit, some higher power, maybe even of demonic temperament, a deadly force, a lightning strike or something else from the sky? Had not her father's penis been a thing imbued with the supernatural?

Zounds! Who would have thought that the mere act of walking would lead to God and the creation of Civilization!

Who would have thought that the mere act of walking would lead to God and the creation of Civilization!

***

Father Malcolm met them at the rectory of the Holy Family Church. He was effusive in his greetings, hugging John first and then Mary and, at the same time, shedding an approving eye on her.

"So many non-believers these days," he said, "John is lucky to have found someone who does believe in God."

"Oh, I do indeed," she replied.

The two men reminisced for a while, and later John asked about the dirt.

"Ah, yes!" the Father replied, smiling broadly. Even though he hadn't been presiding at the church that long, it was obvious that the curative powers of the holy dirt was now a subject dear to his heart. But because the portico that held this power was a distance down the road, he led them first to the parlor where, in between mouthfuls of Mexican pastry his housekeeper had made for the occasion, he began to discuss its holiness. For the moment, Mary forgot all about the Magi.

"When someone feels guilty because they think sex is dirty," the Father said, "I tell them to rub the holy dirt on their bodies, and they won't feel guilty anymore."

"Now that *is* a miracle," said John.

"Not really. It's the power of association, you see. Dirt with dirt— bad dirt with good dirt— holy dirt, that is, the *tierra bendita.* It's almost like magic, how women who are barren rub themselves with it and right away become pregnant."

"Wow!" said John, "God *does* work in mysterious ways."

"He does indeed. I don't think it's so much the dirt that is holy, but the little well which yields it up. Come, let me show you."

They got in the priest's jeep and drove to the Sanctuary. It was a small adobe church with two towers and belfries, wooden doors, walled-in garden and an arched gate. Before entering and looking at the *pocito*, the little well holding the dirt, they toured the premises and surrounding hills where the holy dirt was collected. They were followed about by Rufinus, a small stray Father Malcolm had rescued from the coyotes.

After dinner, the two men drank brandy in the parlor and reminisced about the old days. Mary, who had not yet brought up the subject of Catullus and the incest-loving men of the East—something was holding her back—began to peruse a well-worn paperback that was lying on the table. It was *The Golden Ass* by Apuleius. Father Malcolm took notice at once.

"You've found my favorite book," he said, nodding approvingly. "I don't know how many times I've read it. When you're feeling down and out, when God seems to have abandoned you, there's nothing like reading about a man who is turned into an ass, to bring up your spirits."

"You feel that way, too?" said John.

The priest took the book gently from Mary's hand and began to tell the story about a young man named Lucius who was on his way to Thessaly to study the art of magic. He stopped in a town called Hypata where he ran into trouble. When he rubbed himself with an ointment which he supposed would turn him into a bird and enable him to follow about his mistress, he used the wrong ointment and was instead turned into an ass.

The breadth of his hardships were so heart-breaking. Here was this man in an ass's body, thinking like a man, but being understood by no one, and sorely mistreated by all. The hardships and suffering he endured would have answered the needs of any penitential pilgrimage, the Father said. Or, to put it another way, the suffering of Job paled in comparison to Lucius' suffering.

"But it wasn't *all* bad," said the Father, flipping through to the page which had been dog-eared. It recounted how a noble woman, seeing Lucius perform tricks, had fallen madly in love with him. After paying his master for one night, a chamber had been splendidly prepared with gold-embroidered coverlets and dainty pillows and a soft bed laid on the floor. Then, in softest candlelight, the elegant lady stripped naked.

"*Next she kissed me lovingly,*" said the priest, reading Lucius' narrative, "*not the sort of kisses that pass current in the brothels... hers were the real thing and heartfelt, as were her endearments—'I love you,' 'I want you,' 'you're the only one I love,' 'I can't live without you,' and all the other things women say to excite men... then she took hold of my halter and got me to lie down in the way I had learned. That was a simple matter: what I had to do presented itself to me as neither novel nor difficult, especially when after all this time I was about to go to bed with so beautiful and so willing a mistress...*

"*No, what worried me was how I could mount such a fragile lady with my four hulking legs; how I could embrace such soft and shining limbs fashioned of milk and honey with my hard hooves; how I could kiss such small red lips steeped in the liquid of ambrosia with my huge mouth which was so misshapen and ugly with its teeth like rocks; finally, how that woman could admit my massive penis however much she yearned for it from the tips of her toes. I felt sorry for myself, for if I split the noble woman apart I should be thrown to the beasts... Meanwhile she was repeatedly whispering gentle endearments, pressing constant kisses and uttering rapturous sounds with devouring eyes; and as climax she murmured 'I have you, I have you, my fond dove, my sparrow.' As she spoke she showed that my reservations were needless, and my fear unfounded; for she hugged me as closely as she could, and admitted me absolutely all the way. Whenever I withdrew my buttocks in an attempt to spare her, she would lunge madly toward me, seize my back, and cling to me in a still closer grip...*"

At a noise from John, Father Malcolm could see that he was uncomfortable, and tried to reassure him.

"I think," he said, "that's the part in the book St. Augustine had a problem with."

"St. Augustine?" said John, surprised.

"Oh yes, He had a *big* problem with Apuleius, and I think that's why. I'm writing a paper on it."

It was growing late, and because John had asked earlier for a bit of holy dirt, they returned to the chapel. Father Malcolm's little dog bounded ahead and began digging up the *tierra bendita* from the *pocito*, the little well in the floor, which is always kept full.

"Ah, Rufinus, you are a very naughty boy. Sometimes I wonder why I saved you from the coyotes."

The little dog wagged his tail and sat grinning as the priest scooped up the dirt and replaced it in the *pocito*. A little while later, as they stood in the parking lot of the rectory, Father Malcolm's eyes lingered on Mary's face, illumined by the moon.

"God has given His gift to Chimayo, and this is my gift to you," he said, pressing *The Golden Ass* in her hands. He, too, was bathed in moonlight. As John watched, he thought he saw over each head the glint of a soft glowing halo. But it was only a trick of his eyes, he said later. Being a priest, he had seen too many paintings of the saints.

***

Father Malcolm had thrown Mary a lifeline. Not once, as she had listened to the outrageous story of a woman falling in love with an ass, had she thought of the Magi. I can guess why although I'd rather not. On the other hand, maybe it wasn't so outrageous when you consider that the ass was really a man, and for a child, wouldn't a father's penis seem as huge as that of an ass? But the favor was returned in kind, or at least so she thought, by arriving at Chimayo just when Father Malcolm needed the company of his old friend.

Diary: Our visit to the Sanctuario couldn't have come at a better time. Father Malcolm needed to be consolded. Only a few days earlier, he had, after being persuaded by one of his parishioners, a former voladore from Puebla, Mexico, invited a troupe of professional voladores (flyers) from the same town, to perform a voladores ritual ceremony at the Chimayo church.

The Father had accompanied the troupe and dozens of townspeople into the mountains, to a spot where a 100' tree had been selected. He then blessed the tree and, after celebrating Mass, it was cut down, shorn of its branches, sprinkled with holy water and incense, and hauled back to the church. Wooden steps were nailed to the trunk, and a revolving frame nailed at the top. After it was erected on the adjacent grounds, four voladores climbed to the top, secured ropes around their waists and, to the sound of drums and flutes, leaned backwards and let themselves fall into space.

But as they slowly spun around the pole—"I myself would have liked to join them," said the Father—one of the ropes broke, and the voladore, with a terrible scream, fell to the earth. His neck broken and skull bashed in, he died killed instantly.

Because the pole seemed so phallic-like, I thought of my father's penis and imagined myself hurtling down from its pinnacle. I wonder if there are women voladores. It does seemed just as appropriate for women to fly as for men. And why not, if the truth is a tree and the tree is the phallus?

***

Mary was eager to get back to LA and continue two projects she had started. One was a nude of John, and the other was an almost life-size painting of the mammoth struggling in the tar pit. But at the priest's suggestion, they went to Taos. His enthusiasm for the old pueblo—its art galleries and museums and excellent restaurants in the charming little town, had not been exaggerated.

They had lunch, then drove to Wheeler Peak for what, Father Malcolm had said, was a spectacular view of all the surroundings. After they saw the view, and Mary picked up some pretty stones and colored glass from a magic circle someone had made that was littered with beer cans and cigarette butts, they left the mountain and headed for home.

***

Mary's earliest memory, which I expect is true of many of us, was of her mother. It seems out of character that Mary even put it in her diary—it is such a pleasant one. And so vivid too, after so many years

134

as if it were just yesterday, seeing her first rose as she knelt next to a plant of roses with her mother on a beautiful warm day. She even remembers how blue the sky was, and can feel her mother's arms encircling her. And how soft and velvet the petals and their fragrance: "My brain was perfumed by the sweetest scent."

If only she could have left off with that. But no. Besides associating Helen with the roses, there was also the smell of horse shit—well, more correctly, that mixture of urine and manure one smells at a riding stable. That, of course, going back to the riding lessons at the baron's academy.

Then there were one or two more—I know she read Proust (or, rather, tried to) which must have inspired her to record her own olfactory memories—such as a certain mustiness encircling Helen, a pungent smell—earthy, ripe—that was as deeply embedded and easily recalled as the smell of newly mowed grass or a wet sidewalk.

Well. I have to say that this musty, pungent, earthy, ripe odorous Helen doesn't at all fit with how I remember her. She was almost too clean: never a hair out of place, never a spot on her clothing, never any nail polish starting to peel off.

Poor Helen. But I guess she brought it on herself, being so maligned, if it's all part of the vestigial god-like function of the divine function—the hallucinations of bicameral men and all that—in their right temporal lobes. Mary had a good nose for those sorts of things, I think.

Love/hate coming through the nose! The rose and the manure— sounds like a good title for a book, doesn't it?

***

Paris, it turned out, was good for Margaret. Perhaps it was just the place to go, the right prescription for a soul in need of healing. Her sense of well-being was such that when the last jar of potion ran out, she was in no hurry to return to Athens.

She had been to Paris before. This was when Helen had refused to

135

spend the summer in Glenbrook, and insisted on going to Paris instead. It hadn't been much fun, and young as she was, it was after she viewed Ingres' painting, the *Grande Odalisque* at the Louvre with George that she began to drink wine.

"Yes, that will do it," she wrote Mary. "Standing in front of an odalisque with one's father will always do it."

There was also the gaiety of Paris, the outdoor cafes, the *joie de vivre* and all that. A rainy and unusually cold summer hadn't at all daunted her. Color returned to her face, and toward the end of the summer she invited both Mary and John (Barbara was still at the work camp) to join her. Reluctant at first to go—she was having trouble with her painting of the mammoth, and getting the right expression on his face. But who can resist Paris?

And how nice it was, being with Margaret and her happy children. They had become a bit plump, but that was from all the confection shops around, and all the delicious bonbons that were too hard to resist.

Together they visited Monet's gardens, Versailles, the Eiffel Tower, the Latin Quarter, Monmartre, the Moulin Rouge, Notre Dame Cathedral and the Luxembourg Gardens. At Margaret's suggestion, she and John went to see the famous labyrinth at the Chartres Cathedral, about an hour from Paris.

The labyrinth, which dated back to the 13th century, was inside the cathedral, and beyond it on the west wall, a large rose window with flower-like petals of stained glass, radiated from the center. The labyrinth itself was made, they were told, of the same number of stones it takes for a man to develop in the womb, and the tunic worn by the Virgin Mary at Christ's birth was held in the cathedral's treasury. Many people were traversing the labyrinth, and there was a mysteriousness that seemed to be hovering everywhere.

Diary: As we entered it, I couldn't help thinking that the pathways looked like the cerebral cortex—the convolutions of the brain. Even the color was right, and there at the bottom was the brain stem, its stalk-like portion leading to a flower in the middle. I whispered to John—was that the sweet spot, the holy part of orgasm—God?

Well, the way he walked off, leaving me alone in the sweet spot, was not at all a good feeling. It's kind of what it felt like when George ran for office. I decided to get out of it quickly, and cut straight down the stem, ignoring the glances some people were giving me.

***

The *Phantom of the Opera* was playing at the Palais Garnier, and thanks to the largess of Aunt Lucy, everyone got to see it. Naturally, Mary connected the phantom with her father, and the *Music of the Night* with the magic circle. Later that evening, as they drank wine and discussed the performance at an outdoor cafe, they decided to see the Paris sewers the next day. These were famous long before they became the setting for the phantom's lair and the *Music of the Night*. Indeed, the Senator himself wanted to see them, and had taken his family deep inside when they had visited Paris.

So the next day, after buying tickets, they descended the many steps into the grand labyrinth of tunnels and channels that cover over a thousand miles. After spending time in the museum and learning interesting facts about sewage, they entered the sewers themselves. Who knows what thoughts were going through Mary's head, and perhaps, who would want to know.

There were narrow walkways on each side of the channels. They were wet and slippery from the water ducts dripping overhead, and even though there were grates covering the channels, metal barriers had been added along the way. Eventually they came to a sign that said no entrance.

"I remember going past this gate as a child," Margaret said. "Let's go on," she added excitedly even though the channel was no longer covered with a grate, and barred off only by a chain. The children had run off ahead. Worried they might fall in, Margaret called them back, but they pretended not to hear. Suddenly she grabbed her sister's shoulder.

"Oh my God, Mary, it's started!"

She pointed to the children's buttocks. In the dimly lit passageway, their back pockets bulging with bonbons, it did indeed look like something had started to grow. As she rushed toward them, she slipped and fell over the side. A sudden surge of water from all the rain came roaring into the channel and swept her away. When her body was found at the *Pont de l'Alma* entrance, it was covered in dark waste.

***

Margaret's death hung heavily over her sisters, Mary especially who had been a witness to the scene. For months, the splash resounded in her ears, the color of the water still a vivid impression. Thus, when Aunt Lucy sent her the packet of books Margaret had been reading, Mary began reading them at once, hoping to fill the void of her sister's death. Unfortunately, it only made the loss more acute.

Written by the French philosopher, Jacques Lacan, they talked a lot about desire and such things as an object of desire that can never be obtained. The consequences of that, was that it set in motion the desire for anything.

Well, the sisters knew very well what that object of desire was, and why it wasn't attainable. But Margaret had attained it. Indeed, all four of them had. She had even talked about his ideas the night before she died. Suspecting what Margaret was hinting at, why hadn't Mary told her about herself? If Margaret had known a long time ago that for the Magi—for Balthasar, Melchior and Gaspar, there was no "unattainable object cause of desire," there was only *Khvetukdas*, would she not have dwelt so on a pig's tail? And still be alive?

***

Prof. Barnes' interpretation of the Scriptures—the chaos and void and all that—had made an impression on Mary. But not long afterwards, she began to wonder whether or not the professor's theory of chaos, and her own theory of language needed to be reassessed. This having come during a night of love-making. As the sounds of her voice and John's escaped spontaneously from their lips—spontaneous, uncensored, unmodulated, uncontrolled, unstoppable yet in some way interesting and pleasant to listen to, the timbre and pitch of both voices modulated by their sex, one high and clear, the other deep and low—Mary, thinking (always thinking!) decided next morning that Barnes had missed something. His chaos theory needed more fleshing out. It was not just the rutting and rivalry that caused Genesis to be written. It was the cacophony, too; five or six million years ago, would the bursts of emotion emitted by creatures transitioning from apes to hominids have had the same timbre and pitch and dimorphic frequencies as hers and John's? Or would these poor creatures have set off such a cacophony of noise that the Scriptures could come up with no better way to describe this awesome diorama other than the chaos and void? And did not chaos and cacophony sound like they should both go together?

***

To fill the empty gap in Helen's life (and surely there was one; despite Mary's own personal opinion, Helen was, after all, human)— Margaret was dead, Barbara was at *Puerta La Cruz*, Mary was with John, and the Senator was in Washington—she took hold of Alice. It was an easy catch, not hard to explain. Not since Mary's awareness of late, her certainty that the Senator had had all of them, even Alice. Why else did Alice want to be Gilda and die in her father's arms? Surely the poor child was as afraid of Helen as Mary was, Mary, who was always seeing Helen in terms of the gaping vagina—the GV—and wondering how Alice could be warming up to it. Unless, that is, she was so afraid of it that she wanted to befriend it. That seemed like a very plausible explanation.

***

Diary: Now that makes sense, the GV and all, and explains so many things. Now it's not odd at all that they go around everywhere

139

together—movies, restaurants, shopping. Even trips.

"Where is mother?" I'll ask Marcus.

"Oh they've gone to Las Vegas," he'll answer. And another time, "Oh they've gone to Palm Springs."

Sometimes when they think no one is looking, says Bertha, they will giggle like schoolgirls and binge on sweets and eat whole boxes of Oreos. That's when they act like cats that have swallowed the canary.

Ah, the power of the GV! It can even make you fat. Look at Alice now. She doesn't give a fig newton that all the weight she lost from diet pills is coming back. She just rationalizes it by saying all great opera singers are fat (up and down, up and down—that's how her weight's been going ever since the horses). But wait! Has she been terrified of it, too, like me, way back when? Is that why she used to dress up as Batman or Spiderman at Halloween instead of Beauty or the Little Mermaid or even Mulan the Warrior Princess, and why she threw her arms around Martin when he gave her—was it for her fifth birthday?— a red firetruck?

***

Now some readers, I'm sure, might find Mary being rather catty or callous toward her sister, especially since we know what happens to Alice—her being institutionalized and all. But if it *is* all coming from the vestigial, divine god-like function of the right hemisphere and the injudicious ideas that grow out of it—isn't that why Cain killed Abel?—and that in the end they were merely hopeless bandages— *Khvetukdas* and the Crucifixion—which, like most self-help books, weren't helpful, then how could Mary help it, I mean, being snippy and all?

***

Alice's appeasement of Helen—Mary called it a self-sacrifice to the god Baal—came to an end one evening when she was out walking and met Joe, the security guard who patrolled the park at night, rolling by on his bicycle. She had seen him before and always waved, but this

140

time, as she peered into the glowing windows of neighboring houses, and fantasized about beautiful women and handsome men making love, he stopped to say hello.

This was more than thrilling because, as impossible as it sounds, Joe had a trained voice, a beautiful tenor voice, and he often sang while he was on patrol. One evening as he was riding past her house just as she and Helen were leaving, he was singing the duke's aria from Rigoletto. One need not be surprised that, on the following evening, Alice—on the pretext of wanting to lose weight—went for a walk. Her night strolls paid off, and Alice, for the first time, was dating someone other than her mother.

His parents called him Giuseppe. They, too, were opera lovers, and on the night that Alice was invited to their home for dinner, they were playing *La Traviata* on speakers that carried throughout the house. It was a grand house set in the hills above Los Feliz, and as Joe led her around the garden with fountains and statuary, the strains of the Love Duet reaching even out there, she pictured Joe as Alfredo and herself as Violetta embracing each other on stage at the Met. When is a voice ever just a voice, one might ask?

The two often went to the opera. Mary describes how Alice, during a performance of Rigoletto, began touching Joe's genitals.

"As the hunchback was limping about malevolently," she wrote, "the two left their seats and returned just before intermission. Lots of people have done it in the Mile High Club, but how many can say they've done it in the lady's restroom at the Dorothy Chandler Pavilion?"

After several months, it looked like the couple were serious. While Helen wasn't keen about having an Italian son-in-law, the Senator was delighted. Not only might this stand for more of the Italian vote, but now he could talk opera to someone who understood it.

But for Joe, it was plan to see that Helen didn't like him. The coldness she was famous for was too obvious. Was she jealous? Jealous that Alice was now his and not hers? Or was she attracted to him—he was, after all, viral and handsome—and hiding her attraction by being cold and aloof?

One evening as they were all eating dinner, Alice looked at her mother, then looked at Joe. With a deep sigh, she knew she wanted to get married—to Joe, that is. Whenever he proposed, she would say yes.

It wasn't long after that, that he phoned her and said he wanted to see her, it couldn't wait.

"I hope it will make you happy," he said.

When she welcomed him that evening, his eyes sparkled with joy and excitement. Her own eyelids fluttered and her heart pounded as he took her hand in his, surely to slip the ring on her finger. But why was it the right hand instead of the left?

"Guess what! I'm going to Italy to study with the great Maestro Bernini! He is probably the most famous singing teacher in the world!"

As he was speaking, the baron, who had just returned from Germany, entered the room. He, too, had some news to tell, and was equally excited. But Alice had quietly slipped out the room and returned seconds later with a butcher's knife. As she lunged at Joe, her eyes blinded with tears and rage, she missed and plunged the knife instead into the baron.

***

Diary: Last night I dreamed I was in a temple with beautiful halls of marble and gold, perched high atop a narrow outcropping of rock that reached thousands of feet in the air. But this pinnacle was so phallic-like in structure that I could not help but get aroused even though I was asleep. And when I awoke—oh, how I wished there was such a place!

A few days later she wrote: But there is! It's the Fanjinshan temple in China. Oh how exciting!

How did she know this?! Mary's prescient dream still resonating in my head when I visited John in Rome many months later, he said he'd thought about becoming a Buddhist monk after seeing this picture and showing it to Mary. Mystery solved!

***

CANON VI

"Whether it's Khvetukdas or card tricks, it all starts in the ancient divine function of the right hemisphere of the brain."

"Once you've been in the magic circle, you don't need God. All the shibboleths He stands for are no longer necessary. God in the sky no longer exists, only God on earth, only orgasm."

"'Jesus was made flesh by the Word of God.' Now that we know what the Word is, it all becomes clear."

"Our stubborn refusal to know ourselves, and the unknowability of people: it's all locked up with truth—the truth of ourselves and the truth of others. But if truth is a concept that is rooted in the phallus, and the phallus is the Word of God, how can we know truth when we believe only God knows it, and His Word is off-limits?"

"In order to expound on the virtues of God, His antithesis—orgasm—must be relegated to the fires of hell."

"Is it a mere coincidence that we can experience these attributes of God—terror, death, joy and love—in one fell swoop of orgasm?"

"At the Metropolitan Museum there is on display a biface—prehistoric hand ax—possibly as old as 700,000 BC. Because of its large size, beautiful color and exquisite design, it's thought to have had a purpose other than utilitarian. Perhaps it was man's first attempt to capture God in art?"

"If orgasm is God, then there is no conflict between spirit and flesh since they are one and the same substance, essence, reality. The conflict is totally imaginary."

"The infallibility of the God's word means that men will always rule because the penis is incapable of error."

"Could the configuration of the male genitalia—penis in between two testicles side by side—have led, thanks to the creativeness of the human mind, to the Holy Trinity—Father, Son and Holy Spirit? And if so, could the Holy Spirit be the one in between?"

"Whereas Zeus, god of the Greeks, impregnated many women, the Holy Spirit impregnated only one."

***

On the way back from New Mexico, Mary spent the whole time reading *The Golden Ass*. Hardly did she look out the window and see the beauty of the American west as the car speed past it. No, her mind was too engrossed in the enchantment of the book, and it wasn't just the fabulous scene which Father Malcolm had read aloud. It was many other scenes, many other episodes and experiences—not just the magic ones when Isis came to Lucius the ass and fed him rose petals to make him human again. But ones that were true to life, the ugly part, the true part where people were cruel and murderous, people no different than people today.

What a genius Apuleius was. Not only to have created such a story of magic, but also one as true to life as any story could ever be. But wait! Was it not a story of transformation, of one thing turning into another? What else was like that? Was that where its hold came from, that it was more than a story about people, but one about God, too, and His magical transformation?

The thrill of it all was too much, and it was not long before a package arrived from Amazon, and John began to notice he was eating dried rose petals in the salads, the soups, the entrees and desserts.

"They are supposed to be good for you," Mary answered as a vision of Lucius the ass with his big knobby teeth comping happily on them and giving her an adoring look. "They are full of anti-oxidants."

Ah, if only she were still a child and could still be playing Pin the Tail on the Donkey. But it wasn't too late to move to the country and buy a real donkey. She gazed at John and imagined how he would look with big donkey ears. So sweet! So lovable! But then, why not? Hadn't Titania, queen of the fairies, thought the same thing, too, when she first gazed on Bottom—a weaver from Athens who had been transformed into an ass? Was it just a coincidence, or at Shakespeare, too, come under the magic spell of Apuleius and *The Golden Ass*?

***

Although the world was never their oyster thanks to George, who but Mary, fully aware of the debilitating handicap, would give him a pass? Well, yes, he *was* God, but even so, who but Mary would blame the hominids instead? And the taboos—the unapproachable, unmentionable and inviolable objects, words and acts, and not George, that had sent her and her sisters down the rabbit hole. No, *not* George, only the hominids manipulating people just like the *Wizard of Oz* did from behind a curtain of smoke and mirrors.

Not that she was advocating *Khvetukdas*, but wasn't it monstrous and ghastly and cruel that children who were objects of a father's desire were made to suffer the inequity of it, all because these wizards—these primitive men with primitive minds who were primitively afraid of their unrestrained orgasm, had repurposed it into God? Was it not nonsense to have lives ruined this way, especially since orgasm was the most natural thing on earth? And beyond that, how could there be free will and the ability to choose and act independently, if the wizards were running the show and had created all kinds of crazy things like angels, demons, heaven and hell in order to repurpose orgasm? But if it all wasn't really working, and there was still that unrequited place of yearning in the gonads to break free from constraint and soar like a bird or an angel and take people into forbidden territories that can only be accessed by allegory, allegory that turns some men into murderers and others into the rich and powerful, allegory that the hominids created as the lawful antidotes to men's forbidden desires, allegory which work for some and not for others, then *why blame George?*

Oh me oh my! Are you pulling your hair out, too? Oh well, so much for the power of the mind, the power of love, the power of rationalization and the power of quicksand and quagmires. But it has set my mind to thinking. And the question is, are these truly some insights Mary gained from her childhood and all the magic it produced, or has she gone stark and raving mad? Maybe one has to, to give a man such as the Senator a pass.

***

Shortly after their return from New Mexico, he dropped by the duplex. He wanted to discuss Glenbrook and the investigation. But as he listened, his mind drifted off to the days when he frequented the neighborhood, still a lawyer. Truth be told, he always enjoyed being there. Despite the Jewishness of the neighborhood—it was near Fairfax—it was a part of old LA, and nothing could beat it for charm. The Farmer's Market was nearby, and though the stalls nowadays sold mostly artisan products at high prices, he didn't at all mind, it was such a lovely place to wonder through.

Many a time he'd had lunch at Canter's delicatessen with Walter. They'd discuss court cases and other legal matters, and he always looked forward to his favorite sandwich—chopped liver on rye— while Walter always ordered the pickled herring. Now, while in his heart George knew that Walter hadn't killed Christ, he resented him anyway. This was for always ordering the pickled herring. The raw herring with its silvery skin reminded him of the time he saw, as a young boy, his aunt chop the head off a large fresh fish she had bought in San Pedro. There was not only the horror of seeing it decapitated, but of something else. But that was always too hazy to remember.

He returned his attention to the present just as Mary was describing in great detail the charred remains and how they had still been smoldering.

"The smell was really terrible, and that's because the sheriff said the arsonist had used tons of gasoline. Can you imagine? He could have set the whole mountain on fire."

The Senator sighed. What was the point of chastising the two for not staying longer and learning more about the investigation? Nothing would be gained, and after a few more questions, he got up to leave. As he walked toward the door, he noticed a couple of smallish stones and a few pieces of colored glass on the mantelpiece above the fireplace.

"What's all this?" he asked curiously, picking up the two stones. They were not round and smooth, but oblong, and looked rather like figs lined with little ridges.

"Oh, just some souvenirs Mary brought back from New Mexico," John answered. The Senator turned them over and over in his hands.

"They aren't very pretty," he said, "but they do have a nice feeling. My daughter always knows what she's doing."

He put them back on the mantel and said good-bye.

***

It was about this time that the person who shot Professor Barnes—who had, by the way, recovered and was now teaching mathematics—was apprehended. It was, as his classmates had suspected, Rufus. His uncle the Archbishop had disguised him as a nun, and hidden him at Poor Clare Monastery in Roswell.

The facts of the story had emerged. It was not so much the professor's theory that had set Rufus off, but the professor's remark about ants. A few days before the shooting, a student had asked whether the professor thought there was a connection between the shrinkage of the human brain, which was believed to have happened between 3,000 to 5,000 years ago, and religion.

"Oh no doubt," the professor had answered. "Our brains can be likened to a petrie dish in which magic and superstition are cultured at birth. As civilization advanced upon the bedrock of religion, hierarchies and castes emerged. This created a demand for smaller-brained people who could service the hierarchy and do all the hard work without too much complaint. It's hard to tell which is a more brilliant evolutionary development—this reduction in men's brain cells or the mindless activity of ants. It should be seen, however, as a means to the same ends."

With these closing remarks Rufus, having believed that the professor had implied that it was God who made people stupid, was heard to mutter as he left the classroom, "You'll be sorry!"

But many people thought this wasn't the real reason for the shooting. During the professor's lecture on evolution, he had passed out a drawing illustrating the changes that took place in the pelvis. And, not wishing to leave well enough alone, he had said that in the churches, the font which holds the holy water could have evolved from the bowl-like pelvis from whence came all the magic. Was not the os sacrum—the sacred bone—part of the pelvis?

Rufus had been seen crumbling the diagram in a shaking hand and gnashing his teeth as he left the classroom.

Yes, for many people, Rufus' confession didn't hold water.

***

149

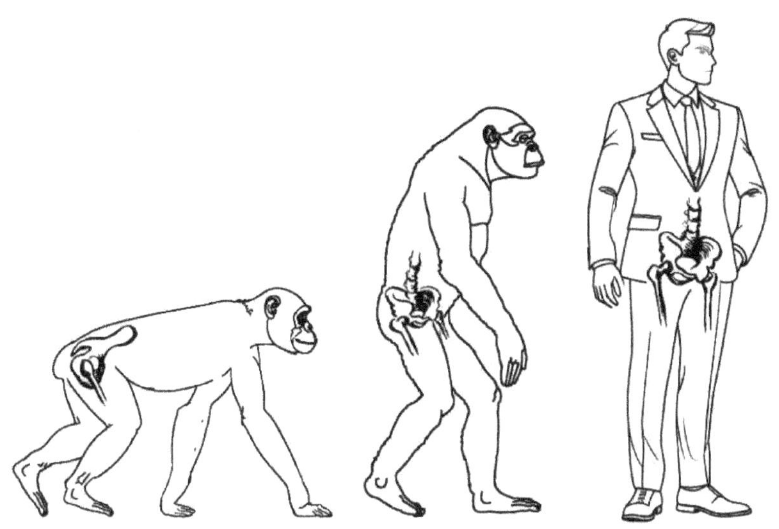

Was not the os sacrum—the sacred bone—part of the pelvis?

***

Diary: Often when I pleasure myself, and feel the kingdom of heaven rising from the soft lips of my vulva, I will wish I was still there in the Garden of Eden, there with my father. But there are other times when the waves are not so delicious and don't come of themselves but must be forced. Then, as I'm awash in fear, I hear a cry for help. But this isn't often, and what brings it on I've never been able to figure out. Perhaps it's a game of dice: will I explode in joy or fear, pleasure or pain? But if Einstein said that God does not play dice with the universe, might that include orgasm, too?

Reminder to self: stop on a high note, don't go for the last one— "one more time"—and fail and be unhappy. Don't be a pig.

***

Diary: I wonder what Dr. Niedlhauf would say if I told him about my latest dream. Actually, it's one I have all the time—well, not *all* the time, but lots of times. But since he hasn't been very good at analyzing Alice's, I don't suppose he'd be any better at mine. Still, I *would* like to know what it means. I can imagine an ancient augur, on hearing the dream, telling the King of Persia or some other such monarch, not to go into battle that day.

But then, why waste my time with the doctor? Don't I know enough about dreams of crashing waves to know where they're coming from? Even so, there's no getting away from it, how scary they are, especially when the waves are a thousand feet high and there's no place to run.

This last one, near the pier at Santa Monica—that's where mother used to take us before dad bought the house in Glenbrook—was full of waves. First there was the one that rose up all along the horizon. A monster, incredible, mesmerizing, unbelievable. How could it be happening? How?

But as I stood paralyzed, more giant waves appeared. They were so close to shore I was afraid they would get me. I thought I should run, but where? The only high ground were the Pacific Palisades, but they were across a dangerous street, and the cliffs were too steep to climb. Just in time I woke up.

Well, come to think of it, maybe the augur would have told the king to proceed to battle. Since I woke up and nothing had happened, wouldn't it be a sign that the king would win?

***

It was the ceremonial opening of the Memorial Gardens at Christ Cathedral in Orange County, and the Senator wanted to be there. While the press was interviewing him, Mary wandered about the beautiful gardens before joining John and the baron inside the cathedral. For those of you who are unfamiliar with it, it was originally known as the Crystal Cathedral—this because it is the largest glass building in the world.

As John put spittle on his finger to wipe off a smudge on the glass pane, the baron stood stock still, like one struck dumb.

"Gott in himmel!" he exclaimed. "Look at all this light! Mithra would have loved this place!"

Mary's mouth fell open. Von Clapp knew about Mithra? A gush of blood rushed to her cheeks, and her hear began to pound.

"I can see them now," he continued, making a broad sweep of his arms, "all Mithra's converts reclining on couches, holding goblets with sacred wine, and before them on tripods, tiny loaves of bread marked with crosses in honor of the sacrificed bull."

As she listened in rapt attention, her respect was growing minute by minute. Was it possible that he knew about the Magi? About *Khvetukdas*? All her resentment—his letting her fall off the horse and bringing *Struwwelpeter* to the house—disappeared. But before she could speak, the ceremony for the opening began, and a solemn procession of men in long flowing robes appeared, led by the bishop. How beautiful they all looked in their ancient priestly dress. She could almost hear them teaching the gonads the same lessons with the same rituals the poor things were taught in times gone by. But why not? Didn't they still need to learn the same lessons? Were they not always hankering after the same forbidden desires? She should know, if anyone.

She tried to catch the baron's eye, but he was busy looking at the cathedral. Well, okay; because now something had caught her eye. It was the bishop's mitre—his hat. And as it glittered and shimmered all gold in the sunlight, why, she wondered, was he wearing a hat that, with its rosy red opening at the top, parting like smiling, beckoning lips, looked so much like a vagina? Ah, could heaven be paved with golden labia? And if so, was there a better way to keep hope in the hereafter alive?

***

Diary: When I told him what the mitre looks like, he took off right away for a retreat in San Bernardino. It's okay. I've had a full week of pleasuring myself without any interruptions. Yes, a full week if levitating and bilocating with interruption. Why not use those terms? Are they not how the church describes those religious miracles when the saints are lifted off the ground, or reported to be in two places at once? What better way to describe the miracle of orgasm when you are both in your body and out of it at the same time?

Sometimes when I pleasure myself, and I hear myself think—It's too beautiful! Too beautiful! No more! No more!—I see the prophets of old covering their eyes, or turning their faces from God because He is too powerful to behold.

Ah, if only this glorious metamorphosis of the body, this unparalleled pleasure of the mind and all the feelings that go with it— the peace and happiness and love that comes over you, the gratitude, compassion, friendship, forgiveness, goodness, mercy, kindness, tolerance combined in that one split second of electro/chemical current—could go on forever! With a god like this, prayer is just a poor substitute, a waste of time and a poor use of the hands when all one needs is a finger! Was consciousness created just for this?

***

Ah, could haven be paved with golden labia?

***

Diary: I'm so relieved! John called this evening and said it wasn't my fault at all, and had nothing to do with what I'd said about the bishop's hat, why he left, that is. No, it was something the baron had said earlier at Christ Cathedral about Mithra and the bull and Jesus. It had really gotten to him, and he needed time off to think.

I burst into tears. Was it because he said it wasn't my fault, or because he asked me if I knew that the vagina hat—I mean the mitra, was named after the god Mithra? (Which I didn't.) Either way, and I don't know why I cried, but I did, it all felt so good what he said. Jeté.

***

The Senator was able to get Barbara an early release. The inmates at the work camp were sorry to see her go. When they hadn't been out fighting fires, they were learning how to do plies and jetés. She hadn't been free long when an internship opened up in Washington, and the Senator said he could get that for her, too. If she'd been able to get the beautiful peacocks at *Puerta La Cruz* out of her head, and how beautiful they were when they spread their tails, almost as beautiful as the Firebird, she might have accepted. But instead she decided on a job at a strip club in Wilmington.

***

Diary: This is all so wonderful! The Senator is embarrassed, and Barbara gets to dance. She uses a lot of ballet technique on the pole. They are billing her as the Firebird, and she has glued these long red feathers to her G-string. She looks sensational and is getting lots of attention. People are constantly tucking bills in her front, but she won't let anyone tuck bills in her tail Her eyes sparkle all the time—I've never seen anyone so happy!

Important people are coming to the club, and there have even been some proposals of marriage, can you believe! But since she's not at all ready for a relationship, all she needs to do is hint around that somebody did something to her when she was little, and they drop her like a hot potato. Which is what she wants. Her dancing career is way too important now that it's back.

"But if I ever do fall in love," she said, "I'll be very circumspect. None of that stuff that Margaret was into—what was it, something about an unattainable object of desire? Unless he's as broad-minded as John. I can't believe that he never reacted badly when you told him about dad. Do you think it's because he's heard worse confessions than yours? Or maybe the same one, over and over?"

***

Oof! Little did she know. Mary's confession had occurred on the way back from the Memorial Gardens. The couple had taken the 5 Fwy on their way home. This way Mary could see one of her favorite things—that amazing old tire factory built to resemble the Assyrian palace of King Sargon II. Now a shopping center called the Citadel, for all intents and purposes, it is still his palace.

What caused this bad decision? Was it von Clapp's surprising revelation in the cathedral? Was it the procession of priests? Was it the mitre on the bishop's head? Whatever it was, it made her take a leap of faith and, as they came up to the huge figures of the ancient kings carved in stone on the Citadel, tell John her secret.

It was met for a long while in silence. Of course, he was concentrating on his driving, but the way he was staring at the road had now taken on a funny look. When at last he spoke, he said, "Gee, it's hard to believe he did all that. Are you sure?"

Uh, duh? Did he not get what she was saying? Was it a guy thing, men sticking together no matter what? As she wrote in her diary, a bit over the top, I think, but perhaps necessary to express her resentment at his cavalier attitude to an event which, in her mind, was as momentous as these:

"What did he expect, the rape of Europa? The birth of a child with two heads and a pig's tail? Joan of Arc burned at the stake? But I *was* Joan of Arc, and I *did* hear the voice of God, only God was orgasm and the stake was a penis, my father's penis as firm and straight as a tree, and I've been burning on it ever since."

***

Diary: Last night, we—Barbara and I—managed to get Alice away from mother, and took her to the strip club We plied her with drinks, hoping she might come to terms with what, we both now suspect, was the same thing that had happened to us. We didn't hit the bull's eye, but we might have come close.

As Barbara pirouetted and jetéd around the pole, her red tail feathers tickling the nose of a certain gentleman and causing another to say, "Ah, c'mon, Barbara, why don't you consider the rest of us goats," Alice, who was watching as if hypnotized by a snake, said, "Barbara's so lucky to feel comfortable being naked like that."

"Yes, but I think there may be a reason."

"Really? I wonder what it is."

"Well, maybe when a person is little," I began, but right away she interrupted me.

"You know," she said, "I've been afraid all my life of being who I am. Or maybe it's what I am, a female. And I don't know why."

"Maybe there's a reason for *that*."

"That's what I've been thinking, but what could it be?

"Well, when I was little..." She interrupted again.

"I think the easiest way is to change my gender. I'd rather go through all the stuff you have to go through—operations, hormones, whatever—to get rid of the fear. Do you know what it's like to be in a body you don't want to be in? To live in constant terror, day after day, year after year?"

I thought of mother, and was going to say yes. But before I could she said, "That way there won't be anyone out to get me."

Oh how I wanted to tell her about the Magi, and what they said about girls sleeping with their father, and boys 'with she who bore

157

them.' Might not *Khvetukdas* help her to stay in the body she was born with? But instead I asked her how her singing was coming along and if she'd found a new teacher. A few minutes later, Barbara jetéd off the pole and, to the cheering and applause, pirouetted across the bar. As money flew from every direction, Alice suddenly got sick, and rushed off to the bathroom.

"What happened?" Barbara asked, taking a quick break. She listened quietly until I came to the singing part.

"Oh let her alone," she said. "She's the same as I am. Do you think she really wants to sing in front of a huge audience and have the world know that she is only singing for dad? I mean, how scary would *that* be? She'd probably poop in her pants."

I thought this rather unkind. Still, I imagined this scene at the Met, and all of a sudden, Alice takes a dump on the stage. Thank goodness, she never got over being told that her voice wasn't worth a plug nickel.

We stayed on until closing. With John off on another retreat, it was a pleasant way to spend time. Barbara took a break and sat down with us. The dancer who took her place hardly looked more than a child, and the gentleman who was giving her the most attention looked about ninety. But wasn't that how old Joseph was when he took the Virgin Mary to wife? And since the Virgin was already pregnant, was that why an angel intervened and brought an end to the unholy alliance—that is, twelve-year-old girls marrying ninety-year-old men—that is, fathers and daughters? Was that whole thing a warning about forbidden love? And why the "incest-loving men of the East" were brought into the picture, and the shepherds, too, because centuries before, it was shepherds who attended the birth of Mithra, god of light, venerated by the Magi? But if this venerating the virgin birth to confirm the new ideology had really worked, why, I thought, were the three of us sitting here?

***

Yes, their father's shadow was long, but his, at least for Mary, caste

158

no unpleasant olfactory memories like Helen's did, only the divine scent of God. Whether or not the other three sisters had similar memories, well, we shall never know. And why be curious about them anyway. There're enough curious things about Mary's memories to kill a dozen cats.

For instance. Now that we know that only rose petals could save Lucius' life, that they had such sacred, magical qualities they were able to transform the ass back to a human, was Mary's olfactory memory of the rose and her mother also something magical, a fragrance originating not just in the rose, but also in the divine right hemisphere? A fragrance of God?

But how could anyone love such a mother? Her iniquity was there to see, plain as day, on an old Christmas card that Helen had addressed but never sent to cousin Jessica. The message *Seasons Greetings From Our House to Yours* was engraved above a picture of the four children standing next to Santa Claus and his reindeer. At the bottom she had written, "George *is* that way," underlining the 'is.'

Ah, foolish woman. Foolish to write it—she couldn't send it now, she'd be giving herself and the magic circle away—and foolish to keep the card. Well, maybe the Deep South had impacted her vestigial divine function with too much dirty soil, and Mary had a reason to hate her. But perhaps that came later? After the magic rose? And if so, was the truth hidden? Hidden by conjuring up only the unpleasant smells?

But lying is as old as the human race. And who knows? Perhaps all lying starts where Mary's did, in the ancient divine function of the brain's right hemisphere. Did Mary love her mother or hate her? I think it was both, myself. The bad smells were only a cover-up.

***

John was no longer getting aroused. This had started shortly after the opening of the Memorial Gardens at the cathedral. No matter how many tricks Mary tried—simple things at first like honey, ice cubes, scented oil and thongs from Victoria's Secret, then later, pumps, vibrating penis rings, bondage restraints and reading aloud from the *Kama Sutra*, the well had run dry, and no amount of coercing either on her part or his could induce the return of Rex the king, the straight measurement.

"Sorry, kid," he'd said, trying to sound like Humphrey Bogart, "I must have paid more attention than I thought to Leviticus and God telling Moses not to masturbate."

This was a horrible mess. How could she have been so stupid? She *knew* she shouldn't have told him, so why did she? Oh, horrible, horrible Mary! If this were like days of old, she would have torn out her hair and smeared herself in ashes. Ah, if only men and penises and love and her own self-worth were not rolled into one! But was that really her fault? I myself would like to blame it on Helen. But then there are the taboos and the hominids that Mary's always talking about.

Anyway or either way, how embarrassing that she couldn't turn him on, that he had to take Viagra, and that that, after a short time, didn't even work. What to do, what to do! Then the lightening struck.

"Let us try the holy dirt!" she cried. If it worked to get women excited, why not the men?

Ah, dear Father Malcolm! Within minutes of taking a tiny amount from the pretty box where John was keeping it on the mantel, and rubbing it on his member, he had an erection. Unfortunately, the Word of God wouldn't stay around without it: eventually, the box became empty.

The priest was afraid to send more. He wasn't sure, but he felt there were eyes upon him. Who knows but that a little thing like sending the *tierra bendita* in the mail couldn't get him in trouble. He heard John's heavy sigh.

"Have you tried the injections?" he asked. "I can tell you they work."

A short time later, the couple came home from the Boston Medical Group with a supply of auto-applicators. The injections worked, just as Father Malcolm predicted, and life returned to normal. Days were spent at the tar pit or the museum, and whenever the Senator needed the two to accompany himself and von Clapp to Newport Beach—"the baron," Mary wrote, "is now rumored to be part of the old Hapsburg dynasty, and people think he should run for governor"—and other venues, they always obliged—Mary the loyal and devoted dog to the last, albeit a snarling one.

Nights, beautiful nights, in the bedroom with the BMG injections. Please don't think they were using the applicators like the mice were using their little levers. But the truth is, that in all this joy and excitement and bliss, they had forgotten the doctor's warning: too many injections, he said, over too short a period of time could cause a prolonged and painful erection known as priapism. And so it happened that on a certain evening, John became Priapus himself, the Greek god of fertility whose penis was always in a permanent state of erection. Many a king would have lost his crown to John during the many hours of his very straight measure. Could Lucius the ass's tumescence been more fascinating than John's?

But eventually, with time and ice, the Word of God, like the wrapper of a drinking straw when it's crinkled up, and a drop of water makes it move, it, too, began to shrivel. And with the end of the injections, the king was dead, and there was no king to replace him.

CANON VII

"Sex will stay dirty as long as orgasm has to wear a mask."

"If the earliest civilizations were settled along such rivers as the Tigris and Euphrates where men could plant crops of barley and wheat and make beer and get drunk, can it be said that repressed orgasm was the catalyst for civilization?"

"Eucharist comes from a word meaning grateful. If we are grateful to God for transforming the body and blood of Christ into bread and wine, should we not also be grateful to the first magicians who were able to transform orgasm into God?"

"Since musical instruments are designed to resonate with desire, it's no coincidence that they are extensions of the human body and often resemble it. In this way, they help close the gap between what is permitted and what is forbidden."

"God is the climactic moment and the divine voice that expresses it."

"God is the greatest shapeshifter of all time."

"The spirits that lived in the penises and vaginas of the hominids now live in the Spirit of God."

"Decode the Bible, and the truth shall set ye free."

"How can an illusion that began a million years ago seem so real, not just to me but to everyone else in the world? If orgasm isn't behind God, then why are people who don't believe in Him still affected by religious iconography—I mean, where is that coming from?"

"Language and culture have covered up the true identity of God. Could that be what they were created for in the first place?"

"The God Particle: for men it's testosterone, for women it's estrogen."

***

*"The spirits that lived in the penises and vaginas of the hominids
now live in the Spirit of God."*

John was glum but seemed content with his renewed state of celibacy. Father Malcolm was sorry to hear it. One day, a package arrived addressed to them both. The note read, "This has worked for many others. It should definitely work for you and Mary." When they opened it, they were surprised to see a jigsaw puzzle. It was a faithful reproduction of da Vinci's *The Last Supper* except that Jesus and his disciples were all Black.

"Oh well," said John, breaking out the pieces at once on their own dining room table, "a puzzle is a puzzle, and I do so enjoy doing them."

Well, imagine this. Before it was even finished, not only had laughter and jokes returned, but so had his desire for Mary. Even before the last piece was put in place, the two were in the sheets again. Ah, dear Father Malcolm, was there ever anyone like him!

But what had happened? Had these black figures helped John expiate his own guilt, the guilt that Mary's confession had brought on? Had it been atoned through the holiness of a Black God? That his own black testicle was not scary anymore, not with a Black Jesus in charge?

But why, then, had the exact opposite seem to happen when Barack Obama was elected President? The boom in gun sales—the Barack boom—as people, even those who already owned guns, rushed out to buy more—Why couldn't they see what a miracle it was to have, for the first time in American history, a *black* testicle was in charge and not a *white* one? To loosen the Bible's grip on the darkness and the light, and all that?

The second puzzle that arrived—Mary had neglected to spread the Good News to Father Malcolm—dear Father Malcolm—was even better than the *Last Supper*. It was a depiction of the Crucifixion, and when John had fit in all the pieces, there was Christ on the Cross, a beautiful Black Christ, very well formed, very buff. Was this not Groddeck made flesh?

"Oedipus, Oedipus, on the Cross we all die."

Who did he remind her of? Ah, yes, herself, and it was obvious that he needed *Khvetukdas* as much as she did.

***

Diary: Margaret's children are here with Aunt Lucy, to visit their grandmother. They seem quite happy, but maybe it's because Aunt Lucy has been taking them to therapy. Poor little things! I know it's silly, but sometimes when they are running about, I will find myself staring at their little bottoms. Of course, there will never be any sign of a protrusion. If they were going to have a pig's tail, wouldn't it have occurred right after they were born? They love to read, and have just finished *Alice in Wonderland.* Now they are starting it's sequel *Through the Looking-Glass.*

As we sat in the garden today, they asked me to read to them. Everything was fine until I came to the part about Humpty Dumpty. One of the twin stopped me and asked, "Will anyone be able to put Aunt Alice together again?"

Yikes, where had they heard that?

"From Grandma when she was ready us the poem."

As the children recited the old nursery rhyme, and how all the king's horses and all the king's men couldn't put Humpty together again, I wondered if Humpty Dumpty had been molested, too. Why not? People do weirder things than that, don't they? Poor little egg!

I started to read again but did not get very far before they stopped me and asked if there was something wrong with Aunt Barbara, too. How perceptive they were! Although if little girls touched by their father are never quite right in the head, maybe it wasn't all that hard.

Thank goodness I have the Magi, *Khvetukdas*, Groddeck, Apuleius and Lucius the ass. The twins will never wonder about me, I'm sure. I don't know why those things are so helpful, but they are. Oh, and John, too, of course. Oh, and the religious puzzles with Black people. I wonder if there is a Black Virgin puzzle—I'll have to ask Father Malcolm.

***

REM Dream—I.E., Very Short

The Queen of Hearts had chased her children into a dark forest.

"Off with their heads," she shouted. Fortunately, the four children found a tree whose girth was so wide that if they kept running around it they were sure she would never catch them. There was a perverse pleasure in the frightening thought that she might.

Faster and faster they all whirled as they raced around the tree. What do they say? A body in motion stays in motion? Soon they were going almost at the speed of light, spinning like a centrifuge. But when at last the large hadron collider slowed down and came to a stop, there was nothing left of the queen and her children but a big puddle of ghee at the bottom of the tree.

Then, straight from the pages of Sophocles and Euripides, an ancient Greek chorus dressed in togas and masks stepped out from the shadows and began this chant:

"Some things are never to be known. Hidden in the tangles and plaque of the brain is a secret that is millions of years old—a secret that has caused all the tangles and plaque in the first place and, after these millions of years, is impossible to discover.

"But when the Apocalypse arrives and the world explodes, the tangles and plaques will also explode. Then the truth will be revealed and the secret uncovered, because that's what an Apocalypse is meant to do—uncover things. Fortunately or unfortunately, everyone will be dead, and no one will get to know what the tangles and plaque were hiding—that it was the ancient divine function of the right hemisphere that started the whole thing off in the first place."

***

Isn't it amazing how Mary could remember all that? I mean, word for word? But I think it was so much in her psyche, that it just came naturally. And who knows if the chorus really said what it said. Maybe she just added it after Helen—I mean, the Queen of Hearts turned into rarefied butter. I kept thinking, as I read deeper and deeper into the diary, why did no one ever guess? And why should I now act so surprised? Because every so often I'd come to their house and her father, if he wasn't taking care of business—I mean official business— would be wearing a terrycloth bathrobe with nothing underneath. I remember once or twice sitting on his lap and wondering about what I saw partially exposed. A great sausage it looked like, the kind that von Clapp so enjoyed—knackwurst, was it? I'm so glad that I never saw my father's. At least I don't think I did, but with such things, perhaps one can never remember?

***

Diary: Von Clapp and Walter don't get along. Well, I shouldn't say Walter. He likes everybody, even father despite shunning him during that first run for office. No, it's all on Wolfgang's side. It's almost like he's sniffing the air whenever he sees Walter, sniff sniff, and what can Walter say after that?

But something really amazing happened today, and I think that's all going to change.

Walter, you see, stopped by to drop off some papers. They were needed that night at the Senator's rally. He turned to leave but I stopped him. How could I let go by, another opportunity to discuss what it is I'm always discussing with him? As usual he listened patiently, a serious look on his face although I sensed that inwardly he was laughing.

"I must say, though, that I like your connection with Mithra and the Eucharist. That is rather tantalizing."

Von Clapp, who was waiting in another room for Helen, came rushing in.

"Mein Gott," he exclaimed. "You two know about Mithra?"

"Mary keeps me informed," said Walter pleasantly. "She says you know about him, too."

"But of course, dear Walter! All Germans know about Mithra. Why, we grew up with him. When I was a boy my parents would take

168

trips through Germany and Austria to see the excavated mithraeums—the temples where he was worshiped. While you people go to Disneyland, we go to Heddernheim, Neuenheim, Friedberg, Osterburken, Linz and Virunum to see the mithraeums. They are all over Europe, of course, but the greatest number have been discovered in Germany. I'm just surprised that any Americans know about him."

Oh how could I ever have despised this man? Little kids fall off horses all the time. Was it his fault that he paid more attention to mother than us? He probably never even heard us screaming for help.

"Mein Gott," he continued, "when I was a little boy, I saw so many reliefs and sculptures of Mithra driving his sword into the bull that I wanted to be a bullfighter. 'Dummkopf!' my mother would scream. 'We Prussians fight people, not bulls.'"

Walter rubbed his chin thoughtfully.

"A lot of people," he said, "drive up and down California to see the old Spanish missions. They are everywhere, too. Maybe it all evens out in the wash."

"No, no," said von Clapp, shaking his head violently. "A Catholic Mass doesn't come close to watching a bullfight in honor of Mithra. A pity Constantine chose Christianity over Mithraism. He had a choice, dear friend, which religion would become the official one."

"Was that because he didn't want to sacrifice anymore animals?" I asked. How wonderful it was, to see the baron and Walter talking to each other.

"No, no," he answered. "It was purely political. It was easier, you see, for the new Christian converts to identify with a dead man than with a dead bull. More converts, more money in the coffers. It's a pity though, that he didn't have the foresight to see that, by putting a dead bull on a cross, you could worship both religions."

"Oh no," said Walter. "That would never do. If the bull were hung from a frontal view, and his huge genitals were in plain sight, people would be too embarrassed."

Just then Helen made her entrance, the baron clicked his heels, excused himself, and the two went off together taking the papers to the Senator's rally. Alice stood outside, looking sadly after them. I wondered if a cross with a bull might have helped her. I mean, surely she wasn't happy with herself, playing that role as she was with mother. And how can anyone ever like anyone if he doesn't like himself? And how can he like himself if he's all screwed up and maybe wants to be a boy instead of a girl, or a girl instead of a boy? I suppose you can still 'love,' but can you really 'like?' And if you can't 'like,' is it the 'not liking' part that leads to unhappiness and eventually destroys the love?

***

It was easier, you see, for the new Christian converts to identify with a dead man than with a dead bull.

Diary: Me and my big mouth. The other night John got very upset because I cried out, "Daddy!" when we were making love.

"For God's sake!" he said, rolling off me. "Will you never get over him?"

His anger surprised me. I thought he'd gotten used to it by now, me saying that. (I really can't help it, you know.) Why was he all of a sudden so upset? As I pondered his question, I heard myself thinking: which sounds better, God the Father or God the Daddy? The former, of course, was more dignified and more what people were used to hearing. But what would happen if the clergy during services started saying God the Daddy? Wouldn't more children understand what church services were all about? And John more understanding, too? I mean, of me?

***

Alice's mistaken attack on the baron came on the heels of his return from Germany. Under mysterious circumstances, or so it appeared at the time, he had gone back to his homeland—that much everyone knew—after being so preoccupied for several weeks that he'd even neglected his horses and clients. Unbeknownst to Mary, it had a lot to do with her.

Yes, that one little conversation that afternoon with Mary and Walter, a conversation that he'd never had with anyone the whole time he lived in America—nobody else had ever seemed interested in Mithra the times he might bring it up—at least not the way Mary had.

In the past at the Senator's fundraisers, etc. hearing the remarks she'd make, he wasn't sure whether she was intelligent or not. But now, now he knew she was of extraordinary intelligence. Of course, it never dawned on him—how could it?—where that intelligence was coming from. But even if it had, just seeing her eyes light up and her cheeks burn bright that afternoon, was this not an indication that it was time to do what he had always wanted to do? Perhaps before, like Gretchen said, it just hadn't been the right time. Or maybe he hadn't talked to the right people. But now, the thought that there were other

Americans just like Mary (ahem. Really?) and Walter the Jew was what caused him to go into action. Yes, taking his inspiration from her, off he went to Germany.

***

When Marcus broke open Alice's door and grabbed away the knife, she had already succeeded in chopping off her hair. A copy of *Struwwelpeter* lay on the floor, opened to the page where the little girl who played with matches is burned to death. Even though von Clapp had given the book so many years ago, Dr. Niedlhauf, the head of the private clinic where Alice was now interred, thought there had to be a connection. And who knows if, in Alice's deranged mind, there wasn't? If thumb-suckers have their thumbs cut off, and children who won't eat soup waste away into wraiths, imagine what awaits the child who has done a deed far worse than that?

But Dr. Niedlhauf had come up with other clues. Because Alice kept saying, "The horror! The horror!" he wondered if she'd ever read Conrad's *Heart of Darkness*. No, thought Mary when the doctor called her up to ask. She was probably thinking of her mother's vagina. But instead she told him that Alice *had* read the book at his clinic. He hung up saying *fuck!*

Oh well, as sorry as she felt for him, how could she tell him that one such as Alice didn't need to read Kurtz's last words *The horror! The horror!* to know what it was all about? Were they not the perfect words for what happens to a child, a creature of nature, of the Periodic Table with its atoms and molecules billions of years in the making, who is punished and crippled for life because she has responded to forces beyond her control?

Oh, she wrote, if only people could see themselves as such creatures! See themselves as victims of clueless hominids. Would that not make them act kinder toward themselves? And make it easier to tell what is real, what is not real? Unless, of course, reality is illusion

173

and illusion is reality. But in the long run, would it really matter, either way?

But if Mary believed all that, and it seems she did, why could she never feel pity for herself? And be kinder toward herself, toward others, too, even the Gaping Vagina? Why the unrelenting search for the Magi, for *Khvetukdas*, for anything that could save her soul? Why, indeed?

She was probably thinking of her mother's vagina

Blame it on the hominids, blame it on the hominids. How many of you have picked up on this and think it sounds childish? But to give the poor girl a break, especially considering what she has gone through, why not give it some consideration?

For instance, up to now, we only perceive them from their bones—prototypes of modern physiology, concrete records of how are bodies evolved over the eons from theirs, from their physiognomies to ours—i.e., everything on the outside, on the looks of things. But how many of us have ever speculated that what was on the inside—their brains, their interior thoughts—might have likewise evolved into us?

Which might explain why we are not just plain stupid, but are as stupid as they were? Yes, stupid because they were stupid—our ineffable stupidity inherited from them just as our bipedalism was, and while we no longer look like them, inwardly we might, in fact, *be* them? In which case Mary might be right after all?

One afternoon, she stopped by Walter's office to pick up some documents that the Senator shouldn't have, Walter thought, left behind. As she waited for him to unlock a filing cabinet, she noticed a postcard that lay on his desk. It was a picture that Walter's cousin had sent of the Temple Mount, a hill in the Old City of Jerusalem that is venerated by all three religions.

"How was Shlomo's trip?" she asked, fingering the postcard.

"Not so good," Walter answered, coming back. "He came down with Jerusalem syndrome, and had to be locked up for a while."

"Oh my God!"

"Oh my God indeed. He had a lot to do with it."

She listened transfixed as Walter explained what had happened. During the last days of the tour in Jerusalem, Shlomo was so overcome by the spiritual experience of being in the holy city that he'd fallen, like do many others, into an acute psychotic state known as Jerusalem syndrome. This, the doctors at Kfar Shaul Mental Hospital had explained, often causes people to identify with someone in the Bible, and in Shlomo's case, it was King David. Wearing a replica of King David's crown and carrying a harp he'd bought in a souvenir shop, he went to the Western Wall looking for Queen Bathsheba. Most everyone was amused until he sat down and began to play and sing. This, you could see, was interfering with the serious Jews who were wailing at the Wall, so the police were summoned and he was taken to the hospital where he was treated with mild anti-psychotic medications and tranquilizers. But when the doctors said that the best way to treat the syndrome was to get the person out of the city and home to their families, Shlomo was released and, with his wife Rebecca, much relieved, was rushed to the airport just in time to rejoin the tour as it headed for home.

It is hard to imagine Mary's excitement as she listened to Walter. What could this syndrome be, but an expression of orgasm's power in the holiest of cities! And how wondrous its power, that it could make people of all persuasions, the doctors had told Walter, psychotic.

Once again she eyed the golden dome and the minaret and the many graceful archways on the postcard, and saw how they all mimicked the erotic zones of a human body—the breast, the penis, the vagina. But before she could expound on this and share her knowledge that Shlomo had succumbed to this paean, to this ineffable beauty of orgasm at the holy site—surely Jerusalem was the sacred symbol of the sweet spot itself—Walter's secretary came in and told him his next client was there. So it was back to business, and with a heavy sigh, Walter handed Mary the documents, gave her a paternal pat on the head and pushed her gently out the door.

"He came down with Jerusalem Syndrome, and had to be locked up."

In Wolfgang's absence, an attachment had grown between Gretchen and Helen. Neither woman knew why he had left, and despite any personal jealousy each might felt toward the other—I'm guessing they did although Mary makes no mention of it—they began to bond over the mystery. The more they talked about him—actually, according to my mother, it was rueful gossip—the less they missed him and the more fun they were having. They often met for lunch on Larchmont, or dinner in Hollywood or Beverly Hills. They went riding together on the baron's horses, and after one such occasion, both their clitorises getting more than unusually excited as their stallions galloped up and down the hills, Helen and Gretchen returned to Hancock Park and, sweaty as they were, lost no time jumping into bed.

No one was surprised about Gretchen. Didn't she always say, "Ich komme aus Berlin?" But Helen? Helen, the virtuous flower of the Deep South, the perfect example of Southern womanhood? Who would have thought! But it was true. Marcus had discovered all after hearing passionate sounds coming from her bedroom and opening the door just a crack.

Yikes! How could this be! How could Helen upend Mary's theory that hanging black men from trees had kept her on the righteous path of Biblical Scripture? Or had Mary simply picked on the wrong sex, and the hangings weren't for the women at all but for the men?

But wait! Could there still be room for Helen in Mary's theory? What if the lynchings had worked so well that the Word of God had backfired and made sex with George too scary? Could the lynchings have turned her on to women instead of men, the divine right vestigial lobe now bathing her clitoris in the Light—woman with woman, virtue with virtue, a delicious relief from the Darkness of men?

Oh! what would the slave owners of yore have said—what would Helen's great, great, great, grandfather have said, the one who owned the 3500 acres and forty slaves, seeing it all go south as this little flower of the South went over to Sappho?

John seemed hardly interested. He was too engrossed in his latest puzzle—*Virgin With Child*—who were both Black. And besides, he reminded her, as he put the final pieces into the Child, hadn't Father Malcolm said something about what did it matter who you had orgasm with as long as you had it?

Diary: Did Father Malcolm really say that? But if he did, why would John still have that weird dream last night? He says it's because he was listening to news reports about all the wash boarding that's going on. But how does he know it's not because of what's going on with Helen and Gretchen?

Dream

John has been mistaken for an Al Quaeda leader, and taken to a black op site in Thailand. The CIA operative has wrapped a wire around his penis, and inserted an electrode into his urethra. Then, while Chinese music is heard in the background—or is it a cat yowling?—his genitals (John's not the cat's) are run through with electric shocks. As John screams, his torturer looks at him kindly.

"Sorry, bro," he says, "don't take it personally, I'm only punishing your genitals so that mine will behave better. They are always angry and trying to lead me astray."

*****

Diary: Why do I always get a migraine when I think of mother's clitoris? Maybe because, since Gretchen, I've been thinking about it too much? And they're still doing it even though the baron is back. I wonder if he knows?

Dr. Neidlhauf is hoping that Alice will start to sing again, now that she's stopped eating and talking. He's been trying to get her to sing while Callimachus plays the piano. He's actually very good. He was a child prodigy and gave concerts all over the world—even Carnegie

Hall. But when he walked on stage at the Segerstrom concert hall—that's the place where you could hear the baron laughing in the audience—and took his seat at the grand piano, all of a sudden he couldn't remember the notes or who he was. He had turned to the audience and asked, "Do you know who I am, and why I am here?"

By this time he was about sixteen, old enough to become a patient at the clinic. But Alice just sits there with her teeth and fists clenched, and not even mother who has come with Gretchen and the Stephen Foster song book has made any difference.

Marcus says the house is too quiet. He even misses the loud *Rigoletto* music. He, Martin, Derrick, and Bertha have all been to visit Alice. Indeed, they were the first to go. The grounds, they told me, were so beautiful, full of trees and shallow ponds with water lilies and beds of flowers—a veritable paradise. But alas, one without roses. Dr. Niedlhauf, in answer to Derrick's question, was thinking of the thorns. But if it was rose petals that cured Lucius of his ailment, imagine what they might do for Alice. Should I tell the doctor about Apuleius?

I know it sounds silly, but I confess it took me a while before *I* could go see her. I felt like I was going to need some kind of strong talisman to protect me. What if *Khvetukdas* didn't work at the clinic? Or the Magi, either, in that atmosphere of lunacy? Yes, they were the Magoi because they had power—*magh.* Wasn't that why magic made the impossible seem possible. But what if "the mutual connection of father and daughter," the connection that makes all kinds of fiends, demons, wizards and witches die, and is the highest good and the surest way of getting into heaven and avoiding hell, didn't work anymore after I saw Alice? Especially since I, more than anyone else, knew why she's crazy?

Blame it on the hominids, blame it on the hominids.

182

PART II

The baron's knife wound, despite the size of the knife, was more successful in loosening his bowels than doing any permanent damage. Indeed, Alice's aim was so off that the slight puncture wound on his arm was barely visible. But for a Prussian from an ancient family, the accident in his pants was very embarrassing. Still he refused to press charges. Not only because he was a friend of the family, but because in that moment of truth, as the shining steel of the knife blade flashed before his eyes, he saw not Alice but the god of light sending him an omen. He knew he had made the right decision to start a cruising business in Germany.

The enterprise, *Tripping with Mithra* (a double entendre, since the restrictions on Cannabis, he was told, were soon to be relaxed—"Ah, to see a mithraeum in a haze of smoke," he waxed lyrically) would navigate the Rhine and Danube rivers. The boat—called a longship—would make stops wherever there were mithraeums, taurobolia and bas-reliefs. And when these ancient remains were inland, the passengers would be transferred to the sites on chartered buses.

Because Mary was his muse, because the idea for this venture had come from her, naturally he wanted her to come along. It was to her credit, wasn't it, that he could introduce the Tauroctonous Mithra— the bull-slaying Mithra—to all Americans, if possible?

Mary was totally unaware of her role in all this. But there was no way that she could refuse the invitation to go. To be in the land where the god of the Magi had been so loved and honored was a dream come true. So what if her enthusiasm might betray her—her secret, that is, and the doctrine of the Three Kings, the Three Wise Men? Did not everybody love them? Why did Balthasar, Melchior and Caspar sing out in the hearts of men long after childhood was over? Was it possible to think that the Magi's secret was somehow known to little children? Because didn't most of them already know that the Christ child was going to wind up dead? Did she really need to keep hiding?

But everyone's excitement was momentarily dulled when Dr. Niedlhauf suggested that Alice also go on the first cruise. Having more or less given up on her—she was the first patient that the truth serum hadn't worked on—he thought that this trip might do her a world of good. The baron was at first reluctant. He was still smarting from the accident he'd had in his pants. But when the doctor said that Alice had shown remorse for that, and that he would be coming along, too, the baron decided to take the high road and agreed. A date was set for the first sailing.

CANON VIII

"The root of every word in the human language has the same danger and beware significance as the warning caw of a crow or the roar of a lion."

"The concept of masculinity, whiteness and religion all have their origin in the Word of God, the phallus."

"Women's uphill struggles wouldn't be all that difficult if we weren't fighting against the Word."

"God is the greatest, most ingenious simulacrum that was ever devised. He is the simulacrum of simulacrums."

"When people recognize that they all come from the same source, the competing visions of God will be unsustainable."

"If it weren't for the Biblical (and the hominids?) theology that good and evil are symbolized by light and darkness, schools would never have been segregated."

"The Bible is an encrypted book which, once the code is broken, reveals man's struggle to overcome his biological urges told through metaphor, allegory, 'fairy tales,' miracles, and laws."

"The leader of any religious cult is indeed doing God's work—i.e., having sexual dominion over all his women."

"There are two ways to look at the saying, 'Cleanliness is next to godliness:' (1) either to have clean (pure) thoughts about orgasm, hence sex; or (2) to keep the anus clean since it is so close to where orgasm originates."

"If we always act, consciously or unconsciously, for a reason (as some scientists think), and there's a reason for that reason, and so on, could the ultimate reason—the reason behind all reason—be control of the gonads?"

"If the nativity of Christ—hence Christianity—is theologically the renascency (rebirth, renewal) of man, and the Latin word renascent means that which is "springing or rising into being again," is the renascency of man really about him, or about his penis?

"The veiled inner sanctum of the ancient Temple of Jerusalem: Was it called the Holy of Holies to honor the vagina?"

***

Diary: I've gone several times now, to the Niedlhauf Mental Health Facility. Alice is letting her hair grow and doesn't so much look like a man. Even Dr. Niedlhauf has seen the difference. He said that he'd never been able to figure out why some girls want to be boys, and some boys want to be girls. To find out, he had given Alice some sodium pentothal. But all she said was that she'd overpaid Helen and wanted her money back.

***

I used to think that Mary's carping about her mother, especially after being around mine whom she liked, came from being spoiled and privileged.

"Thank God she only dropped four."

"Oh, do stop criticizing her," I said one day. "So you didn't have the perfect parents. Well, who does? You could have been born in the Congo and gotten your arms chopped off. Or the Middle East and sold into slavery. Or how about India? Wasn't a little girl just sacrificed so that the farmers would have a better harvest?"

But how was I to know where her anger came from, and the hard feelings and inability to distance herself from the past, which now seems so understandable? The pitiless lure of Helen's vagina and the omnipresence of George's penis would make anybody crazy. And for all the angst, the inner suffering these disabilities caused her, she would never be able to forgive them. Or herself, multiple orgasms notwithstanding.

***

Diary: Von Clapp has sold his riding academy. The horses were sad to see him go. A lot of whinnying went on as he went from stall to stall and fed them their last lump of sugar.

"I will come back to see you, meinen liebschen," he told them. But they could tell he was lying, and several horses turned their backs and went to the other end of the stall. Mother laughed when she heard the story, but I thought it was sad, and you could tell that the baron's feelings were deeply—not by mother but by the horses.

If only they knew, I thought, why he was selling the academy— that we were all going to Cologne and the Shrine of the Magi, the golden cabinet in the Cologne cathedral that holds the remains of the Three Kings. Surely they would forgive him! Oh, if only we could be there on Epiphany! That's when you can see the three skulls through an open screen—up close and personal—wearing their golden crowns. Surely it makes it easier to imagine how they looked on the very day they brought their gold, frankincense and myrrh to the manger.

John has put together a puzzle of the scene. The Three Wise Men are all Black, they look very beautiful.

***

Being mad at one's father's penis does not make for a good relationship. Despite Mary's wish otherwise, John was on the verge again of leaving. Not even a trip down the Rhine would make him change his mind. Once again, Father Malcolm saved the day.

Once again he was in trouble. He had himself begun applying the holy dirt to the bellies of pregnant women who hoped the *tierra bendita* would assure them of healthy babies.

Well, it is one thing to place a wafer on the tongue of the faithful, or a smudge of ash or sprinkling of water on their forehead. But to smear dirt, even if it's holy, on the stomachs of women? This seemed, when news of it got to his superiors, not right. Indeed, some went so far as to use a Jewish word and say it wasn't kosher.

When the news reached him, the Archbishop of Santa Fe was very angry. A thorough search was made in Catholic doctrine and, finding no precedent to allow or excuse it, he was on course to having the priest suspended. But John, looking for a way to save his friend, came up with an idea and flew to Santa Fe to present it to the Archbishop, Rufus' uncle, if you remember. A priest, John told him, on such a voyage as von Clapp's, would be needed to answer any questions from the passengers. His presence on board a ship with such a controversial program (the way John put it, it sounded like the baron was trying to resurrect Mithra), would be of great service to the Church. If anyone needed convincing as to which was the superior religion, it would be Father Malcolm's job to do so. The Archbishop sent this on to the Vatican, which had the last word. The decision was made that as long as the Father stayed on board where he could be watched, and John accompanied him as a watchdog, it was a very good idea. John agreed that he would, and Mary needn't have reminded him of all the kindnesses the Father had shown them such as the *tierra bendita* and the puzzles.

Father Malcolm soon afterward bought his ticket and booked a flight to Budapest with money donated by the many new mothers in Chimayo.

***

The maiden voyage was scheduled to begin in June. It would embark in Budapest where, by happy coincidence, the passengers could visit the well-preserved Aquincum Mithraeum, then continue up the Danube to the Rhine and eventually end in Amsterdam. This was the typical route of the longships, but as the travel brochures promised, *Tripping with Mithra* would not be your typical journey. The usual time spent strolling along picturesque streets and buying souvenirs would instead be spent following in the footsteps of Mithra. Like the footpaths that pilgrims still take in Spain, this would be a waterway pilgrimage. The dissemination of the Mithraic Mysteries would be at the passengers' fingertips as if by magic.

And they would get their money's worth, too; the land between the Rhine, Danube, and Main, known in antiquity as the Agri Decumates, was fertile with Mithraic discoveries. And as they followed the god of light from one city to the next—Dormagen, Cologne, Bonn, Neuwied, Mainz, Strasbourg, Xanten—the all-inclusive price included classic cuisine prepared by award-winning chefs, and lectures by acclaimed scholars.

Unlike some of the river cruises, there was no beverage package. The baron was not yet solvent enough. Nevertheless, the trip quickly sold out. Dr. Niedlauf and Alice were lucky to have bought in ahead of time. But as their luggage was being loaded into the Uber, Callimachus and his lady friend came hurrying over.

"Beware, beware!" he cried. "The Rhine is full of danger, *full* of danger!"

"Bah, let her go," said his friend. "She's a vegetarian."

All the way to the airport, Dr. Niedlhauf couldn't get Callimachus' voice out of his head. He'd been in the psychiatric business long

189

enough to know when someone was right. As they drove up to the Lufthansa unloading zone, the doctor, looking at Alice's pallid face and limp body, took a deep breath and, giving her a gentle pat on the hand, told the driver to turn around. His own enjoyment would have to come another time.

***

Despite the pain of leaving his horses behind, the baron knew he hadn't made a mistake. Before the cruise left Budapest, the passengers had explored the excavated ruins of the old Roman town, and returned to the ship heaping praise and encomium after encomium for the temple of Mithra and its beautifully restored altar. Now the Americans would learn that Germany had more to offer than beer and sauerkraut. But there were also Europeans on board, and Asians, and people from the Middle East including some Berbers—actually they were Amazighs who had been visiting their relatives in Budapest. Pretty soon, thought Mary, the whole world would know about *Khvetukdas*. Zounds!

The *Happy Bull* (like other longships, von Clapp had given his a name) stopped first in Vienna. Here the passengers went to visit the Carnuntum Archaeological Park nearby to see the remains of a Mithraic temple. That evening, von Clapp, in his desire to bring Mithra into better focus, invited his old friend, Joseph von Balthasar, to give a lecture on the genesis of his surname. They had both gone to the Spanish Riding School in Vienna and shared the same love of horses. But a horrific fall Joseph had taken when he tried to best Alberto Larraguibel's record jump of eight feet plus, urging his bewildered and terrified mount over a nine-foot jump, had left him a cripple.

This was more than obvious as he limped and hobbled about, going from one chart to the next, each delineating various lineages of Balthasars. During the lecture, he mentioned all the Balthasars and von Balthasars who had, over the centuries, proliferated throughout Austria and the Rhineland. Indeed, they had their origin in Austria. One of them, Hans Urs von Balthasar, was a famous theologian. How

190

regrettable it was that he had died two days before becoming a cardinal. One never knew, did one?

More names and histories were discussed. This pleased the baron as it was his intent to show the influence of the Magi all over Germany. He was less pleased when a passenger said that Balthasar was a common name everywhere—even in America—and that many people gave their animals that name. His own dog was named Balthasar.

There was loud laughter, but Mary barely heard it. Indeed, she had barely heard anything during the two-hour lecture—not the von Balthasar family's coat of arms nor their lineage going back to the 1600s. For from the moment he had limped into the lounge to the moment he limped out, there was but one thought in her mind, one thought consuming her: How could a man with the name of a Magi have fallen off a horse?

Thus, when he invited her later that evening to have drinks back at his hotel—it was near the Schonbrunn Palace—and what an honor ir would be (this because the baron had told him she was his muse), Mary, out of character, I think—the limp and all—despite wanting to see the palace—declined.

The next stop was Linz. Here the passengers were able to view the Mithra stone at St. Martin's church. Von Clapp warned the local guide to refrain from mentioning the fact that Hitler had grown up in Linz— there was going to be no connection, ever, between Hitler and Mithra.

***

Everyday the Chief Officer printed out a two-page newsletter for the passengers. It was called *The Happy Bulletin*, and it had, not only the day's itinerary, but also news and sports from around the world.

One day an item appeared about a neuroscientist and ethologist in Europe who had placed EEG electrodes onto the heads of dogs in order to see whether their recognition of words would help determine how and why only humans excel at languages, and help construct a theory about how language evolved. An angry response had followed from an academic in New Mexico.

"Bah!" he was quoted as saying. That whole idea was a waste of time and money. There was no mystery at all to it, how language evolved. It was not the component parts of language shared with other animals—if there were any—that mattered. Only an animal whose orgasm had, thanks to that dynamic alignment—pelvis, vertical spine, brain—gone out of control (as was the case with our primate ancestors) could learn to speak. The need to control it would, out of necessity, create that complex system called language.

"If only more people would listen to me!"

A response from the scientist in Europe had come quickly.

"I'm listening and I'll tell you this, that even if your preposterous idea is right, and all the animals could talk, from lizards to lions, if they had that same dynamo alignment, it's surely by the grace of God that they don't. Do we really want Homo sapiens to share the planet with, say, Canis sapiens? Aren't things bad enough as they are?"

***

The *Happy Bull* next stopped in Regensburg. The Romans had built a fortress there in the 2nd century A.D., but all that remained was the Porta Praetoria, the north gate. Von Clapp thought it important for his passengers to see it anyway. This would help them get over the notion, if they had one, that the Romans had only lived in Italy.

The city itself had escaped the bombings of WWII, and while John went to visit the diocese that was founded in the 8th century, Mary and Father Malcolm just wandered about, enjoying the sights. As they passed an outdoor cafe, they noticed much excitement taking place. A group of bystanders were trying to help a woman in the throes of an epileptic seizure. It was a terrifying sight to behold. Father Malcolm nodded his head knowingly.

"The ancient Greeks called it the 'sacred sickness,'" he said, "and associated it with the divine. It was induced by the gods."

One could see why. As the poor woman convulsed and twitched, her back arched in a position Mary was very familiar with, she wondered how the throes of so terrible a disease could so perfectly mimic the throes of passion and ecstasy. But only the gods could attest to that if it was all part of the divine.

***

The third or fourth night on board, Father Malcolm gave a lecture on the Magi. He wanted the passengers to learn that there were other things they did beside following the star to Bethlehem. For that he had turned to *The Histories* by Herodotus, and told them about the Magian priests, Smerdis and Patizeithes. They happened to be brothers, and in 521 BC, Patizeithes persuaded Smerdis to rebel against the king of Persia while he was away in Egypt. He succeeded in taking the throne, but when the plot was discovered they were both killed. So great was the Persians' anger that they began to kill every Magus in the country, and if night hadn't fallen, not a single one of them would have been left alive. After that, a great festival called the Magophonia—the killing of the Magi—was held annually throughout Persia, and no Magus was allowed to leave his house during the celebration.

"Isn't that interesting?" said Father Malcolm. "If not for Herodotus, the only Magi we would know about would be the Three Wise Men."

"No, no, not if you are Persian," said one of the passengers. "We know all about the brothers. In fact, there's a Persian rock band that wrote a song called *Magophonia*. It's really great."

A few nights later—Father Malcolm's lectures and the baron's alternated in the lounge—the passengers learned again from Herodotus, how much the Magi liked to kill animals. Other priests killed them only as offerings in sacrifice, but the Magi liked to kill anything they could lay their hands on—literally—from ants on the ground to insects in the air. Only dogs and men were allowed to escape their zealousness.

The baron was not pleased. These ancient priests of Zoroaster and Mithra were coming off looking pretty bad, next to the Three Wise Men. Hopefully the passengers would have forgotten all about it before the voyage was over.

The next day the *Happy Bull* docked in Cologne.

***

"Jawohl, a paean to orgasm!" said one of the German students wearing the Phrygian hat he had bought in the ship's gift shop. "The American woman is right."

Evenings in the lounge had loosened Mary up, and as the passengers had entered the cathedral, its naves, arches and sinewy columns had a more spell-binding effect than usual.

"Ja, it's a womb, just like she said!"

A local guide led them to the Shrine of the Magi. This was a beautiful three-tiered cabinet made of wood but covered in copper, silver, gold and precious gems. Since the 13th century it has been home to the bones of the Three Kings. This was what Mary had been waiting for. This is what the horses would have forgiven the baron for, had they known.

But as she, like the others gazed upon it in awe of, if nothing else, its intricate decoration, and was finally face to face (almost—the shrine was placed high up on an altar) with the descendants of *Khvetukdas*, she found herself thinking how much more wonderful it would be, if Apuleius lay inside instead of the Magi. Or even better, the bones of Lucius the ass. Yes, a golden shrine to the Golden Ass. And on Epiphany, when the shrine was brought down and the screen opened, there he would be, a golden crown atop his long boney skull with his big nobby teeth. How much more exciting that now seemed than the skulls of the Magi.

The guide moved the group to the old sacristy to see the Cathedral Treasure, a collection of staffs, swords, and jewel-encrusted monstrances displayed in glass cases. He gave the histories of some of the treasure, such as the monstrance, not as elaborate as the others, which held the links from a chain that had once kept St. Peter a prisoner.

"But what a strange name for such beautiful receptacles," said Mary. "It sounds so much like monster."

"Das Fraulein has much insight," he said admiringly. "Over the centuries they have morphed from the monsters people used to believe in—the supernatural beings and objects that imposed the will of the gods. There is hardly any difference between the words monstrance and monster, because they both come from the same word which means to warn."

As she listened, George's face flashed before her eyes. A few minutes later, as the group shuffled out of the room, a woman next to her said, "And all this time I thought they were just part of the pageantry. I wonder what they are warning us about."

When the tour ended and people were left on their own, John and Father Malcolm wandered about the splendid building, and Mary went back to the golden shrine. As she gazed at it reverently, she was joined by a young man wearing a white gabi draped over his shoulder. It was decorated with an embroidered border, and on his head he wore a white kufi that was also embroidered. He was frowning so at the shrine that she wondered if he could see what she was seeing, a beautiful donkey lying inside.

"You're lucky you still have these relics," he said, breaking the silence. "Ours were taken away when the British invaded my country."

These, he went on to describe, were small tablets called tabots that represented to Ethiopians the dwelling place of God. These relics were so holy, they could only be looked at by a priest. One of his uncles was in Britain at this very moment, trying to negotiate their return.

"Maybe they will, maybe they won't," he continued, "but I doubt we'll ever get back the one that's inside Westminster Abbey."

This seemed odd, but when he said that the tabots were so holy that they not only couldn't be seen, they could also not be named, was this not because, like the Ark of the Covenant, they were the dwelling place of orgasm? And why one was sealed behind the altar in Westminster Abbey?

***

That evening Father Malcolm came aboard with a stray dog which looked very much like Rufinus—a brown and white mixture of all sorts of things. An argument broke out between the priest and von Clapp.

"I don't have insurance for dog bites or rabies," the baron said. The Father put his hand on the baron's shoulder.

"My son, what is a dog but an unfortunate creation of man? Without a second thought, with no selfish motive that by doing so he will go to heaven, he is always ready to give of himself. What cares if he be loved or punished? He has no choice but to play out his role which, in any of the above situations, is always the victim. Why, he suffers for man just as much as did Christ, maybe even more."

The baron, remembering how his horses turned their backs on him, quickly relented. Malcolm named the dog after his previous one,

Rufinus. Under his eye, he allowed Rufinus to run about the ship. It wasn't long before people could see how smart he was, and many who had read the article in the bulletin, including an old rabbi who had joined the cruise at Regensburg, agreed that if orgasm had not given people language and civilization, then, as far as organisms go, dogs might have become better and smarter than humans.

"Indeed," said the rabbi, "while the Bible says that he who lies down with dogs gets up with fleas, why not the other way around?"

Poor Mary! What with Herodotus and the words too holy to speak, and the tabots too holy to be looked at, and now a rabbi on board, the Ineffable Word's spiritual leader, was it any wonder that we should find a rendering of the Tetragrammaton in Mary's diary, and below it these words? "Growing hard beneath her, she has seen the holy of holies, the magic four letters, the Tetragrammaton, the Sacred Root, her father's penis."

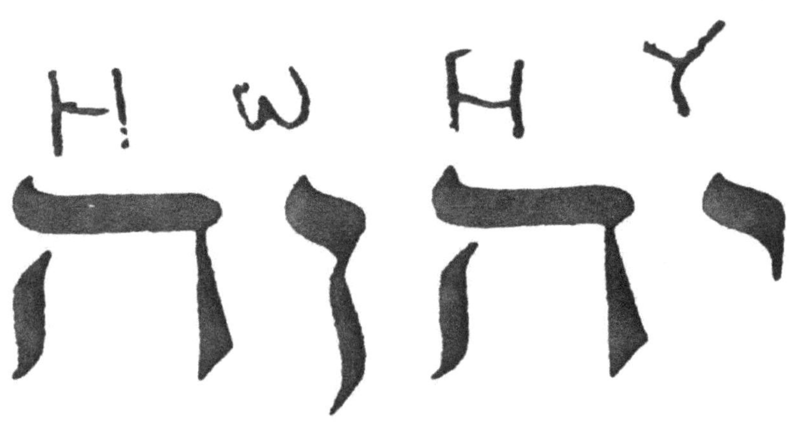

***

The *Happy Bull* stayed in Cologne overnight, thus allowing the passengers as much time as they needed to visit the Roman-Germanic Museum adjacent to the cathedral. It was full of Roman artifacts and, said von Clapp, the Dionysus mosaic floor was not to be missed. It was past midnight, but Mary, who had gone to Father Malcolm's cabin to play with Rufinus, was still not back. John checked his watched, sat up in bed and thought of jumping ship. No, it wasn't anything Mary was doing. Even he might have dreamed of Vadim, the handsome Russian passenger they had gotten to know, and spoken his name while sleeping. No, it was the pagan aspect of the trip that had gotten to him and was making him feel uncomfortable.

As he sat in the dark thinking, he suddenly remembered the Aachen Cathedral. It was only an hour away, and therein was the Marienschrein which was famous for its four relics—the Virgin Mary's cloak, the blood-stained cloth in which John the Baptist's head was wrapped, the swaddling clothes of the baby Jesus, and jumping ahead some thirty-three years, the loincloth he wore on the cross. Every seven years it was exposed to the public, and although it was folded into a triangle, a woman in John's parish in Boston who had seen it, had told him she could actually see the imprint of the Lord's genitals. Surely seeing this would bring him back to the true religion and restore his faith in the one true God. But just as he was about to put his plan into place, Mary came in and jumped into his arms. It didn't take long before the desire to see Jesus' genitals was lost in the glory of Mary's vagina.

***

"Ah, Mary, you should have come with me."

It was Father Malcolm, who, in a state of ecstasy, was describing the rose windows he'd seen at St. Gereon's Basilica while they were still in Cologne. He had not stayed to visit the sacristy, but had slipped away from the Magi's shrine and, by chance, happened upon the basilica, not far from the cathedral.

"The entire narthex is one rose window after another," he continued, "some plain ones, some with wonderful purple petals. I can't imagine a more beautiful tribute to Isis and the roses she fed to our Lucius—the magic antidote to his metamorphosis. What a beautiful world, there is so much magic in it."

Our Lucius? Why had he said that? But never mind that. She had come to his cabin to return *The Histories* which she was determined to read after his lecture, and had found something exciting. No, there was nothing in it about *Khvetukdas*, but there was something just as good if not better.

When Herodotus was in Egypt, a priest told him that he was forbidden to speak God's name—Osiris that is—the Phallus, the Word of God, and instead had to use such phrases as *"whose name I'm unwilling to mention,"* or *"I think it not right to mention."* Well, wasn't that what the Jews had to do, too? Use the Tetragrammaton YHWH because God's name was too holy to pronounce? Zounds! What would Walter say to that!

She recalled how nervous he'd looked when they first talked about the Tetragrammaton.

"Shem ha-meforash," he said in a low voice.

"What?"

"Shem ha-meforash," he repeated. "It means Ineffable, and is another name for the Tetragrammaton."

Already knowing what ineffable meant—incapable of being expressed in words—i.e., indescribable—she had wanted to ask, was that not a perfect rendering of orgasm? But at that moment, he'd had a violent attack of hiccups, and rushed off for a glass of water.

In her diary she wrote the following: I think I have stepped on Walter's toes. A few days after the hiccups, he gave me a book which he borrowed from his rabbi, called *The Sword of Moses*. Unfortunately, it hasn't done what he hoped—in fact, just the opposite. For instance, the power of that Ineffable Name was explained in this passage: "There is no greater mystery than this. It leads your soul to the light of lights, to the places of truth and goodness, to the region of the most holy, to the place where there is neither man nor woman nor any definite shape, but a constant an inexpressible light."

Dear Walter, can there be a more poetic description of orgasm than this? And look at how many ways there are in the book to express the inexpressible, and forgo mentioning the Ineffable Name of God! But beside the strings of mystical names and numerous combinations of numbers, there is the Sword of Moses itself (Moses spoke of it just before he died) signifying the Divine Name, and deemed so effective that its power was used to invoke all kinds of magical recipes such as these:

"To remove a rich man from his riches, say No. 45 upon the dust of an ant-hill and throw it in his face."

"For diarrhea write No. 47 on a red copper plate and hang it round his neck."

"If thou wishest a woman to follow thee, take thy blood and write her name upon a newly-laid egg and say towards her No. 55."

But why not, if the Sword is what I think it is? Naive or not, what better way for the servants of God to acknowledge the power and magic of orgasm?

***

When the baron learned that two passengers had been arguing for several days, whether or not it was the Nibelungenlied or Mithra behind the Holocaust, he decided it should stop. The argument had gone back and forth, and each man was adamant about who it was and why.

It was the Norse gods, said one, that got it started, not Mithra. Why did Richard Wagner, who hated the Jews, write four operas on the Nibelungenlied? Was it just a coincidence that he was Hitler's favorite composer?

"My friend," said the other, "gods are gods. They are all unconscious

200

archetypes of one sort or another. Yes, your Nibelungenlied story was composed by some Austrian from the Danube region a thousand years ago, and, yes, Wagner grew up in towns where the remains of monumental temples probably built for these gods might have influenced him. But if the German legions were worshiping Mithra centuries later, how do you know that he is not embedded in the German psyche? Didn't our guide say that Hitler used to play on the Mithra stone when he was growing up?"

The baron, as he hurried over, cursed the Linz.

"Gentlemen, gentlemen," he interrupted. "I can assure you that Mithra had nothing to do with the Holocaust. He was a good god, not a bad one."

"Like Wotan, you mean," said the man protecting Mithra.

"Our guide said that back in the Middle Ages, the Germans used to paint their houses in bull's blood," said the other man.

"Gentlemen, I think you are both wrong," said the baron. "Just look at all the countries that have never had mithraeums or legends about the Norse gods. Don't they hate the Jews, too? Take Russia. There are no mithraeums there, and look at all the pogroms they've had. No, there is absolutely no connection between Mithra, the god of light, and the underground race of evil dwarfs, you may be sure."

Neither man looked convinced.

"Do you happen to know," said one, "if there are any mithraeums or taurobolia in Poland?"

"No, why?"

"Well, after the war ended, the Poles were still killing us. I thought that maybe the death camps were built on top of some taurobolium or other, and the Poles were slaughtering us instead of the bulls."

It now became apparent that the man was Jewish even though he didn't look Jewish or have a big nose. Likewise with the other man who, seeing how uncomfortable von Clapp looked, said kindly:

"Dear baron, it's as you said. "We are slaughtered everywhere, even where there are no taurobolia. It's only a coincidence, I'm sure, that there are so many of them here in Germany."

***

The stillness of the night had carried the men's voices up to the Persian's balcony. The next day when he saw the baron was alone, he approached.

"I hate to tell you this," he said, "but I think that man may have been right about Mithra and the holocaust."

"My good sir, I'm sure he wasn't."

"Well, here's the thing. I myself am a Zoroastrian and I think I know what I'm talking about."

The baron's mouth fell open, as did Mary's as she sat listening nearby.

"In our sacred book the *Dinkard*, there is a famous discussion—controversy, you might say, between a Zoroastrian theologian and a Jewish dissenter, about an ancient practice—or a doctrine, you might say, called *Khvetukdas*. This discussion took place a thousand years ago."

And he quoted: "On a grave attack of a Jew upon a priest, which was owing to asking the reason of the custom as to *Khvetukdas*."

My friends, I need not tell you what went through my mind when I read her diary. Was her heart beating like a drum? Had her ears stretched as big as a donkey's? Was there boundless joy in her heart, or sheer terror as the Persian recited almost verbatim the passages from the *Dinkard*, the same ones she had read, and going beyond how it diminishes the power of demons. Indeed, light flashed from such unions, and the offspring were like those born of swift Arabian horses. Zoroaster himself said so, and that to terrify the demons and bless the body with holiness, *Khvetukdas* was to be practiced.

Many couples had proliferated the earth from the union of Mashya and Mashiyoi who were brother and sister. The demons who were

202

enemies of man—in striving for their non-existence through the practice of *Khvetukdas*—distress, anguish and fear were all eliminated.

But the dissenter had disagreed. What Maysha and Mashiyoi had done was a sin. Hadn't Adam and Eve, siblings themselves, been cast out from the Garden of Eden for the same sin? How diametrically opposed he was. Because *Khvetukdas*—the surest way to get to heaven—was for him the surest way to get to hell. Hadn't the serpent, the snake proved it? Once a phallic symbol of fertility and the earth mother and desire, in Genesis the serpent—the Phallus, the Word of God—had been turned into Satan, the adversary of man. Could this Judaic reinterpretation of the Phallus have caused a backlash of hate that had gone on to this day?

The baron admitted that it did sound like the Jewish dissenter might have had a problem with Mithra, but since it was only one man's opinion, and that formed such a long time ago, he thought the argument was specious. With a polite nod, he excused himself and left.

Well, dear reader, had this conversation taken place a few days before, Mary's ears might indeed have become as big as Lucius'. In fear and trembling, she might have jumped overboard. But ever since the vision of Apuleius or the ass lying inside the golden shrine, the doctrine had loosened its grip. Now, as she listened to the learned Zoroastrian, and visualized the serpent, Adam and Eve and even Osiris and his magic penis, she only smiled to herself and continued her painstaking and loving illustrations for Father Malcolm's treatise.

***

CANON IX

"Through nature (orgasm), the mind took shape (grew) and became aware of itself."

"God created man in His own image. Of course He did: you cannot separate man from orgasm, or orgasm from man."

"Was the last World War really a drive for empire, or a desire to exterminate Jewry from the world and the worship of God along with it?"

"Killing animals at the altar, killing humans who worship a different God—magic circle or not—it's all rooted in the gonads."

"Marriage vows taken before God are only meant to keep husband and wife from having orgasm with other people."

"Is it war which leads men to kill, or the holiness of orgasm? How many wars have been fought in the name of God (George Bush invoked Him most recently), and how many are still to come?"

"In worshiping the monarchy, we are, in a sense, worshiping orgasm because for centuries it was God who appointed the kings to rule. The public's rabid interest in the Royals today is very prurient, indeed."

"Having an orgasm is like having a cipher to decode the Bible."

"Orgasm is the amorphous shape of God."

"Mine eyes have seen the glory of the coming of the Lord every time wave after wave of it sweeps over me."

"If God's flesh is cleansed by being sprinkled with cleansing water, then is baptism but a ritual to make semen holy, too—in the cleansing waters of repentance? Are the waters themselves the semen, and people are baptized in its holiness?"

"From the Theban Triad (the Egyptian gods Amun-Ra, his wife Mut and their son, Khonsu) to the Holy Trinity (Father, Son and Holy Ghost), only the names have been changed to protect the gonads."

***

Father Malcolm's treatise was turning into a major work. Indeed, why not—there was so much ripe material at hand—the ass, *The City of God*, Jesus, Apuleius the magician, but who wasn't back then? Magic was magic, was it not? And then there was the disdain, the disparagement by the Father of Christianity who had written his book 350 years after Apuleius died, yet was still finding fault with a statue that the contemporaries of Apuleius had erected in his honor. Etcetera, etcetera. The priest already had a title: *Philosophiae Naturalis Principia de Aurelius Augustinus Hipponensis et Lucius Apuleius Madaurensis*. Asking Mary to make illustrations, she had jumped at the chance and had already finished several splendid drawings of the ass.

Diary: "This," said the Father when he finally noticed me, "is the most exciting thing I've ever written."

In search of Rufinus, I had gone to Father Malcolm's stateroom. The little dog was curled up on the priest's bed. I sat down and began to pet him, wondering what his life had been like, before he followed Father Malcolm back from St. Gereon's Basilica.

It must have been difficult; one could see that in his eyes as they kept me in focus. So near, I thought, and yet so far, were he and I to and from each other. So similar and yet so different. But was it Rufinus I was thinking about, or myself? I lived with me, but was it really me I lived with?

"Isn't it wonderful," I said, "how a dog can love so despised and reviled a species as the human female?"

"What?"

"Oh, nothing."

My thoughts went back to the treatise since I was now a part of it, and really wanted to get the drawings right. I listened intently to how, in *The City of God*, St. Augustine took Apuleius to task for every little thing he did—even his writings on Plato. But it was only because he himself believed in magic and, he'd harbored the thought that *The Golden Ass* was autobiographical and had been turned on by the ass.

Well, whether this was normal or not, the thing was this. In his youth he had led a rather wild life. He had mistresses and all kinds of things. So after he converted to Christianity and left his pagan days behind, what better way to cleanse himself of dirty thoughts than to come up with the doctrine of Original Sin? After all, if humans have inherited a tainted nature through the act of birth, then is it his fault that things like the ass lying with a woman turned him on?

As I pictured him in the womb—the saint, not the ass—I wondered: could some ancient vestigial memory of masturbating in his mother's womb have been Augustine's inspiration for Original Sin? Did not the act of birth include not only the womb but the birth canal, too, and the vagina? And at the very start, orgasm, too? Or was *The Golden Ass* behind Original Sin, as the Father thought?

"For a man of God," he said, "this is a very dangerous way to be turned on."

But allowing that no one is perfect, not even a saint, all that people needed to do now, was look at Augustine's oeuvre in a new light. That was why he was writing his treatise.

Even so, how, I wondered, could a man who believed that Apuleius might actually have turned himself into an ass, be credited as the Father of Christianity?

***

"For a man of God, this is a very dangerous way to be turned on."

The baron had taken Walter seriously. The Mithra and bull necklaces—similar to the cross necklaces—proved to be very popular, as did the Phrygian caps. They were made of soft red material, and looked exactly like the ones Mithra and the Magi used to wear. The excursions to the mithraeums were exciting, the scenery was gorgeous, and the food was delicious. But why not? The baron had hired a Michelin star chef, and the apple strudel, Black Forest cake and noodle kugel were overseen by the baroness herself.

At the baron's request, none of the food was deconstructed. The meat came out looking like meat, not like pureed pieces of puff surrounded by pastry. Indeed, there was such a surfeit of meat that the ship's toilets began to feel the effect. The *Happy Bull* being an old ship, the engineer was kept busy going from one stateroom to the next.

This wouldn't be happening, thought Mary dreamily, with Alice's toilet. As she waited for the engineer to arrive, she thought of the old witch who had hovered over Alice's plate of vegetables. As she replayed the scene, she began to wonder if there was more to meat-eating than just the sacrifice. Was this woman consuming it not only to eradicate the animal—deny the fact that they were her brothers under the skin (or better, under the fur) like maybe the Paleolithic people were doing 50,000 years ago when they began using shells and flint blades to shave off body hair, but also, by consuming it, was she not becoming one of them and they, magically, her, and maybe, that being such a paradox, helping to make her crazy?

***

Other lecturers came on board at various stops, and when it was learned how popular being baptized in the blood of a bull used to be, Father Malcolm, wanting to get into the spirit of things, came up with the idea of anointing the passengers, in imitation of the Hindu custom, with a spot of vermilion on their foreheads. John didn't think this was wise.

"Remember what happened in Chimayo," he said. "Not everyone is as open-minded as we are."

But the priest continued to argue. Whether it was stigmata blood or bull's blood, didn't it all come down to doing the work of God?

This made sense, and anyway, how could John say no to his friend? At the next stop, they went together to look for an artist's supply store where they could buy a tube of red pigment.

***

At Mainz, the passengers were bused to Heddernheim where they stumbled around the excavations of three temples. Afterward, they came back to the city and saw the Roman theater. That night they were bused to the Staatstheater for a performance of Mahler's Symphony No. 2, the *Resurrection*. Indeed, as the violinists and cellists furiously manipulated their bows back and forth in the final movement, their tremolos like the furious speed of a man giving himself an urgently needed hand job, Mary thought of her father's penis. But why not? In the end, weren't all resurrection symphonies about resurrecting the Phallus of Osiris, the Word of God?

But not all people were equally impressed or exhilarated. Several passengers had fallen asleep, and during the intermission the wife of one began berating her husband.

"I'm sorry, dear," he replied as they sidled in next Father Malcolm's group at the bar. "But you know how I feel about Mahler's music. I especially can't stand it when I hear a motif or refrain he has borrowed from some other composer."

There was such a crush at the bar, that as he rattled off the list of such men as Strauss, Beethoven, Brahms, Schubert, Schumann, a robust-looking German standing next to him couldn't help but chime in.

"You'll never fall asleep with Wagner," he said. "What is more thrilling than the ride of the Valkyries? Or when Brunhilde throws herself on Siegfried's funeral pyre? My wife always gets excited by that."

"Ja, but what about Die Gotterdammerung?" said his friend. "What is better than the ending when Valhalla goes up in flames and all the

210

gods with it?"

"Don't let's talk about it, I get too emotional."

"Ja, me too. Why? I don't know."

"Well, warum nicht? It's the collapse of the world, the magic gold goes back to the Rhine and the earth returns to its natural state without any gods around to dictate the rules. Who wouldn't be affected? It's really just too powerful."

Everyone was exhausted when the bus returned to the ship. After one last night cap, and playing a little with Rufinus, Mary went to bed. Since he was the last thing she thought about before going to sleep, perhaps it was only natural, then, that she should have dreamed that night about the Vietnamese Humane Society rather than Rhine maidens and Wotan and his magic gold ring.

The Society wanted her to make a donation, and she was about to send them a check when she remembered that the Vietnamese like to eat dogs. Considering that the more money they received for the shelter, the more dogs they could eat, she tore up the check. She awoke next morning feeling lighthearted and happy because, on reflection, it was really her mother who wanted the money, and it wasn't the dogs who would have been eaten, but Mary herself.

Now, if some of you are wondering, as am I, whether Helen would have eaten her off a plate or devoured her in that perennial gaping chasm of fear, either way, one can see why Mary felt happy when she tore up the check.

But why has this whole thing about vaginas freaked *me* out? I have to admit it has. Because if it hasn't, why have I had this unsettling dream of my own?

I'm in the Armstrong house looking at the portraits Bruell painted of the family. I go from portrait to portrait, first to Margaret's, then Barbara's, then Alice's. When I come to Mary's, even though it looks the same as always—the distant look, the parted smile—I read it differently, now I see the truth: *She knew.*

When I come to Helen's, I stop. No longer the portrait I

remembered, it has become encrusted with thick layers of impasto which begin to crack before my eyes. I can even hear the sound—it's a sort of grinding sound—slow, methodical, rhythmical—it's like the rolling movement of an earthquake. When the movement and cracking stop, her portrait has changed into the abysmal opening of a vagina. The Senator, too, has changed, but not into the grinding, impasto-layered phallus I expect to see, but to a small rodent which scurries down the canvas and jumps into Helen's pink pastiche. When I look closer I see it is Mickey Mouse. I cover Helen's portrait with the same velvet cloth Dorian Gray used to cover his own grotesque portrait.

Oh well. What did Christ say? Judge not that ye be not judged? And if it weren't for the treachery of her parents, Mary's fantastic ideas would never have evolved, probably, and I wouldn't be chronicling her diary. But do we draw a line somewhere or—God forbid—cross over it like the Senator did and be done with it. Who is to say? Not me, I'm only the narrator of this story.

***

It hadn't taken long, once the journey began, for rumors to fly: it was not just to see the archaeological sites—the real purpose was to restore the once high-standing of Mithra and make trouble for the churches. Thus it was not surprising when prelates began showing up at the quays wherever the *Happy Bull* was docking. Some held up the cross as passengers disembarked, others simply looked on and wagged their heads in disapproval. Naturally the baron was annoyed, but after talking it over with Father Malcolm, decided it was best to ignore them rather than make complaints.

At one such stop, the boat was met by a prelate who, unlike the others, politely invited everyone to his church to see the replica he had commissioned, of a mosaic floor believed to be from the world's earliest Christian prayer hall. It had been discovered in Israel, at a Roman-era village.

The baron was taken aback by this show of kindness, and happily accepted. The prelate whose name was Father Odonskey led the way to his church which was nearby. The mosaic was of various abstract designs. In the center of the floor were a pair of fish inside a medallion. With their mouths gaping open, they looked like they were gasping for breath. When someone asked about it, the priest replied that the Greek word for fish, *ichthus*, was also the acronym for Jesus Christ Son of God Savior.

Not even Father Malcolm had known that, and complimented Father Odonskey for a job well done. Von Clapp thanked him profusely, saying that those early Christians must have indeed been inspired to have created such a masterpiece. Hoping his sentiments would end any further problems with other prelates, he clicked his heels, made a slight bow and said Auf Wiedersehen.

In the afternoon, Father Malcolm went to the upper deck with Rufinus, to work on the treatise. A copy of the *Apologia* was on the chair next to him.

"Ah! You know him?"

Startled, the Father looked up. It was one of the Amazighs from Budapest. His face was wreathed in smiles.

"Who?" the Father asked.

"Apuleius," the Berber answered, pointing to the book. "Next to *The Golden Ass*, his *Apologia* is one of my favorites."

The excited priest invited the young man to join him. For the next several hours they discussed their mutual admiration for the writer— how clever he was and how witty. Was there anything better than how he parried the accusations that he had used magic—a capital offense— to win the affection of a rich widow? When one of the accusers, who himself had wanted to marry the widow, saw Apuleius cutting up a fish to make into a magic potion to win the widow's love, hadn't Apuleius countered it brilliantly when he said that, even if it were true, even if he did practice magic, could he, Apuleius, be in better company than the Magi, since they, the priests of Zoroaster, used their magic to teach people to worship the gods? That the *Apologia* was now acknowledged as one of the most remarkable speeches in existence, both men agreed to heartily.

"I must confess," said the Father, coming up for air, "how surprised I am at your knowledge and enthusiasm."

"But why not?" the Berber answered. "He was the greatest Berber that ever lived. We Amazighs call him the Amazigh philosopher."

"A Berber, you say?" said the surprised priest. "I thought Berbers were all nomads."

"That is the problem. Everyone thinks that all we do is herd sheep and live in tents. They cannot conceive that one of the greatest writers of all time was actually one of us."

"Ah!" said Malcolm, "that is why he could see so deeply into the mind of an ass!"

The Father had meant it as a compliment, but the young man, whose name was Mustapha, was offended. He stood up and said, as he turned to go, "We are planning to erect a statue of Apuleius in Budapest. But perhaps it would be better if it were of Lucius the ass."

Father Malcolm felt terrible.

"Rufinus," he said, knowing there was no point in sending the Berber a bottle of Champagne, "we must go and apologize."

Off they went to Mustapha's cabin. They both received a cold reception, but the little dog, not to be put off, soon won him over. And eventually, the priest, too. How could Mustapha hold a grudge against him, knowing he had named Rufinus in honor of the *Apologia*?

But why has the whole thing about vaginas freaked me out?

***

Diary: Dr. Niedlhauf radioed me with some good news. Alice is beginning to open up. No, not to him but to Callimachus. When the Uber had returned from the airport, she went straight to him and thanked him for his warning. The doctor doesn't see any problem in their hanging out together. In fact, he thinks it's rather sweet.

Father Malcolm wants us to get together with Mustapha. The three of us have so much in common.

***

With the ship having spent so much time in unscheduled repair stops—yes, that is what happened—Father Malcolm had plenty of time to work on the treatise. In fact, it was nearing completion. Much of the fodder for his thesis came from the large tome St. Augustine had written in the 5th century in defense of Christianity and its detractors. But because there was so much heavy-handedness in it toward Apuleius—indeed, two of its twenty-two books were directed against him—Father Malcolm, perplexed by this, hoped in his treatise to get to the bottom of it. It seemed so unnatural, he said, all the attacks and name-calling as in "your Platonist co-sectary Apuleius." And in referring to him as the African philosopher, Augustine said that not all men "who are called philosophers are lovers of true wisdom."

But whence, the Father wanted to know, the attacks came from? Yes, Apuleius was of the belief that the messengers that mediated between men and gods were similar to men, being of an animal (i.e., humanistic) nature with the same passions as men: "For they are capable, just as we are, of being affected by all that soothes as well as all that moves the mind."

But since he was only subscribing to the Platonic view, why was he singled out from the other Platonist philosophers of the time? Why did St. Augustine say that Apuleius' book, *On the God of Socrates,* in which these celestial beings were discussed, could not have been written by a sane man? True, that with messengers having bodies and minds of

216

men, some who went by the name of Sleep and Love, and "who possess powers of a different nature; Love, of exciting to wakefulness, Sleep of lulling to rest," men could be lulled into sinful behavior. But wasn't Apuleius only adhering to the views, the philosophy of others? Why was he singled out? Was it because St. Augustine believed in the story of a man who had fallen asleep for several days and, on waking, had been transformed into a pack horse and sent to Rhoetia to carry provisions for the Rhoetian Legion—a perfectly believable story, he said, especially since it had been verified?

Was it through Lucius that the Platonic daemon—the same aerial being as the angel who carried the messages between gods and men—became the evil demons we know today because they could arouse desire in men? And in Augustine, thanks to Lucius the ass?

But if God had transformed Lucius into an ass, would Augustine have felt better about his fellow Maduran? Would he have spared Apuleius the hatchet? When the two men had so much in common—both Africans, both coming from the same cities and studying at the same places—would such a nasty piece of work ever been written? Would the Church Father have given more ground to his fellow compatriot even though his messengers were different from the saint's? Though Apuleius' beliefs came from Plato, would he have been bludgeoned for them? Where was this all coming from? Where was this terrifying idea that men, without the right kind of messenger, would easily be corrupted? Go astray? And do the same things that Lucius the ass did, and that St. Augustine, thought Father Malcolm, could never get out of his mind?

"Yet their mind did not become bestial, but remained rational and human, just as Apuleius, in the books he wrote with the title of The Golden Ass, has told, or feigned, that it happened to his own self..."

Because St. Augustine, like others, believed in magic, was *The City of God* all about this? Was the great seduction scene—the soft pillows, the velvet coverlets, the candlelight and the woman reaching for the beast's scrotum—just too memorable, just too too much?

Feeling the satisfaction that comes with a monumental job well done, that evening Father Malcolm went off to a beer hall with the students. After awhile the hall broke into a German drinking song. It was *Ach du lieber Augustin,* in honor of the patron saint of beer, another St. Augustine, all together.

***

Many people came to Father Malcolm seeking answers to perplexing questions. For instance, one evening when he was sitting up top, he was approached by a young deckhand. His family, he said, was very poor—they had migrated to Germany from the Middle East—and despite the poverty, he was one of fifteen children.

"But there are many families like us," he said. "Do you know why that is, Father, why so many poor people have children?"

"Because, my child, orgasm is what makes life worth living."Rather astonished, the deckhand asked, "Would that be why there are billions of people in the world?"

"Oh, indeed. Rich and poor alike—you can never have enough."

The young man, feeling his question had been adequately answered, thanked the Father and went back to swabbing the deck, a big smile on his face.

Then there was the little boy who wanted to know which cheek Jesus meant him to turn, the one in the front or the one in the back, whenever his older brother was teasing him. Since it was obvious that the child already had gay tendencies, Father Malcolm laughed and said he would know the answer when he was a little older.

Right after he left, another passenger sought him out. It was a woman whose husband had, she said, been deceiving her for years. The priest, though tears were streaming down her face, told her that she might as well ignore it.

"Deception," he said kindly, "is what it's all about. People deceiving one another and, in doing so, deceiving themselves. It's what makes the

218

plot of a book or a movie. It's only when people are moving about, doing some physical labor like driving a car, watering the garden, working an assembly line, that there is no deception. But the minute they stop, the minute they speak—ah, then it begins and really, never ends."

"What is your advise, then?"

"Just go with the flow, my child, and perhaps practice it yourself."

Well, why not, thought Mary. If the Word is the phallus but we say it is God, isn't that where it all starts?

Before leaving, the grateful woman, astounded by his knowledge, asked him if there was anything he didn't know.

"My child," he answered, "even if I knew everything, I still wouldn't know anything."

***

During a particularly rowdy evening of drinking and singing—a favorite was an ancient Sumerian drinking song to Ninkasi, the goddess of beer (it had a catchy refrain that was easy to learn—"Kase kase kase kase"—"beer beer beer beer")—one of the German students fell overboard. He was fished out with little trouble, but von Clapp blew up and threatened to throw all the students overboard.

"Dear baron," said the Father, helping to dry the boy off, "people have been getting drunk since the beginning of time. They've told me that the song goes back five thousand years."

"Ja, ja," said the boy's friend. "Doesn't the baron know that the first crops planted on earth were the grains that men could make into beer?"

"Ja!" said another. "Und where would all the agribusiness billionaires be today, without those first farmers needing to get drunk?"

The baron, being of fair mind, and remembering that much of the money for his new enterprise came from his own investments, thanks to advise from George's brother, in Anheuser-Busch, apologized for losing his temper and gave all the boys a round of *Gomez* (more on that later).

***

Father Malcolm was on the way to his cabin when he ran into Mary.

"You are flushed, my child. Is everything all right?" he asked.

"Mustapha has invited me to Budapest to see the new statue when it's finished."

"Ah, that is wonderful! I knew you would like each other."

He hurried off to finish the notes for the night's lecture. They were the result of a chance meeting with an archaeologist at Hedderheim, and learning that there existed about thirty miles south of Rome a fabulous mithraeum. Not only was it well-preserved, but it was thought that Apuleius himself had built it next to his own house.

What a great opportunity, Father Malcolm had thought, to slip in his treatise—*vis-à-vis* Apuleius and his mithraeum in Rome—and see what the reaction might be. In the daily bulletin, the lecture was announced as "Is *The Golden Ass* the bedrock of Christianity?"

To his great joy, the audience was spellbound. Point after point, they listened to with rapt attention; how easily it would be, for instance, for anyone, whether they believed that metamorphoses could take place or not, could not fall into Lucius' place.

For who, he had said, could read about Lucius and not become an ass himself? Were not the trials and tribulations of Lucius a perfect showcase for the human condition? Were there any in the audience who couldn't understand what it meant to be locked in a foreign body, crying out for help in a bray no one understood, mistreated by humans—father and mother alike?

Mary, herself, was thinking that, had the people on the Montessori board known what laid below the surface, would they have said those horrible things about her? And the horrible things her art teacher said about her sculpturing ability?

220

"But whether you agree with this assessment or not," the priest concluded, "on a final note, as for an ass having sexual intercourse with the lady, penetrating her with his huge member—is that not a perfect vehicle for Christian redemption? Far faster, anyway, than using chickens, goats or pigs?"

Many people came up afterwards and congratulated him.

"Your insights into Lucius and St. Augustine are amazing! Where do they come from?" someone asked.

"I wish I knew," said the priest. It was an honest answer.

***

Diary: How much fun it is to be on this trip. There are so many museums around, and so many old masters who liked to paint motifs that clearly divided the world between the black gonads and the white gonads.

Just today, I saw this seventeenth-century painting of a light-skinned king defending himself with a jeweled monstrance, against a dark-skinned infidel. Here in broad daylight, well not exactly, was this excellent example of the good gonads fighting the bad gonads. And since the king was standing at the right side of the monstrance, while the infidel stood on the left, couldn't one assume that the good gonad was on the man's right testicles, and the bad one on the left?

In another gallery, there was this polychrome statue of St. Michael vanquishing the Devil. There was St. Michael standing astride a dark-skinned Indian whose befuddled face seemed to be asking, "Why am I here?"

"Well," I told him, "you're here because of the gonads. You are the dark one, and you need to be taught a lesson by the white one."

I wonder if my *Tale of the Testicles* ever got published. I should write Jessica and ask.

***

221

Diary: The old rabbi is very interesting and fun, too. When I told him about Dr. Niedlhauf's patient who thinks he is Moses and got angry when his staff wouldn't turn into a serpent, he laughed.

"Yes, everyone was a magician back then," he said. "How else could the Red Sea be parted?"

He and Father Malcolm are getting along famously. The rabbi was amazed at how much effort St. Augustine had gone to, to convince his early converts that when Jesus fed 5,000 people with two fish, the power came from God, not from the kind of magic that Apuleius practiced.

As the rabbi scratched his head, I could not help but stare at the Star of David he wore around his neck. Was it, indeed, a six-pointed star, or the triangular symbols that represent the female sex?

They were both pleased to learn that the rabbi had also read the magical papyrus of London and Leiden when, as a young man, he had delved into Jewish mysticism and studied the Kabbala. What fun they had, recalling the many Egyptian formulas for making love, and wondering whether some might have worked better than others: the dung of a hyaena, pounded with honey and rubbed on the phallus? Or what about hawk's dung pounded with salt and, if too dry, mixed with wine? Or was it the more elaborate compound made of barley, apple seeds, blood from a black dog, and semen poured into wine, then given to a woman?

As I was wondering whether Moses might have used such formulas, too—well, why not? Even he, before he became a famous prophet with a long white beard, must have had blood stirring in his loins—Father Malcolm reminded the rabbi there were many formulas and rituals for death and resurrection, too, and he was glad that the Catholic church wasn't adding dung to the sacramental wine offered during Mass.

***

222

CANON X

"It's hard to leave the trees when the fear of God is everywhere."

"The hatred of Blacks and all people of color is rooted in fear. It begins in the Bible, the home of God and the magical metamorphosis of orgasm."

"Why do they say we should never discuss religion, politics, and money in polite society? Because all three are rooted in the gonads, and the gonads are always an unsafe place to be."

"The persistence of loss and regret. Where does it come from? The end of childhood and its magical connection to orgasm?"

"We are all little beings alone in the dark."

"If orgasm has been transmuted into God, then Divine Protection is but orgasm protecting us against itself."

"Is the linguist's search for the origin and meaning of words an unconscious desire to know who and what we really are? Because none of us really know as yet, do we?"

"Utopia is a place where men and women can have orgasms all day without having to blow their brains out on methamphetamines."

"To continue to revere any sanctified god is to continue to be a savage."

"What is the battle to subdue nature but a battle to subdue ourselves?"

"Why bicker with the religious notion that humans are made in the divine image? Are we not made in an explosion of divine orgasm?"

"The Metamorphosis of God: this story has yet to be written."

"Orgasm without Him, without the magic. Would people be less cruel?"

***

The *Happy Bull* was not a new ship. This is why the baron got such a good price and had little difficulty pulling in funds to buy it. The many unscheduled stops it had to make for repairs were just part of the norm.

At one such stop—it was a Sunday—Father Malcolm learned that an Episcopal church near by always allowed pets to sit in for the services. Many people who would not otherwise have gone to a service came with their pets. Thus the pews were almost always full, and it was with difficulty that Father Malcolm squeezed in with Rufinus. There were mostly dogs and cats, but iguanas were there, too, and ferrets and a few other species.

Hardly had the service begun when a mouse ran out from behind a pew. One of the cats saw it and, escaping from his owner, rushed down the aisle in pursuit. Rufinus, aware that Father Malcolm had already drifted off into a beatific sleep, slipped from his arms and chased after it. The cat, seeing it was about to get cornered, jumped onto the altar and began to hiss and spit. But despite its defensive posture—arched back, bristling fur and hissing, Rufinus jumped at it. In the ensuing melee, everything was knocked over—the chalice, the candles, the cross all went flying.

Imagine Father Malcolm's distress. He could not begin to apologize, and left more than enough money to cover the damages. But the Reverend himself was so shaken that, even after the holy pieces were set back in place, he couldn't continue and, after giving a quick benediction, disappeared behind a curtain.

Needless to say, on the way back to the ship Rufinus was severely chastised. Even after he was back on board. But Father Malcolm's severe expression and displeasure soon melted away as he saw how stricken Rufinus looked. The priest scooped him up on his lap and said, "Linnaeus named your species *Canis familiaris*, but a better name might have been *Canis unfortunatis*."

At the sound of his voice, Rufinus wagged his tail happily.

***

Of the 200 passengers on board, many women, fearing cold weather, had brought their fur coats. Only a few were amused when the rabbi passed on Mary's remarks about fur coats and hominids. A woman from Tennessee—the very same cousin that Magnolia had written to Jessica about!—had wondered what her rabbit fur had to do with hominy, one of her favorite dishes. But the German students, missing the dead seriousness of Mary's ideas, thought everything she said was very droll, and were always amused. As in the following:

"Must you gonadalize everything?" John said to her one evening after drinking several glasses of the new beer. Named *Gomez*, it had just come aboard and was being consumed by the minute. It was an artisanal golden lager that the baron had contracted specifically for the ship. In preparing for the tour, he had learned that bull's urine was called *gomez* by the ancient Persians. And because it came from the same place as his semen, when the *gomez* was mixed with water and sand, it was used by the ancient Persians in purification ceremonies.

The Zoroastrian knew all about this. He also knew that the mingled urine of a man and woman who had performed *Khvetukdas*, when mixed with sand, was also used in purification ceremonies. But because he didn't want to upset the baron, he kept it to himself. The picture of a big black bull—Mithra's bull—on the label was, probably, better than a brother and sister making love.

"But why shouldn't she," said one of the students, picking up on John's remark. He and the others were wearing the Phrygian caps, and whether it was the pot they were smoking or the new *Gomez*, they were all very jolly, and began to have fun with Mary's word. Running it this way and that, within minutes they came up with the idea of "gonadalism"—a philosophical doctrine in which all ideas have their origin in orgasmic sensation and perception. Comparing it to sensationalism, the theory that sensation is the only source of knowledge, and that feeling is the only criterion of good, they said that gonadalism went far beyond that because was there any better criterion of good than the feeling of orgasm?

"Das Fraulein is right," someone said. "Like Euclid's axiom, it is a self-evident proof that requires no proof because it is the source of proof."

"And what could be more self-evident than an orgasm?"

"Jawohl, but what about Kant and transcendental idealism—how one can systematize the appearance of things but cannot apprehend their inner reality? *I* think God is like a balloon. The outer part—the skin—is God, and the gaseous invisible part inside is orgasm."

"But if it's not Kant," said someone else, "then it has to be Schelling. In Idealism, Schelling said, mind and nature are different aspects of the same Absolute. Through nature, the mind is able to recognize itself and take shape."

"Either way, it's amazing," his friend said. "Combining them both into a balloon—wow."

"But the idea that God is not separate from nature is pure heresy," said someone else.

"But of course. If He *is* like a balloon, who wants to give the joke away? Humanity what a mess!"

***

Ah, to be finally understood! Or was she? Not sure, after saying "Danke shoen" to everybody, Mary left to find Father Malcolm. Right away, a student turned to John.

"Why do you chastise das Fraulein?" she asked. "Your Henry Adams was even more fanatical about the gonads, maybe make him crazy as—how you say—a loon?"

"Henry Adams, the President's grandson?" asked John, surprised.

"Ja, and great-grandson of John. He was so fixated on their power that in his biography, he wrote a whole chapter on it, The *Dynamo and the Virgin.* You must read it, it's quite insane. *'The greatest and most mysterious of all energies.'* That's how he put it. Ja, and it is sehr schon the way he compared their force not only to religion and cathedrals—places like Lourdes and Chartres—but to goddesses like Venus and Diana, and sexy people like Adam and Eve before the fig leaves, and Michelangelo, Rubens and Sir Lancelot and forces that were just beginning to be known, forces both seen and unseen—steam engines, trains, electric currents, vibrations, radium, X-rays, dynamos. Can you not see the hidden allusions to orgasm? Ja, I think I know more about American history than you do."

***

Mary found Father Malcolm sitting up top looking at the stars. They twinkled brilliantly in the dark night sky. There were no sounds at all to break the peacefulness, only the soft ripple of the ship as it glided down the river, and an occasional nightingale off in the distance.

"I was looking for John," she lied, knowing full ware where he was. The priest smiled kindly and, nodding his head, offered her a chair. As he continued to gaze heavenward, Mary broke the silence.

227

"I always feel blue on Monday."

Without dropping his gaze, he replied, "'Los lunes ni los gallos cantan'—'On Monday, even the cock doesn't crow.' That's what my parishioners used to tell me back in Chimayo."

Rufinus, who was lying at the Father's feet, wagged his tail. A moment later, he sat up and scratched rapturously.

"I must get him some flea powder at the next stop."

A nightingale had landed on the railing and begun to sing. There was no way Alice could know the words to that, or was there? Mary had never talked much to the Father or, for that matter, anyone else, really, about Alice, but now all of a sudden she wanted to. Was it the students' attachment to gonadalism that had given her courage? One had even said, "You mean we are worshiping our own genitalia? How silly! No wonder humans are confused."

"And so fucked," said another. "Not literally, either."

Her courage notwithstanding, she now opened up; certain details she left out, such as the Senator and the magic circle. But Rigoletto was there and Dr. Niedlhauf's most recent assessment that Alice's case was hopeless.

"She has stopped speaking again, even to Callimachus."

"Ah, that is too bad," said Father Malcolm. "I would have hoped the priest could help her."

He put his finger to his nose in thoughtful repose. Then, after looking around to make sure they were alone, he said, "My child, what the girl needs is a good dose of ayahuasca. Take my word for it, it'll set her straight in no time."

He smiled benevolently at Mary's surprised look.

"When I was being investigated in New Mexico and waiting for the ax to drop, one of my parishioners told me I might feel better about myself if I went to Peru and tried some ayahuasca. The idea seemed like a good one. But why, I asked, Peru? Aren't there ayahuasca ceremonies all over New Mexico? Yes, they said, but the best shamans are in Peru.

"At first I said no, not wanting to leave Rufinus behind. But when so many of my flock said they would look after him, I changed my mind. Nothing but the best, I said to myself."

He paused and shook his head sadly.

"In my very first trance, I saw Rufinus being eaten by a coyote. Can you imagine my shock when I later learned that a coyote *had* eaten him? But the shaman didn't give me this news until all the ceremonies were over. And I give thanks to God that he didn't, because look at me now—a new man, happy, optimistic, open to whatever comes. The shaman told me all would be well—and look, here I am, sailing along on this beautiful river, with a charming artist at my side."

A thrill went up Mary's spine. Did he mean *her*? As she tried to stay calm, she said, "I don't see how we could get Alice to Peru. I think she's under some judicial order or other, having tried to kill the baron."

"If I tell the doctor about the hallucinations, he might see the imperative of her going."

When the Father had described the hallucinations to the shaman—blinding images of grids and circles and lines that were squiggly, straight, curved or like tendrils—putting him in such a state of euphoria that he wasn't sure whether he was seeing God or visualizing in the wavy gasoline colors, an orgasm—it was such an awakening of divine love and light—the shaman had jumped up and down in excitement, saying that only a chosen few had ever seen them. It was these six geometric patterns—the shaman called them entoptic visions—that had initiated magic and religion and, in this hominid state of awareness, the separation of the human species from the apes.

"My child," said the priest, "I must confess that this information caused me to have a crisis of faith. When the shaman said that religion was a neurological disorder, and that art was electricity and electricity was art, which was why, when I had reached out to touch God in my visions, my hand hit a cold hard surface, something like a rock—how could I continue in my profession?"

"'Not to worry,' said the shaman. 'You will still be able to help people as a priest, I should know.' And look how right he was. Here I am, ready to help Alice."

He leaned back in his chair and patted his lap. Rufinus jumped on, and Mary's thought that the lap was meant for her, lasted only for a second.

"You know, " he said, clasping his hands behind his head and looking again at the stars, " what a privilege it is to be alive? To go from caveman to man on the moon and be part of all the inventions and intentions along the way, all the beauty, all the horror, the good people, the bad people, the in-between people—wonderful and horrible both? Yes, a real privilege to be part of a ride that's not over yet. And all that from six electrical patterns!"

As an afterthought he said, "Life is beautiful, isn't it?"

Was he right, she wondered? Maybe. If only the magic circle didn't zap so much energy from it!

***

"Guess what?" said John, "St. Joachim finally got the new bathrooms."

The mail had just arrived, and John was in Malcolm's room reading a letter that Rose had sent. 'I'm sharing the good news,' she wrote, and had included a clipping from The Boston Globe.

At the time her son was about to leave the priesthood, his parish was in the middle of a fundraising drive to replace two unisex bathrooms in the church, that had only one stall apiece. Upon his departure, however, the funds that had been so forthcoming had suddenly dried up, and the project was put on hold.

"Mother was quite upset," said John, "but how was I to know that my leaving would have such an impact?"

But enough funds had finally come through, and the old bathrooms finally replaced. A ceremony had taken place, and there was a picture of the current priest blessing the new bathrooms. As he sprinkled them

230

with holy water, he prayed that health and healing would abide within the stalls.

"Ah," said Father Malcolm looking at the clipping, "what better place to use an aspergil than when blessing a bathroom."

***

The argument about who was to blame for the Holocaust—Mithra or the Nibelungs—had gone viral. Thus, when it was being one evening hotly debated in the lounge, John, in a foul mood—but why not, when someone keeps moaning 'daddy' when you're about to climax, or you hear the name Vadim from the sleeping person next to you—Vadim?—although there was no question that this big fellow with his hair in a top knot wasn't sexy—blurted out, "Why don't you ask Mary? She knows everything."

"Das ist richtig!" cried an enthusiastic student. He was now a member of a newly formed group who called themselves the balloonists. "Someone go find her!"

"No need," said John, suddenly taken by a wave of jealousy. He knew, having heard it before, what she would say, and if there was any truth to it, why not take the credit?

So, to everyone's relief, particularly the baron's, John said it was neither Mithra nor Wotan who was to blame, it was the hominids. Were they not the first to dream up the gods? Who would ever have thought of weaponizing anti-Semitism and wiping out the Jews, without them? Or equating evil to the darkness of a man's skin? Yes, the Jews were not dark, but to the gonads, wasn't their god? Who else had eaten up all the other gods, the pagan gods that used to encourage the licentiousness of the gonads? Ate them up and spit them out, or simply let them dissolve in his mouth? To the gods of the gonads, was not Jehovah an evil god and, by association, the people who worshiped him? But by sending the Jews to the grave, would it not also be sending Jehovah? And ending the monotheism of Judaism, a religion which the gonads couldn't stomach and reacted against viscerally and violently? What is Armageddon but the hope and desire for the end of God and

His reign over the never-to-be-tamed gonads? Does not this final battle take place at Megiddo in Israel? Is not every pogrom against the Jews their punishment for God? Where else could the irrational hatred be coming from? No, the blame should be laid at the cave entrance of the hominids, not here along the Rhine and the Danube. Or something like that, said John, ending rather lamely.

***

When the news came back to Mary, that the students were elated, thinking they had been let off the hook—it was the hominids not Hitler—and the rabbi, taking it to mean that the Holocaust was the Jews' fault—"Oh well, what else is new?" he had said, Mary went to the sun deck to find Father Malcolm. He was there, his hands folded comfortably across his stomach, his black cassock tucked neatly around Rufinus at his ankles, a smile played upon his lips as he looked contentedly at the heavens.

"This has become your favorite place," said Mary.

"Yes, the sky is so clear, I've seen a lot of shooting stars. Every time I see one, I make a wish. There goes one now."

She sat down next to him. The heavens were full of shooting stars, and on one of them she wished John would go to hell.

"Can you love someone even though you don't really like them?" she asked.

"Ah," said the priest, "I've heard this question so many times. In the confession box and out. 'I love him but I don't like him.' Or vice-versa. How can that be, they ask? And I was always at a loss to explain it. But one day I asked them my own question: 'Do you like yourself?' And after a moment's silence, they said, 'No, not really.' And I said, 'Well, how can you like someone if you don't like yourself?' And that, dear Mary, I think is the crux of the problem. Love comes easy, it's part passion, part affection and need and fairy tale make-believe. But *liking* someone—now that's a different story. That's something you can't lie to yourself about because you feel it too deeply. It's probably the *not liking yourself* part that leads to people's unhappiness, and eventually destroys the love."

This made a lot of sense. Where, she wondered, had such wisdom come from? Apuleius, perhaps? Or the pregnant women at Chimayo? The incest-loving men of the East? She still wanted to talk to him about that, about *Khvetukdas*. It seemed so much a part of the whole thing—why a priest is called Father, why he calls his flock his children, and why it is so easy for him to get them into bed. Fear of his own raging hormones, he had told John, was what had turned him, like many other young men—bouncers, chemists, whatever—into priests. But ever since her epiphany at the Shrine of the Magi, it didn't seem so important. So instead she tried another approach.

"Why should people not like themselves?" she asked. She knew what caused her own dislike. But what about people who knew nothing about the magic circle? Father Malcolm shrugged.

"Only God knows the answer," he replied. "Only God, my child."

***

The *Happy Bull* remained all night in port. Mary, unable to sleep, threw a coat over her nightgown and went to the upper deck. The railing was moist and slippery. In the water below she could hear the fish splashing about, and there was enough light from the ship to see them jumping in and out of the water.

Earlier that evening she had gone to the Father's cabin with her latest drawings. She had found him in a perplexed state. Despite the ease Rufinus had in making friends, there was often a troubled look on his face. Even in relaxation, stretched out with his head resting on his paws, the trajectory of his mouth often pointed downward. It was only in sleep that it didn't, and that his lips formed into an actual smile. Thus it was now as he slept in the folds of the priest's cassock, and as usual, Father Malcolm was wondering about it. It was a perplexing idea that the little dog was smiling about something, and if so, then what was it?

233

As the priest continued to contemplate, his index finger pressed firmly against his lips, why Mary thought he was thinking about her, one can only wonder. Do you think she was disappointed when he at last spoke, and she learned he was only thinking about Rufinus?

"You know," he said, "He is just like the Mona Lisa. You can't tell what she's smiling about, and you can't tell what Rufinus is smiling about."

That was man's greatest shortcoming, he continued, to never know and never be able to know the thoughts behind a dog's smile.

But could he have, if God had not given man dominion over the animals? Of course, this master and slave business was to keep man's own animal side in order. But what if the fish of the sea, the birds of the air, and every living thing that creeps upon the earth had dominion over man? Would they, he wondered, treat us as cruelly as we treat them? But how could they, for, being without sin, where could the concept of cruelty come from?

Ah, imagine being ruled by anteaters! Think of it! How amazing that would be, to be licked at will—theirs, of course, not ours.

Now, as she stood by the railing and peered down at the fish, she hardly noticed the slight drizzle starting to fall. They were playing, were they not? The fish of the sea? Playing, having fun, just like humans? Perhaps it was not such a stretch to see them and all the other animals having dominion over man. And there would be no need for them to eat us because, like dear Father Malcolm said, their souls were free of sin, and their gonads free of repression. Perhaps they were making love now! Why not? How delightful it was to see them jumping gaily in and out of the water. Even the sound of their splashings about was delightful. It wasn't hard to see why they were used for magic love potions. But if they, the fish of the sea, had dominion over us, would they have made us into love potions? Would they have fed five thousand people with two loaves of bread and God's only son?

Ah, so many things to think about. It was best just to close one's eyes and listen to the beautiful sounds of the water as they penetrated the night.

***

Besides the books and playing cards in the ship's library, there were also dozens of jigsaw puzzles. John's appetite for them had not lessened even though they were now scenes of bullfighting, these being a substitute for the Mithra puzzles von Clapp had ordered and were still on the way.

He was now at work on a matador in a red brocade costume, and a bull pierced with lances. It was almost, although not quite, as fulfilling as the other ones had been—the religious ones—what with the piercing lances and all—for reasons which he knew not why.

As he was piecing together the matador's tight breeches, he was joined by Father Malcolm returning from the lounge. A discussion had just taken place, he said, between the baron and one of the Greek passengers. Lifting his glass of *Gomez* to the baron, the Greek had said, "Why baron! This is almost as good as *Minotaur!* Almost!" Since he was the son of Spiros Apparaticus, a shipping tycoon, the baron had decided not to argue.

But others did. And since both lagers were of the same golden hue and equal fullness, it had come down to whose bull was better, Mithra's bull or King Minos' bull.

"Anyone can kill a bull, but how many people can perform acrobatics with them?" said the young Apparaticus. That seemed to move the majority in favor of the *Minotaur*. But when one of the students said that Mithra's bull had died for men's sins, everyone agreed that it was the *Gomez* that couldn't be beaten. Judging by the overall enthusiasm onboard and the nightly gaiety in the lounge, the baron's red face had beamed with happiness at the thought of how successful these voyages were going to be.

235

"As far as I'm concerned," said John, listening to the priest's recap, "they're all the same, these bulls—even down to the matador's."

"No, no," said his friend. "They each have their own special place with God."

He had begun to help with the puzzle, and was just fitting in a piece of the bull's tail when the ship gave a sudden lurch, scattering the puzzle onto the floor. It took a while to pick up all the pieces, and as they crawled around on their hands and knees, John was somehow reminded of how he and Malcolm used to put the Nativity Scene together at the church where they had both served as altar boys. A need to confess now took hold.

"I've never told anyone," he said, "that I was molested by Father Arnold."

"Ah! I think he molested all the boys in the choir."

"Not you, too!"

"Oh yes. He'd tell me that if I went against his desires, I was going against the will of God. So of course I obeyed and soon realized that the greatest reward of all was in doing God's will."

As an afterthought he added, "I guess that's why most of us never said anything."

CANON XI

The hostility of religion to science is easily explained: religion doesn't want us to know that orgasm is just orgasm, and not God."

"All the goodness in life comes to fruition in orgasm. Is that where are concept of good comes from?"

"What a different world it would be if all could have sex without guilt."

"To all you Conservatives who believe that tradition and custom are the true bearers of wisdom, let me remind you that the original bearer of wisdom was Aphrodite, goddess of love. From her groin springs every structure of human life.

"'In God We Trust.' And what is more trustworthy than a good orgasm?"

"Money doesn't buy happiness, but it buys forgetfulness. The bigger the mansion, the bigger the yacht, the less we remember things that might have been but can never be."

"There are two ways to look at the saying, 'Cleanliness is next to godliness:' (1) either to have clean (pure) thoughts about orgasm, hence sex; or (2) to keep the anus clean since it is so close to where orgasm originates."

"If orgasm has been transmuted into God, then Divine Protection is but orgasm protecting us against itself."

"The Metamorphosis of God: this story has yet to be written."

"Why bicker with the religious notion that humans are made in the divine image? Are we not made in an explosion of divine orgasm?

PART III

Helen was missing Gretchen terribly. She would even have left her post as the newly elected president of the Ebell Club—that's how much she wanted to be with her. Luck was with her.

The Senator's popularity was now at an all time high, and some of his colleagues were talking about his trying another run for President. Feeling the generosity of spirit that comes when all is going well, he wanted to do something for his wife. Thus, knowing how much she had wanted to go on von Clapp's first cruise, and also knowing that the *Happy Bull* was soon to make the reverse journey from Amsterdam to Budapest, he decided, now that the Senate had gone into recess, to take the trip.

A welcoming committee waited for their arrival at the Schipol Airport in Amsterdam. It consisted of the baron and baroness, and the mayor and members of the city council. After they were greeted by the mayor, he turned to the baron and said, "Thanks to you, we are hoping that our city will not only be known for its red light district and cannabis cafes, but also for the beautiful reconstructed mithraic temple in Heilig Landstitching. As far as I know, nobody ever goes there."

"Ah, dear Burgemeister, I shall definitely change that," said von Clapp, bowing politely.

How happy everyone was that evening. The *Gomez* flowed freely all through the night. Even Mary was happy. Ever since she had seen Lucius the ass lying in the Shrine of the Magi instead of the Three Wise Men, she hadn't felt angry at the Senator. Indeed, she was very happy to see him board the bus the next day and the next day, the new passengers boarded the buses going to the Mithraic temple, which was on the first day's itinerary—windmills and tulips toward the north, and the Mithraic temple about an hour away to the south. By the time the excursion returned to Amsterdam, most people were exhausted.

***

The last stop was Vondelpark in Amsterdam. It was a lovely place to wander in, full of trees and lakes and flowers. Mary sat down with Helen and Gretchen on the grass, while Father Malcolm and John took off to explore with Rufinus.

"That dog is no good," said Helen, watching them disappear. Rufinus, so out of character, had nipped at her at her heels. While Mary was dwelling on this, the Mayor, who had just arrived, went with George and the baron to look at the statue of Joost van der Vondel, the 17th century poet for whom the park was named. It was made of bronze, and sat atop a very tall plinth with four angels carved at each corner.

"Look at the size of that," said Helen. A deep sigh heaved from her breast. "We used to name lots of parks after General Lee. But now all his statues and monuments are being taken down."

Gretchen patted her hand affectionately.

"Don't worry, liebchen, the South will rise again. When Wolfgang and I visited his brother in Tennessee, we saw lots of Confederate flags. Everywhere we went, we saw them."

But what could that mean, all those flags? Why was Mary, as she watched her father, thinking that it wasn't the South rising again, but General Lee's penis? Because slavery and the gonads were so inextricably connected? But why, even though it was so high up, was she seeing Vondel's penis, too? Because her father was standing in front of him? Why, all of a sudden, did she see Vondel's statue as a tribute to the sacred phallus? Was it possible that that was why there were so many of them—statues, that is, and most always male statues— everywhere in the world? Yes, and why the world was permeated with them? Because they were all tributes, all these statues, to the sacred phallus? Tributes to the hominids who created good and evil, dark and light, good gonads and bad gonads? The Doughboy and Beethoven—both were in Pershing Square. Opposites they were, but what matter, as long as they had a penis? Was it the hero, poet or martyr who was being honored, or his penis, his phallus, the Word of God? Bronze statue or greased-up obelisk—was it not all the same magic?

Ah, should not the Senator have a statue, too? Was not his phallus—God be praised—the truly magic one? It wouldn't be hard to raise the money from his rich supporters in Newport Beach, and how glorious it would look at the entrance, perhaps, to Lido Isle.

No, what he needed was an obelisk like the Washington Monument at the National Mall. They called it the Pencil. But why not, since both words—pencil and penis—came from the same gods, the Penates, that were held sacred in Roman households. Some people even called it God's pencil—perhaps the best name of all, capped, as it was, with an inscription too far above the eyes of men to see—*Laus Deo*, Praise God. Was this not the Word of God, the Phallus of Osiris—exposing all 555 feet of itself in the nation's Capitol?

That evening she met her father in one of the narrow corridors. After a quick greeting, they were about to pass each other when Rufinus came bounding along and jumped gleefully at Mary. It caught her off balance and she fell into the Senator's arms.

"No no no no!" said Father Malcolm, quickly scooping Rufinus up. He and John had stayed on in the park. They had only just returned in time to eat, and hurried off to the dining room.

***

241

Was this not the Word of God, the Phallus of Osiris—exposing all 555 feet of itself in the nation's Capitol?

242

The *Happy Bull* made its way serenely toward Dusseldorf. Father Malcolm kept busy with his treatise as did John with his puzzles. Helen threw all discretion to the wind—isn't that what happens when you are in another country?—seeing how busy the Senator was, making friends with all the passengers. He was also too flummoxed to notice. What had happened to his daughter? He could hardly recognize her, she had changed so. So many opportunities she had to bring him down, with so many passengers who spoke to him, mostly on politics. For instance, there was that fellow from Fiji who had started up a conversation about cannibalism. Mary, who was standing right there, could easily have embarrassed George. Wasn't all culture rooted in the gonads, and the differences in cultures—why one culture ate people and another culture worshiped Jesus Christ—were rooted in the various approaches—that is, rituals—used to worship orgasm? He'd heard it so many times before. Had she finally come to her senses, was she ready to forgive him for the past?

What do they say, all good things must come to an end? And so it did for this idyll. The Senator had become violently ill—it was his old problem with seasickness. Oh, why had he forgotten? How many times had the family crossed the rough waters of the Catalina Channel without him? It was only twenty-six miles, but even that was impossible. Nothing could help, not even Dramamine. Now, unable to keep the delicious food down, he decided to get off at Dusseldorf.

"I will book you a flight right away," said the baron, almost too quickly.

"Nein, nein," said Gretchen, putting her arm protectively around Helen. "Just book one. His wife didn't come all this way to see only one mithraeum, and a fake one at that."

The discussion was loud enough to be overheard by some of the passengers. One of them, the Duke of Calle de Olvera, who had already become friendly and knew that the Senator was Chairman of the Foreign Relations Committee, put aside all airs despite his noble heritage, and invited the Armstrongs to visit his brother in Spain, Don

Francisco. He owned a large estancia in Andalusia and was one of the biggest bull breeders in Spain.

"There is no doubt, Señor," said the duke, "it would be a great honor for my brother to show you, not only his bulls, but Madrid, also. It is such a beautiful city, and I'm sure he will introduce you to King Felipe, who is a personal friend of his."

The king? It was obvious from George's excitement at this proposal that he had never read Walt Whitman. Helen, too, became animated.

"Go, liebchen," said Gretchen approvingly. "When George flies home, you can fly back to Germany and pick up the ship."

***

CANON XII

"If the morphing of God began millions of years ago at the beginning of the hominid's reign, why is it so hard to believe that it actually happened?"

"In the final analysis, might the ends to which all words serve—be they recipes for cookies or equations to send rockets to the moon—be in order to keep orgasm at bey?"

"To see how powerful the fear of orgasm is, one only has to look at our fear of God. But if it weren't for this fear, there would be no Calvinist notion of predestination, no Protestant work ethic, no capitalism and no stock market."

"Here's a conundrum: How can the bad feel so good, the wrong feel so right, and the horror of it all feel so glorious? Does the answer to this mystery lie somewhere in the magic of childhood?"

"Religion is the control of orgasm. But orgasm can't be controlled. That's why religion is hypocritcal and doesn't work."

"What is Armageddon but an unconscious desire to blow ourselves up because in reality we really can't stand ourselves?"

"Language and culture have covered up the true identity of God. Could that be what they were created for in the first place?"

"If it weren't for the Biblical (and the hominids?) theology that good and evil are symbolized by light and darkness, schools would never have been segregated."

"God created man in His own image. Of course He did: you cannot separate man from orgasm, or orgasm from man."

"The beauty of God, the beauty of orgasm — is there any difference?

Whenever a passenger with the surname Gomez came aboard—there had been a Gomez family from Gibralter on the first cruise, and now there was a well-to-do family, originally from Mexico but now living in Los Angeles—they had flown First Class with the Armstrongs—the baron always treated them with great deference. Whether there was any connection between their name and bull's urine didn't seem to matter. That there could be—didn't bullfighting come from their countries?—was enough to put them in a rarefied atmosphere, and he always comped them with free *Gomez*.

This is what he was doing when he learned that his friends had accepted the invitation.

"You have made the right choice, Señora," the duchess said that evening. "There are much better mithraeums in Spain than in Germany."

"That is nonsense," said Gretchen, putting down her drink. "The best ones are here in Germany."

"Forgive me, baroness," said Calle de Olvera, "but my wife is right. Not far from my brother's estancia is the mithraeum at the Villa del Mitra. And there are others that, if you like," turning to Helen, "my brother can take you to see."

"And besides," said the duchess, "the German mithraeums are like a dead language. But ours are still breathing. Has the baron told you about the taurobolium—how a bull would be slaughtered above a grate, and those lying below it, receiving his blood, would have their sins washed away? Well, we in Spain have kept that tradition alive. In the bullfight when the bull is killed, he has given us his blood so that our sins will also be washed away."

"And that," said the duke, "on top of the blood of Christ, should cover all bases."

By a happy coincidence, the baron had already planned for an overnight stop in Dusseldorf. Rameau's opera *Zoroastre* was being performed at the opera house, and it was a great chance to imbue the new passengers with the spirit of Mithra. Composed in 1749, *Zoroastre*, they read in the *Happy Bulletin*, was the first opera to write about Persian mythology. Was that not an indication of how important this trip was? If Germans didn't truly love their Mithra, then why did they so often perform the opera?

George, who had never seen it, felt well enough to go, now that the ship was at dock. It was a merry group that sat in the reserved seats, and became even merrier as they watched the performers play out the battle between Good (Zoroaster) and Evil (Abramane), in slacks and jeans and baseball caps and all kinds of modern clothes. Indeed, it was all very campy; there were gay men dancing on the rooftop, people drinking beer, and two sisters (Amelite and Erinice) fighting (at times even in a bathtub) over their love for Zoroaster, "the father of the Magi." As George watched him, he had the uncanny feeling that he had seen him before—no, not Zoroaster, of course, but someone else, someone he knew. But who was it? He was still trying to think who the high priest reminded him of when the performers came on stage with real pieces of cake. As they held the thick slices layered with pink icing, George began to feel ill again and, with apologies to all, excused himself and took a taxi back to the ship.

The next morning, just as the sun rose and the dawn sky turned from darkness to light, he and Helen disembarked, and the *Happy Bull* sailed on to Cologne.

***

The Armstrongs were unable to meet the incarnation of God—that is, the Royal Phallus, the Word of God and, also, Apuleius might have said, the daemon of Socrates who carried messages between men and gods, while they slept—because King Felipe was out of town. Instead the limo had set off at once for the estancia at El Escorial which was not far from Madrid.

But George, in expectation of the meeting, had put his beloved Reyn-Spooner shirt aside, and in a formidable business suit and red tie, this was how he greeted Don Francisco. Helen, on the other hand, had worn a delightful summer dress that showed off the whiteness of her skin and the softness of her arms. Even kings, she knew, were susceptible.

"Ah, Senator, you have a most beautiful wife," the Spaniard said, taking her hand and kissing it.

"Yes, that I do," said George proudly. He was still feeling unwell, and tugged at his collar that was becoming uncomfortably tight in the heat.

A heavy lunch had been prepared—gazpacho, paella, fish, meat, poultry and vegetables. The Senator bravely dug into it even though the lobster of the night before had still not fully evacuated the premises. Glass after glass was lifted in salutation to each other's county. The don's wife, Doña Maria, listened patiently as Helen chattered on, interjecting every so often, and always with a smile: "Ah?" "So?"

When the meal was finished, and the Senator had stoically polished off his flan, Don Francisco rubbed his manicured hands together in happy anticipation.

"Now we will go off and see my bulls."

It is unfortunate for the Armstrongs that they had only just commenced the river journey. Had the don's invitation come at the end, perhaps they would have been overly surfeited with bulls—mythical ones, that is—and George, at least, would have excused himself and gone to lie down. Which is what Doña Maria did, saying she would join them later before politely excusing herself.

Don Francisco led his guests to his private bull ring. Several young men were standing about, waiting to put on a *capea*, a bullfight with a young animal who has never seen a cape. They had chosen a young bull named Ferdinand who, though inexperienced, was full of vim and vigor. He was looking forward, you could tell, to having a good time.

"How magnificent," said Helen as the young men took turns putting Ferdinand through his paces, their graceful cape work as smooth as butter.

"Yes," said Don Francisco, looking at her arms. They glistened with sweat, and reminded him of marble veined in pink. Neither of them noticed that George, whose face had turned a pasty white and was dripping with sweat, was in bad shape. Actually, he was about to be sick, so he began, unnoticed, to edge away. Unnoticed, that is, by all but the bull. The young brute had spotted the Senator early on, struggling, as he was, to open his collar button and yank off his tie. What, the bull thought, was that thing flapping in his face? It was as red as the cape, smaller, too, much easier to get past.

And the man behind it… who was he? He looked sick. Had he done something wrong? Ferdinand had never seen anyone like him, and his interest grew so much that he barely paid attention to the cape. How much fun it would be to stomp on him! Ah, was this not his chance? He knew he could never pinion the young Spaniards, but this clammy, sweaty, sickly-looking man was an easy mark. So, with a snort of happiness, he turned from the cape and charged toward the barrier where George had gone to be sick. With an effortless leap Ferdinand was over it. In this moment of truth, the Senator forgot his illness and began to run. But it was no use. Even without a gimpy leg, what man has ever outrun a bull?

The horror that ensued, not even a hardened criminal deserved. Before Don Francisco's men could reach him, the bull had caught George on his horns. Shaking him like a dog shakes a cat and tossing him in the air, whenever he came down, the bull would toss him up again. He was having so much fun! Up and down, up and down as if George were no more than a rag doll. What do they say about a body in motion? Once it starts it never stops? That was what the young toreros might have been thinking as they tried to subdue the bull.

When they finally did, and George had come down for the last time, there was not much left of him.

***

An unperturbed, unrepentant Ferdinand played happily with his friends, romping here and there in the green meadow once again. As he playfully locked horns with his peers, he was, naturally, unaware of the thin red line on which his fate was, at the moment, hanging. Once a bull has killed a man, should he not be treated, Don Francisco had argued, like the tiger who has tasted human flesh? And besides, to the don's embarrassment, and Helen's too, and all who had watched it happen, the bull seemed to be enjoying himself too much. But it was Helen who saved his life.

Doña Maria, who loved the bulls and always cried when they were sent to the bullring in Madrid, had spoken to her privately.

"You know, Señora, to die on the horns of a bull is very classic—or, how do you say it, classy? Many a matador who has died that way has had a statue erected in his memory. Your husband is among the chosen. He might even become part of a mythology about what can happen to a great senator from your beautiful country, and have a statue erected to him right here in El Escorial. Or maybe even in Madrid. But not, of course, if Ferdinand is killed. People who understand all this would not tolerate a statue."

Ah, the thought of the Senator as a statue! Helen could see him in the Capitol Rotunda along with the other great men of America. And she would make darn sure that his shortened leg would be the same length as the other one.

Thus, between the two women, Ferdinand's life was spared.

***

Minor engine trouble had delayed the *Happy Bull's* arrival in Cologne, and it was still on its way when news of the tragedy reached the ship. Everyone reacted with disbelief. The Senator? Killed by a bull? How impossible was that?

251

Everyone gathered around Mary and did their best to comfort her. Words of sympathy were already pouring in over the wireless.

"It's amazing how many are from Orange County," said John, looking at the messages. He had stopped working on his puzzles to be at her side. And how comforting that was! The loss of her father, the loss of the Word—it was all inconceivable.

Naturally, there were people onboard who held the Duke of Calle de Olvera responsible.

"The least you could do," Gretchen said to his wife, "is help Father Malcolm get a pet passport."

The priest, as much as he wanted to accompany Mary to Spain, but having learned from past experience, was too afraid to leave Rufinus behind. The duke, only too happy to grab at a chance for redemption, did this at once.

Father Malcolm locked the *Philosophiae Naturalis* in his room safe, and the four of them—he, Mary, John and Rufinus, as soon as the boat docked in Cologne, flew to Spain.

***

With his eyes closed and a slight smile that played on his lips, tight as they were, he looked, thought Mary as she gazed at him in the viewing room at the funeral parlor, just like he used to look after he'd fallen asleep in her bed. The funeral director looked at him proudly.

"You would never know, Señorita, that he was gored by a bull," he said. "Our *funerarias* are very good at fixing that sort of thing."

An assistant standing by made a coughing sound and looked away in embarrassment.

"Que paso?" said the don. "Is something wrong?"

"Well, you see," said the director, sighing, "there was one little problem. The señor's penis had been stomped on so badly that it was impossible to reconstruct it, as we were able to do with his arms, legs and face. We saved what we could though, and have it here in this little box."

252

He picked up a small container hand-painted with colorful flowers. Alas! thought Mary as she pictured the mutilated pieces inside. And it had once held so much magic! What a way for it to end. She half expected to see the box begin to glow magically.

"But please don't discount this as a misfortune," the director continued. "If it were a saint's, it would be a holy relic."

"Yes, yes," said Doña Maria passing Helen a knowing look, "and if not a saint, then a mythological hero."

Not knowing that this was Helen's intent, Father Malcolm, hoping to help her get through the tragedy, took refuge in Plato. Why things like this happen, he said, Plato had explained beautifully in his theory of forms and realm of ideas. Everything, he said, whether it was a physical object like a bull, or an abstract concept such as love or beauty, had a perfect form outside of reality which was timeless, unchanging, and perfect. The physical objects that imitated them were merely imperfect copies of the perfect ones. Ferdinand, therefore, like all creatures on earth, was an imperfect form of his perfect form. And being an imperfect form, he had only been doing the thing that bulls often do, which was to gore people. It was, of course, unfortunate that he was showing his imperfection by killing the Senator.

Don Francisco shook the priest's hand.

"*Thank you*, Father, thank you. If something happens like this again, I will bring up Plato. I think my brother definitely needs to hear about him. He is so broken up for suggesting that the Senator come to Spain, that he and his wife, instead of going home, are flying from Budapest to Merida so they can go directly to the bullring at San Albin. Since it was built in the same spot where the Romans used to worship Mithra and the bull, it is probably the purest bullfight of them all, they say, and the best place to purge oneself of guilt."

Mary, however, felt confused. Plato notwithstanding, how, she wondered, could such a thing as bullfighting ever come from his realm of ideas? If the Duchess of Calle de Olvera was right, and the bull was being sacrificed to wash away men's sins, and with each shout of "ole!" there would be one less sin to justify the picador driving in his lance, perhaps in imitation of the Roman soldier who drove in his lance at the Crucifixion, and justify the matador driving his sword between the bull's eyes (even in Mithra's day, the sacrifice wasn't nearly so cruel), and Plato's realm included abstract ideas, too, was there really a perfect form up there to explain all this?

∗∗∗

Since it was built in the same spot where the Romans used to worship Mithra and the bull, it is probably the purest bullfight of them all, they say, and the best place to purge oneself of guilt.

Ferdinand seemed to be enjoying having his picture taken. The cadre of photographers and camera crew who normally would have been standing at a safe distance, had inched forward and were now at a not-too-shabby distance from where he stood under a tree and calmly munched the grass.

Mary had only just learned that a statue of the Senator might actually be in the offing. It was not the way she had envisioned it. Indeed, she had not really envisioned it at all but had only played with the idea of her father and God's pencil being one and the same. But then Doña Maria had said there were many beautiful parks in El Escorial, and he would be seen by the many tourists who came to visit the famous monastery and tombs of the kings.

As the limo drove past the meadow on its way to the airport, a smile played on Mary's lips. Yes, the magic penis was inside a box, but what matter that? For now, thanks to the bull, the Senator might soon be standing in a park as a bronze representation of the Word of God, and wouldn't that be glorious?

***

Doña Maria had been right. The stories about the Senator's death reached the far corners of the earth. In a blog called The Tundra Times, even the Eskimos had learned of his spectacular end. Helen glowed and was making plans for a big funeral. The Senator's death had not in any way diminished Mary's divine experience of God. Indeed, it had only lent further proof that John was wrong, and she'd not mixed the two up—her father with the Divine Spirit—because now that he was dead, how could she?

One night, a giant manta ray swept across the ceiling with such force that it woke her up. It was the Senator! Yes, he had made his appearance to her and frightened her to death. Boom! Boom! he went, and swish! Swish! But why was his spirit in this form—this huge gray shape flashing across the ceiling from one end to the other—and why did it go boom! Boom! And frightened her so? Was he angry with her? Was he blaming her for what had happened? But it was his fault too, wasn't it? Would she have pursued the incest-loving men of the East, otherwise?—would she, that is, if there'd not been, to begin with, a magic circle? Or, likewise, have pursued Mithra, or read all those books about him, or gone with von Clapp down the Rhine? Surely George was not blaming her for his disastrous trip to Spain, although if you thought about it, possibly you could.

Either way, she was too afraid to go back to sleep and, to John's annoyance, kept the light on for the rest of the night.

***

The fatal accident I mentioned at the beginning of this narrative occurred on the 5 Freeway, also known as Golden State Freeway. Even a year after it happened, it's hard to write about. I often wonder if it would have happened at all, had Martin not been sick, and Mary not been driving. And what's so sad, too, is that both women, Helen and Mary, seemed suddenly to have become friends. How else could they have chatted so freely, as Helen had recounted from her hospital bed, about subjects which, before George's death, would have brought only pain and anger?

But why should they not? Doña Maria had called that morning with news that the Mayor of El Escorial had allotted money for the statue. Artists had already been invited to submit sketches. There was debate, said the mayor, whether it should be a single statue—George standing very senatorial-like alone—or, as in a tableau, with Ferdinand beside him. What might Helen's opinion be, the mayor had wondered?

And what, Helen asked, was Mary's? They were on their way to Forest Lawn to make the preparations for George's funeral. Forest Lawn, in case you haven't heard, is a very grand cemetery, perhaps most famous for the stained-glass window of *The Last Supper*. But there are many other attractions besides, such as the Hall of Crucifixion-Resurrection, the Court of David with a bronze statue of Michelangelo's *David*, the Mystery of Life Garden, the Court of Freedom with a mosaic reproduction of Trumbull's *Signing of the*

257

Declaration of Independence, the Great Mausoleum with Michelangelo's *Pieta*, and a museum with paintings by such famous artists as Matisse, Goya and Rembrandt. There are also three nice churches—the Little Church of the Flowers, the Wee Kirk O' the Heather, and the Church of the Recessional—where you can go take a rest when you get tired. Yes, this grand cemetery makes for a nice outing, a pleasant place to pass the day even if nobody in the family is dead. Hundreds of famous people are buried there, and the Senator was soon to be amongst them.

"I still can't make up my mind," said Helen, "whether the little box from the funeraria should be buried with your father—of course, during the funeral I will ask the director to hide it in the folds of the casket—or cremated and kept in an urn. Of course, only the family would know what's in the urn, and if anyone ever did ask, well, since the urn is small, I suppose we could say it was some little pet—a little mouse, or something."

Mary said that it should be buried with the Senator. That way the Word of God, the Phallus of Osiris wouldn't go up in smoke and be destroyed forever. Of course Helen didn't know what she was talking about, and admitted to my mother that she didn't care to know since she was really trying hard to be friends and a good mother. So she ignored the remark and skipped into another subject: how she wished she had taken better care of all the pets the children had had. How many died!—goldfish, turtles, chameleons…. she remembered how Mary cried when the last one's string got caught in a branch, and strangled to death.

Then she said how she would never forget the time she held Mary on her lap, but the child wouldn't stop crying and instead kept asking for her mommy—where was her mommy?

According to Helen, Mary had been listening to her intently. She had never, she said, heard her mother speak like this. Had Helen actually had feelings for her? And maybe even suffered because the child didn't want her? And was even suffering now from the memory?

"I think I missed the exit," Mary said a minute later. "I'll have to turn around."

The next exit was Zoo Drive. When she went to switch lanes, she didn't see that a semi-truck was there in the same lane already.

***

At the time, Helen's description of what happened that day meant nothing to me other than the tragedy, sadness and loss of it all. But later, after I entered Mary's world of magic and all, it took on new meaning. I kept picturing my little friend sitting on her mother's knee, and feeling lost and motherless. No wonder she hated her. The magic circle wasn't all about the Word of God, or was it?

Helen had, for a moment, harbored the wild idea that the accident was intentional. Where did *that* come from? So mind-boggling, so inconceivable that Mary, of all people, would have chosen the exit to the zoo to kill her mother, and wanting, knowing only too well how impressionable children are, to have their thoughts of giraffes and elephants and monkeys and all the other wonderful animals at the zoo, marred forever by the memory of a body lying under a white sheet, blocking off the entrance.

I myself remember seeing, as a child, a terrible accident on the same freeway—police cars, ambulances, two smashed-up cars, and the bodies of two small dogs lying dead on the road. And a woman walking towards them as if in a trance. Some things you never forget.

By a strange twist of fate, Lucille and Don, just back from France, had planned to take the twins to Griffith Park that day. But the weather had turned foul, and the thought of being in the cold while the children rode the merry-go-round, the ponies and the little train wasn't pleasant.

"Imagine," said Lucille watching news coverage on TV, "after seeing their mother disappear in the sewer, what it would be, if they'd seen the body and found out later that it was their aunt lying under a sheet. How much can a child take?

***

Because Mary's death occurred so soon after the Senator's, a memorial service was held for both at the same time. The baron and baroness flew back from Germany, leaving Father Malcolm and Rufinus (who had become the ship's mascot—and why not? "Though he is not part of our world, is that not what made him perfect?" the Father had said) in charge of the boat. So far they had done a good job even though progress—he was in the midst of revision—had slowed down a bit on the *Philosophiae Naturalis Principia.*

Don Francisco flew over with doña Maria and his brother, the Duke of Calle de Olvera. The duke had gone to San Albin and, after watching some bullfights and shouting dozens of "oles!" was feeling much better. His wife however, even though the matador had presented her with the tail and two ears from the bull he had killed, still didn't feel absolved, and decided to stay home.

The presence of so much royalty had brought many people who hadn't intended to come. Almost everyone from Lido Isle was there, and many others from various parts of Orange County. For those who had at first hesitated, well, you can't really blame them—the 405 Fwy is no fun no matter what time of day. Others came all the way from Washington, not just the senators but their wives, too, most of whom barely knew Helen. If the words of Walt Whitman had ever made an impression, they were now lost in the annals of time.

Among those who had always planned to pay their final respect were Walter and Sarah, their nephew Thomas, Helen's cousin Jessica, Mary's old friends from college—the art professors and some others she had slept with, and other people who were sincerely saddened by the passing of both father and daughter. Paying tribute to Mary were the students from her Montessori class. They talked rapturously about the great impression she had made, and brought up such examples as the dell'Arca sculpture. This surprised John because Mary had told him she'd decided against discussing it.

"Her class was never boring," said a young man.

260

"Never," said another. "I remember when she showed us Albrecht Durer's *Praying Hands*, and said, 'What can you *not* do when pressing your palms together?'"

While they were still giggling, someone else said, "And what about her saying that all the cathedrals in the world owe their origins to the genitals because if our ancestors hadn't included them when learning how to count—the one on the left and the one on the right, along with the fingers and toes on the left and the fingers and toes on the right, where would architecture be today?"

"And Bernini's *Ecstasy of St. Teresa*! Remember her saying, 'What is that spear of gold tipped with fire, but the saint's beautiful poetic description of a penis? Bernini understood this—the nature of her religious ecstasy—and, through his own genius, captured her orgasm and his own in stone.'"

As John stepped nervously from one foot to the other, a young woman tearfully presented him with one of the prints Mary had made for the class. Beautifully framed, it was of Luisa Roldan's terracotta, *Ecstasy of Saint Mary Magdalene*. It showed her lying supine in the arms of two voluptuous angels. Her eyes shut, her mouth open, as are the mouths of the two angels who hold her firmly. Mary had written at the feet of two winged cherubs, "Even the angels are having orgasm!"

Meanwhile the duke, who had been upset by his wife not coming, was, after meeting Barbara, glad that she hadn't. He promised to see the Señorita dance before he went home. There was such a crush of people that when Dr. Niedlhauf tried to steer Alice and Callimachus over to the refreshments, someone accidentally stepped on the priest's long tunic and caused it to rip.

"Fear not," said the priest. And, giving the peace sign, took Alice by the hand and pushed his way to the food table. The doctor looked pleased. Both patients, he told an apprehensive baron, were benefiting from each other's company, and seemed well enough to make occasional excursions into society.

"I only wish," he said, "I could get her to stop cooing."

***

The memorial took place in the courtyard of the Ebell Club. It was a beautiful afternoon, and as the eulogies were given by the Senator's colleagues in Washington, the splashing sound of water could be heard coming from The Fountain of Honor. Many kind and moving words were spoken. If Mary had lived longer, said someone, she would have become a great artist. John said that she had led him closer to God than anyone before. And if it weren't for her, he said, he would never have known the joy of doing puzzles intended for Black people. More white people should give them a try.

Don Francisco said that the Senator died bravely and, had he been a Spaniard, would have made a great matador. Walter got up and said there was not, contrary to rumor, a bigoted bone in George's body. And von Clapp, when it was his turn, said he could vouch for that. If there had been, would the Senator have taken him, a German, to Newport Beach and Huntington Beach, as he did so often?

John's eulogy, though surprisingly short, had brought tears to people's eyes. He himself was overcome, as were the students from Montessori. They got up, one by one, and spoke of their love for her and how she had opened their eyes to all kinds of things. What rude fellow then, had uttered "Arrgh?" But it apparently prompted the professor from Chapman, who had already eulogized the Senator, to speak again, this time for Mary.

He could still remember all the evenings at the Senator's house, and how he had enjoyed the discussions she and he had had. There was no denying she was very bright, even though he always disagreed with her. Who, for instance, in their right mind could ever agree with her ridiculous views about Venus and Aphrodite, how they were behind everything in men's life, from the sublime to the mundane—"I mean, can you imagine the idea that things like video games and food stamps are conceived in the groin? X-rated movies, maybe, but Mary Poppins

262

and Mickey Mouse? Or that Francis Scott Key was a racist, and Billy Graham's evangelism came from the gonads, and the Bible is why policemen shoot down the Blacks?"

As he recalled all this and more, and wondered how the Senator had ever put up with her, the tears began to roll down his face, and he had to sit down.

***

Mary's portrait and her father's stood next to each other on tripods. Most of the mourners were still eating, and before the eulogies had begun, John and I had the pictures to ourselves.

"I wish I had been more understanding," he said, looking at the little girl sitting in an apple tree.

"That's the problem with humans," I replied. "We have all these regrets after someone is gone."

"I mean about this crazy dream she had right after George died. But it wasn't a dream, she said, it was real. A swooshing sound had awakened her just in time to see a huge grayish-blue manta ray fly across the ceiling. It was her father. I got really angry because she was so frightened, we had to keep the light on all night."

As I thought about this, I remembered something that had happened only a few months ago. I'd gone with Mary to a travel agency to renew her passport, and while we were waiting for her photo, we looked at the different travel posters lining the walls. She stopped in front of a large one advertising South Africa. It was the photo of a young lion cub playfully rubbing its face against the whiskers of its father. The king of the jungle, lying supine like the Sphinx, submitted patiently to the cub's foolishness. And as he stared into the distance, his huge mane crowning him with power, one had the feeling that he was going to be a good father, and that the cub would come to no harm.

Mary stood there for a long time, and when she turned toward me, I can still remember how taken aback I was. I had never seen anyone looking so sad.

***

POSTSCRIPT

My father wanted Helen to see the manuscript before I submitted it to a publisher.

"She needs to be prepared," he said, after reading it. It was good advise because Helen went ballistic.

She barged unannounced into Walter's office and threw the manuscript on his desk.

"It's lies, all lies!" she shouted, throwing her dignified reserve to the wind. "If George had done those things, I would have known about it!"

My father then told her that, pursuant to all the collateral damage, it was likely that he did. There was Barbara, for instance, who could testify to the veracity of Mary's words. And there was Alice, too, whose personal vicissitudes were enough to bear witness that a crime had been committed.

My mother, who was waiting to have lunch with Dad, tried to reason with her friend.

"There is a dark web in all of us," she said. Helen's tone softened.

"Can you at least wait," she said, "until the unveiling of George's statue?"

The work had gone swiftly, and the ceremony was only a few weeks away.

"I've been invited, and King Felipe will be there, too."

Despite his friendship with George, my father said no. Pulling her shoulders back and looking defiant, she stormed out, but not before saying in a tone of vindictive righteousness, "As for that time Barbara and I were having lunch, and I told her I was prettier than she was? Well, you know what? I *am* prettier!"

She went back to Decatur, and a short time later, an attorney named Jared Mulligan preempted the publication by initiating a lawsuit against Matheson, Morley and Weinstock.

In the meantime, the *Happy Bull* had completed several more successful voyages. Rose had been on one, and by the time the trip ended, and she had seen all the mithraeums and tauroctonous reliefs, she tried to convince her son, who had returned to help Father Malcolm, that he was doing the work of the devil.

"Why can't you become a priest again? Look at Father Malcolm. After all the things he's done, he's still a priest. Just because you leave the order, doesn't mean you can't return."

"That's right," said Father Malcolm, who had been in on the conversation. "With a dispensation from the pope, I believe it's possible."

John shrugged his shoulders indecisively. His friend took his arm and said gently, "Even Rufinus wants you to go. Look how his tail is wagging." That was enough for Rose, and shortly thereafter, she flew to Rome.

Somehow she was able to gain a private audience with the pope. The Holy Father listened politely as she spelled out all the good things about her boy, and how popular he had been with his parish while he was still a priest, and how he was not afraid of controversy.

This interested the pope, and he asked her to explain.

"Well," she said, "a little while ago when you told a gay man that God made him that way and God loved him that way, my son agreed with you even though his friends didn't."

The pope clasped his hands with joy, so pleased was he to hear he was not the only one who thought so. But Mary had thought so, too. The pope was right, she had said to John. God did indeed make men gay if they preferred to experience Him—i.e., orgasm—from behind.

Yes, since orgasm is God, and gay men like to do it from behind, then to experience God from back *there, that* is what makes men gay. As much as John didn't want to agree with her, there was something about this argument that felt right. (He knew not why.)

It was not long after Rose's private audience when news came that the dispensation had been granted. By happy coincidence, once he was reinstated, he was appointed to his parish in Boston which was once again in need of a priest. One can only imagine his surprise when he learned he was to be appointed instead to the American parish in Rome. Father Malcolm received the wireless as he sat up top gazing at the sky.

"God's ways are indeed mysterious," he said to Rufinus, and carefully folded the wireless.

***

It is there in Rome that I went to see John several months later. I had some questions about the diary I wanted to clear up. He welcomed me warmly and began telling me all that had happened since his appointment in Rome; how the pope had warmly welcomed him and later, sent him on a delicate mission to Vladivostok; how, while he was there, he'd met Father Ivan of the Mother of God church, an amateur photographer to boot; how the two had set off to look for Siberian tigers; how they'd gotten lost in a snowstorm; how, somewhere near Durmin they'd seen pugmarks in the snow and followed them and turned a bend and seen a real tiger lying asleep in the snow.

"Man, was he big!" said John.

I listened politely. When he was finally finished, he asked me how things were back home. After a while he asked about the lawsuit. At first I was surprised, forgetting that, being in Siberia and lost in the snow and all, Father Malcolm probably wouldn't have been able to reach him with the news.

"Helen and Gretchen were both killed in a boating accident."

As he sat in stunned silence, I told him what happened. After returning to Decatur, she'd flown off to Germany to be with Gretchen. Then, when it was time for the unveiling of the Senator, they would go together to El Escorial.

In the meantime, the baron had added a new port of call at Koblenz so that the passengers could visit the mithraeum at Saarbrucken, a sanctuary to Mithra built inside a natural cave. It was a two-hour drive, and after the passengers went on their way, the baron had stayed behind and rented a speedboat.

"Kommst, liebchen," he said to his wife. "Let us show Helen the Lorelei Rock."

The ship was not far from the famous rock where legend had it that a beautiful maiden had thrown herself off the rock, and afterwards lured sailors to their death when they heard her enchanted singing. It would be Helen's only chance to see this famous rock, since she and Gretchen were flying to Madrid from Koblenz the next day.

"Ja wohl," Gretchen had replied. "Why not?"

Within minutes the speedboat had reached Sankt Goar, and was whizzing past the Lorelei rock when the accident happened. From his hospital bed, the baron swore, on regaining consciousness, by all that is holy, that he had seen the Lorelei on top of the rock, and when he heard her singing, he lost control. But according to witnesses, it was really the women who were screaming for him to stop.

This, the baron refused to believe. Why, just a few days before, while he and Juan Gomez were drinking beer on the deck, one of the Rhinemaidens had suddenly appeared in the water, and before she disappeared, he had caught a glimpse of the Rhinegold she was guarding in her hand. (Walter, on hearing all this, had wondered if there were such a thing as the Niebelung syndrome, and whether or not it might have affected other Germans, as well.)

"And the baron? Has he gone back to work?"

"Yes, but after being evaluated, he may lose his license to operate the *Happy Bull*. But Father Malcolm says he can handle the job if push comes to shove."

"So the lawsuit is dead in the water?" said John, apologizing for the unintended pun.

"Yes."

His troubled look surprised me. I knew he had never been a fan of either woman, so I assumed it had to do either with the baron's predicament or Father Malcolm's who was now in charge of the passengers.

"No, no," he said. "It's about the lawsuit. I was hoping your book would never be published."

"But why on earth..."

"You know, guilty by association."

Could he ever, he said, knowing how much Mary liked to record things, become a cardinal, let alone God's spokesman on earth, if what he'd said about the Old and New Testaments coming from the testicles, and the penis connected to the Roman gods, was made public? Pagan or not pagan, God was still God.

It was early afternoon when I finished my questions. Most of them remained unanswered, and John apologized for not being very helpful.

"I understand," I said. "But whether you agree about the earthly father and the Heavenly Father, if Mary could still love either one after going down the rabbit hole, does her story not show how wonderfully strange and tenacious is the power of orgasm?"

"Even so," he said thoughtfully, "how can you expose God without paying the price? Maybe some doorways should never be entered."

I wondered if he was right. Mary herself, writing so often about the magic circle, had said that those who enter it are lucky to get out. But I think now that she never did. I think she didn't want to, the little girl in the apple tree. She was there alone with God, and what a privilege that must have been. But I think I would not want that privilege. Like John said, the price she paid was far too great.

I was about to leave when John asked me if I would like to visit the Vatican gardens.

"You have never seen anything so beautiful," he said.

It was no exaggeration. Fifty-seven acres (a magic number, Mary had said, in the *Zend-Avesta*) of pools, fountains, grottoes, forest, gardens all scattered about with sculptures and walkways—a veritable Garden of Eden. As we meandered along, we were joined by a young priest. After a few minutes of friendly conversation, John said, "And your visit to Ravenna—was it productive?"

"Yes, most productive."

As he spoke, he threw a suspicious look at me.

"It's all right," said John, "she knows everything."

The priest nodded and continued.

"It's just as you said. In the Byzantine mosaic at the Basilica of Sant'Apollinare, the three Magi are wearing red Phrygian caps instead of crowns, Should I tell the others?"

"No, no, let's keep it under our hats" (another pun) "for now."

Later, as we rested on a bench, I barely listened as John chattered on about his work at St. Patrick's and the excitement of Rome. The gardens exuded a sensuous beauty, and as the clerics strolled past us, their comings and goings indelibly marked by the blackness of their dress, Mary's voice came to me from the pages of her diary: "The world is built on lies."

Her voice followed as John led me to the Vatican Museum. Inside was a display of silver and gold reliquaries, and monstrances covered with all the precious gems known to man. Can it indeed be that the beauty of religious ritual is orgasmic in nature? And why these resplendent objects glittering with jewels are here to warn us? Orgasm is beautiful but it is also dangerous? Did the clergy who paraded them around know that? Somehow I doubted it. I asked John if such things were still affecting his libido, and he said no, not after Mary.

On our way to the Basilica, he pulled a small box from his pocket.

"Do you know," he said, handing it to me, "what these are?"

I opened it and saw dozens of little black eyes staring up at me.

"Oh my God! This is Mary's old lobster eye collection."

It was still in the same box she'd had as a child. They were the lobster eyes she used to save whenever the Senator cooked lobster.

"She never threw them away?"

It was amazing how alive they looked, disengaged as they were, from their bodies. There was something accusing in their look, like, why did you do this to me? And I thought of Mary, and felt sad.

"Maybe you'll remember this, too," said John, handing me something else.

It was a rosary, and yes, I did recognize it. The Senator had bought it for her at the old Spanish mission in San Gabriel, a Hispanic community where he sometimes took his family during the religious holidays.

I thought she had liked it because the blue-colored beads were pretty. But now I think it was because, to her, they were magic. And why not? Did she not already know what the real magic was, and where it came from? Was it not from the little Crucifix dangling at the end, the naked man wearing a towel? Could He not also have been George, perhaps, wearing a towel after a shower? I wondered if Groddeck had gone far enough, and it was, to a child, beyond Oedipal, just a man whose overt sexuality was undeniable.

Sweet child, to have connected it all up, and not even be Catholic!

"You know, confessing to the lobsters' eyes might really be redeeming," John said as I handed her things back. "Being boiled alive is much worse than being crucified."

He put the mementos in his pocket, and looked around to see if anyone had been listening.

"It's touching that you kept them."

I was never sure if he loved her all that much. As if he read my thoughts, he said, "I loved her very much, but she wouldn't let me in. There was always something in the way."

"Being boiled alive is much worse than being crucified."

"Her father."

"Yes, her father and his magic orgasms. You've read the diary, so you know that mine, I guess, weren't magic enough. The ones I gave her were always his. His and God's."

As we walked on, he added a second thought.

"But now that she's here in my pocket, there's nothing in my way."

We arrived at the Basilica, and joined the people looking at the *Pieta*. One of the tourist groups was American, and when John recognized a couple he'd met in Newport Beach, he slipped away quickly. But I decided to stay, hoping that the group would soon leave and I could get closer to the sculpture. Unfortunately, this was not happening. One of the women could not stop criticizing it. Indeed, she seemed to be obsessed. There was, for instance, the Virgin's youth— she looked like she was the same age as Christ. Then there was the way she was holding his body. It was way too erotic, not least because the cloth barely covered his genitals.

"What do you expect," said the guide. "Michelangelo was only twenty-three when he made it."

She didn't think that was an excuse, and asked if that was why the statue was so high up, so you couldn't see whether he'd carved any pubic hair or not.

After she made a few more remarks, the group moved away. I could now get close, and, after admiring the great artistry of the sculptor, as I found my eyes following those of the Virgin's to where she is gazing, Mary's words came back to me: sex is religion and religion is sex. I also thought of Groddeck's words, that upon the mother we all must die. Was that Michelangelo's dream as he chiseled away at the marble, to lie naked in his mother's arms? And why it imbues the marble with such beauty and splendor? And pity, too, because such things can never happen outside the magic circle?

It may not have been right, her story, but right or wrong, she was always true. And how many of us can tell, or even know, what *is* true?

But then, how many of us have had the Phallus of Osiris and the Word of God to ride on?

***

That evening before we went to dinner, John made a stop at his apartment. While I waited, I noticed a small piñata on one of the shelves. It was a bull all decorated in different colors of crepe—blue, orange, green, yellow, purple. It had a ring in its nose, and its little horns were made of pink. I was holding it when John came into the room.

"Ah, that is my Papal Bull," he said, laughing.

"It looks like the piñata Mary wrote about, the one Father Malcolm brought with him from Chimayo and left in the lounge."

"It is. He gave it to me as a going-away present. 'To remember the *gomez*,' he said, 'and keep you honest.'"

"Do you think the pope knows he's in the business of selling magic?"

Right away I regretted my remark. John looked hurt, and, not having read the diary, how could he know?

275

At the trattoria, we ate spaghetti and drank wine. Naturally, we talked mostly about Mary. The more we drank the more lucid we became, and after reviewing the recent past, we came to the lugubrious conclusion that the events that had propelled the Armstrongs to their untimely deaths were not arbitrary but were, in fact, preordained by the hominids when they took over the earth and nullified the laws of nature.

"If a butterfly's wings can set off a tornado in Texas," said John, "well then, why not hominids and the Armstrongs?"

The next day he drove me to the airport. Just before I boarded, he asked me if I knew what had happened to Mary's portrait of him in the nude. I was surprised because I thought he had it. It was the best thing she ever did. He nodded. It was after spending several minutes wondering where it was, when he said, "She used to sing this catching little song while she was painting it."

"About an apple tree?"

He looked at me guardedly. "How did you know?"

"Just a guess. Her father used to sing it to her when she was a little girl."

"I always thought," he snorted, "it looked more like George than it did me."

"Well, when you're the pope, it will just be a picture of one father and another."

The plane gained altitude, and the land below receded into a miniature, toy-like landscape. When it disappeared below the clouds, I settled back and closed my eyes and let my thoughts drift. Yes, you certainly had to hand it to her, to Mary and her vision of God—who He is, what He is—a peculiar vision true or not true but certainly unique, and I am not at all unhappy to be bringing it to light.

Los Angeles, 2019

PUBLISHER'S NOTE

In memory of Mary Armstrong and their mutual understanding of *The Golden Ass*, Father Malcolm has pledged the proceeds from his *Philosophiae Naturalis Principia* to a non-profit charitable organization he is starting, the Fallen Families Foundation of America. In its mission statement, the FFFOA (pronounced "phiphfoa" with the accent on the first syllable "phiph"—an uptake of breath is necessary for the correct sound which is similar, said the Father, to that of smoking a joint) will provide all the assistance necessary to help people avoid the kinds of pitfalls that befell the Armstrong family, such as being sucked into a sewer or gored by a bull.

The organization is still pending approval of a 501(c)(3) rating.

A Helpful Guide to
Mary Armstrong's Diary

- *Sacred Books of the East*, edited by F. Max Muller
    - *The Zend Avesta*, I-III, Motilal Banarsidass, New Delhi, India, 1980.
    - *The Pahlavi Texts*, I-V, Ibid, 1977.
- Herodotus, *The Histories*, transl. by George Rawlinson, Everyman's Library, Alfred A. Knopf, 1997.
- St. Augustine, *The City of God*, transl. by Marcus Dods, Digireads.com Publishing, 2017.
- Henry Adams, *The Education of Henry Adams*, The Modern Library, New York, 1996.
- *Myth and Law Among the Indo-Europeans*, ed. by Jaan Puhvel, Berkeley and Los Angeles, 1970.
- Lucian, *Lucian*, transl. by M.D. Macleod, Loeb Classical Library, Vol. VIII, Harvard University Press, 1967.
- Plato, *Phaedrus*, transl. by Benjamin Jowett, Digireads.com Publishing, 2019.
- Apuleius, *The Apologia and Florida*, transl. by H.E. Butler, Oxford at the Clarendon Press, 1909.
- Apuleius, *Apvlei Apologia, Sive Pro De Magia Liber*, by H.E. Butler, Ibid, 1914, Forgotten Book Series.
- Eric Partridge, *Origins, A Short Etymological Dictionary of the English Language*, The Macmillan Co., New York, Second Edition 1959.
- *Encyclopedia of Religion and Ethics*, ed. by James Hastings, Charles Scribner's Sons, New York, 1925.
- Apuleius, *The Golden Ass*, transl. by P.G. Walsh, Oxford University Press, Great Britain, 2008.

- Apuleius, *The Golden Ass*, transl. by E.J. Kenney, Penguin Books, Great Britain, 2004.
- *The Demotic Magical Papyrus of London and Leiden*, transl. by Francis Llewellyn Griffith, Legare Street Press, an imprint of Creative Media Partners.
- Catullus, *The Poems*, transl. by A.S. Kline, Poetry in Translation, London, 2007.
- Catullus, *The Carmina of Gaius Valerius Catullus*, transl. by Leonard C. Smithers, London, 1894.
- Apuleius, *Apuleius on the God of Socrates*, transl. by Thomas Taylor, Holmes Publishing Group LLC, Sequim, WA.
- *The Sword of Moses, An Ancient Book of Magic*, transl. by M. Gaster, Ph. D., One-Eye Publishing, 2018.
- Walt Whitman, *Leaves of Grass*, Barnes and Noble Books, NY, 1993.
- Adventures with the Missing Link by Raymond A. Dart, Harper & Brothers Publishers, NY 1959

www.ingramcontent.com/pod-product-compliance
Lightning Source LLC
Chambersburg PA
CBHW041042310726

48978CB00011BA/404